Ennis Public Library
501 W. Ennis Ave.
Ennis, TX 75119-3803

The CONTRACT SURGEON

Center Point
Large Print

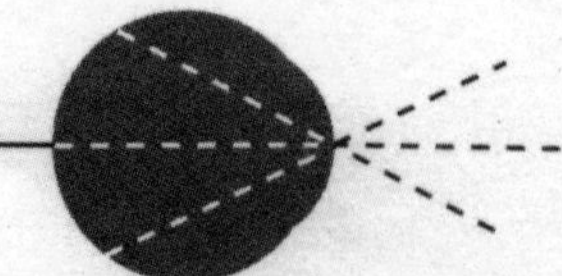

This Large Print Book carries the
Seal of Approval of N.A.V.H.

The CONTRACT SURGEON

Dan O'Brien

CENTER POINT PUBLISHING
THORNDIKE, MAINE

Ennis Public Library
501 W. Ennis Ave.
Ennis, TX 75119-3803

This Center Point Large Print edition
is published in the year 2006 by arrangement with
The Lyons Press.

Copyright © 1999 by Dan O'Brien.

All rights reserved.

The text of this Large Print edition is unabridged. In other aspects, this book may vary from the original edition. Printed in Thailand. Set in 16-point Times New Roman type.

ISBN 1-58547-703-6

Library of Congress Cataloging-in-Publication Data

O'Brien, Dan, 1947-
The contract surgeon / Dan O'Brien.--Center Point large print ed.
p. cm.
ISBN 1-58547-703-6 (lib. bdg. : alk. paper)
1. Crazy Horse, ca. 1842-1877--Fiction. 2. Indians of North America--Wars--Fiction.
3. Oglala Indians--Fiction. 4. Great Plains--Fiction. 5. Large type books. I. Title.

PS3565.B665C6 2006
813'.54--dc22

2005020662

Dedicated to the memory of
OLD HEMLOCK MELVILLE
(1991-1999).
He slept by my chair as I typed.
He was a good critic.

CONTENTS

Many people helped with the historical details in this book, but I'd like to especially thank Bob Preszler, Director of the Minnilusa Pioneer Museum, and Julie Moore of the Sturgis Public Library. Thanks also to Alrene Swift for translating my jibberish into proper Lakota.

AUTHOR'S NOTE

With a few exceptions, the people and events of this book can be found on the pages of the scores of history books written on the subject of the Great Sioux War. In many cases I have appropriated characters' exact words from government documents or firsthand accounts. But although the vast majority of *The Contract Surgeon* is historically accurate, it should not be read as history. Literary license has been exercised, especially in evoking the sense of place that is often lacking in military documents and scholarly histories. The story, because of the requirements of fiction, has been simplified. The events portrayed in this book, their causes and ramifications, are terribly complicated; to understand them fully I recommend the following books as a start: *On the Border with Crook*, *Indian Fights and Fighters*, *The Fetterman Massacre*, *The Killing of Crazy Horse*, *Son of the Morning Star*, *Boots and Saddles*, *The Sioux Wars*, *Hokahey! A Good Day to Die!*, *Red Cloud's Folk*, *Blood on the Moon*, *Red Cloud and the Sioux Problem*, *A Good Year to Die*, *Crazy Horse: Strange Man of the Oglalas*, *Black Elk Speaks*, *Fields of Battle*, *To Kill an Eagle*, and *Crazy Horse and Custer.*

INTRODUCTION

The Sioux Indians of the nineteenth century were a loosely connected group of nomadic horsemen made up of several subgroups speaking a language with common roots. After acquiring the horse, the most tenacious subgroup, the Lakota Sioux, pushed the less aggressive inhabitants of the Great Plains south, west, and north. Within a hundred years they ruled a great portion of the high plains, from the Missouri River to the Rocky Mountains. By nature the Lakota were a combative people and, even before the United States took possession of the Louisiana Purchase in 1803, had made mortal enemies of nearly all the other tribes on the plains.

From their first contact with representatives of the United States the Lakota were defiant. With the exception of a few incidents of petty thievery by West Coast tribes, Lewis and Clark had trouble only with the Lakota, who blocked their progress along the Missouri River and made war on Indian nations with whom the United States was making alliances.

Between the Lewis and Clark Expedition and the opening of Montana's gold fields, the Lakota concentrated their energies on keeping the Crows, Shoshones, Arikaras, Pawnees, and others in a subservient position with regard to the fertile buffalo hunting grounds of the northern plains. But once the people of the United States began to move into that same territory, the

Lakota were forced to divert increasing amounts of resources to stemming the flow of pioneers.

In the 1860s a chief of the Oglala band by the name of Red Cloud rose to prominence and led the Lakota and their allies in a successful war against the United States that stopped pioneer emigration into Montana over the Bozeman trail. After two years of war, Red Cloud, along with Spotted Tail of the Brules Sioux band, signed the treaty of 1868 that excluded whites from their territory and, after trips to Washington, settled in northwestern Nebraska on reservations named for them. They became known as "friendlies," living on the reservations and, in exchange for their passivity, receiving their subsistence from the United States government. Red Cloud and Spotted Tail had won their war and had been recognized as supreme leaders of their people by the U.S. But the political structure of the Lakota was very different from that of the United States. A Lakota leader was only a leader when the people followed him, and the fact that two chiefs had retired to reservations did not mean that the Lakota would cease hostilities toward the United States or any of the other nations on the northern plains.

The Lakota, under other chiefs, continued to wage war on their neighbors, red and white. Two chiefs who emerged during the 1870s were Sitting Bull of the Hunkpapas band and a charismatic young warrior named Crazy Horse of the Oglalas.

What were known as the northern Sioux or the "hostiles" fought the United States Army nearly to a standstill in the Great Sioux War of 1876. But the superior resources of the United States finally wore the Sioux down. In the winter of 1876 Sitting Bull retreated into Canada, but Crazy Horse, with his defiant band of starving Oglalas, remained hostile in the north until the spring of 1877. Crazy Horse became a symbol of resistance for the Sioux, and though his position as chief was not hereditary, he ascended to that position and was, at once, held in increasing esteem by some of his people and loathed or envied by others.

On the United States side the war was executed by an array of generals who had won their fame in the Civil War. At the head of the army was General Sherman. Under him was Sheridan. And under Sheridan, among others, were Generals Crook, Gibbon, Terry, and Custer.

Perhaps the most experienced of these generals, in both Indian fighting and management, was Crook. He had served throughout the West and recently secured the surrender of the Apaches in Arizona. He was a fair man, respected by the Indians, but he was rugged and a dogged adversary in battle. He was known for uncommonly efficient supply trains and relentless winter campaigns and was comfortable with long night marches and early-morning attacks. Among his handpicked officers for the campaigns of 1876 was a young civilian surgeon, temporarily contracted to the U.S. Army, named Valentine Trant McGillycuddy.

McGillycuddy would go on to become Indian agent at the Red Cloud Agency (later known as the Pine

Ridge Reservation) in the new state of South Dakota. He would also be a signatory to South Dakota's constitution, the first president of the South Dakota School of Mines, a businessman, the chief medical insurance inspector for the state of Montana, one of the first licensed doctors in the new state of California, and a volunteer to the natives of Alaska during the influenza epidemic of 1919; he would finally retire as the house surgeon for the Claremont Hotel in Berkeley, California.

Crook, who had his choice of any officers or surgeons for his Sioux campaign, called the newly married McGillycuddy from Washington. It was true that McGillycuddy, although still in his twenties, had been with the geological survey teams that mapped most of the country over which Crook planned to campaign, but Crook never tapped that expertise. The two men were not old friends. Their paths had crossed only a time or two. But Crook was known for being a prophetic judge of character. He must have seen something that told him the young surgeon could play a key role in the turbulent years that were just beginning.

CHRONOLOGY OF EVENTS

1841

Autumn—Crazy Horse is born to the sister of Spotted Tail, chief of the Brule band and an Oglala holy man, at Bear Butte on the northern edge of the Black Hills in what is now South Dakota.

1849

February 14—Valentine Trant McGillycuddy is born in Racine, Wisconsin. Soon after, his immigrant Irish Presbyterian family moves to Detroit, Michigan.

1854

August 19—Lt. John L. Grattan, twenty-nine soldiers, and one civilian are killed in an attempt to arrest the Indian responsible for the theft of a single cow. The Brule chief, Conquering Bear, is mortally wounded. The massacre is witnessed by thirteen-year-old Crazy Horse, then known as Curly.

1854

Summer—Crazy Horse kills his first human being, an Omaha woman.

1858

Summer—Crazy Horse is wounded in open combat. He kills two Arapaho warriors in view of the entire raiding party and earns his name.

1865

April 9—End of the American Civil War. Rebels surrender at Appomattox Court House, freeing the world's largest army to pacify the western frontier.

Summer—Crazy Horse becomes a "shirt wearer" and vows to lead warriors in battle, preserve order in camp, and make sure the rights of the weaker members of the tribe are respected. His shirt is decorated with 240 locks of hair, each representing an act of bravery.

1866

Spring—The United States decides to protect the Bozeman trail, which services the Montana gold fields, by building and maintaining a series of forts. The Oglala chief Red Cloud organizes resistance. The beginning of Red Cloud's War.

September—Valentine McGillycuddy enters medical school at the Marine Hospital in Detroit, at age seventeen.

December 21—Capt. William J. Fetterman and eighty men are decoyed by the Sioux, probably led by young Crazy Horse, and massacred.

1867

The Bozeman trail is effectively closed by Red Cloud's warriors.

1868

April 29—Fort Laramie Treaty (treaty of 1868)

signed, ending Red Cloud's War. The treaty calls for a cessation of hostilities, punishment by the United States government for persons committing crimes against the Sioux, surrender of any Sioux committing crimes against U.S. citizens, and opening of any roads deemed necessary by the U.S. (except the Bozeman trail). The treaty provides for annuities to be paid to the Sioux in return for peace. Indian children are to be educated by the U.S., and farmable land and farming implements provided. A reservation, made up of all lands in the present state of South Dakota west of the Missouri River, is established. The reservation includes the Black Hills and provides that no white man "shall ever be permitted to pass over, settle upon, or reside in the territory. . . ." In addition, the treaty provides for the country north of the North Platte River and east of the Big Horn Mountains to be considered unceded Indian territory with no white presence allowed unless agreed to by the Sioux. Not all Sioux sign the treaty. Warriors under Crazy Horse, Sitting Bull, and others continue to harass settlers and to wage war on tribes friendly to the U.S.

June—Valentine McGillycuddy graduates from medical school and joins the faculty at the Detroit Marine Hospital.

November 27—Gen. George Armstrong Custer destroys Chief Black Kettle's Cheyennes on the Washita River in present-day Oklahoma. The village is attacked without reconnaissance, at dawn while the

Indians sleep. Over one hundred men, women, and children are killed as they emerge from their tepees.

1871

McGillycuddy joins the Great Lakes Survey and directs a crew that resurveys Chicago after the Great Fire of 1871. He begins courting Fanny Hoyt.

1873

April 6—Gen. George Crook accepts the unconditional surrender of the Apache-Mojave chief Chalipun. This pacification of the Southwest was achieved by using Indians as scouts and fighters against their own kind. Crook is recognized as perhaps the premier Indian fighter in the nation.

Spring—McGillycuddy accepts a position as topographer and surgeon with the international survey of the boundary between the United States and British America. It is his first contact with the Sioux and their way of life.

1874

July 2—The Black Hills Expedition, under the command of Custer, leaves Fort Abraham Lincoln in present-day North Dakota. Their purpose is to survey the Black Hills for mineral deposits, a direct violation of the Fort Laramie Treaty.

July 25—Custer enters the Black Hills.

July 27—Custer finds gold in the Black Hills and spreads the word to the nation.

August 2—Red Cloud moves his people to the agency named for him. They settle near Camp Robinson, Nebraska, thirty miles from Spotted Tail—who settled on his agency six years before. A line of demarcation is established between reservation Indians under Spotted Tail and Red Cloud and the hostiles, or northern Indians, under Crazy Horse, Gall, Sitting Bull, and others. Clashes continue between white settlers and hostiles (with occasional aid from the reservation Indians).

1875

June—McGillycuddy, as a member of the Newton Jennings Survey, enters the Black Hills for the first time. He is the first white man to climb Harney Peak, the highest point in the Black Hills and a holy site for Lakota Sioux.

Autumn—McGillycuddy and Fanny Hoyt marry in Detroit, Michigan.

Autumn and winter—Miners stream into the Black Hills, a blatant violation of the treaty of 1868, and conflicts between whites and Indians increase.

December 6—Hostile Indians are advised that they must move to reservations or face military action.

1876

January 31—The deadline for all northern Sioux to be on Dakota reservations. Few have complied.

February 1—Driven by rumors of an eminent attack on the miners in the Black Hills, all Indian affairs are turned over to the War Department. Agents are replaced by military men and war is declared on non-reservation Indians concentrated in what is now southeastern Montana.

THE YELLOWSTONE CAMPAIGN

February 21—The Yellowstone Campaign begins. General Crook and eight hundred men push north from Fort Laramie to engage hostiles. They are one of three columns that intend to descend on the hostile Sioux and Cheyenne camped somewhere northeast of the Big Horn Mountains.

March 17—Col. Joseph J. Reynolds attacks and destroys Cheyenne Village on the Powder River. Crazy Horse supplies the survivors with food and shelter from subzero temperatures.

April 3—Col. John Gibbon and 450 men begin to march east from Bozeman.

May 17—Gen. Alfred Terry, with now Lt. Col. George Armstrong Custer and 925 men, begins to march west from Fort Abraham Lincoln in Dakota Territory.

May 26—McGillycuddy leaves Washington, where he is making maps from his field notes of the Black Hills survey, to join Crook's column—which has withdrawn to camp east of the Big Horn Mountains.

May 29—Crook again pushes north.

June 9—Crook engages the enemy on the Tongue River.

June 16—Crook engages the enemy, led by Crazy Horse, on Rosebud Creek. Crook is driven from the field and McGillycuddy, who has just caught up to the column, takes charge of fifty-six wounded.

June 25—Custer attacks a huge hostile village on the Little Big Horn River without proper reconnaissance or prudence. A counterattack by the hostiles produces many wounded; Custer and his entire immediate command are killed and mutilated. Among the leaders of the successful counterattack are Crazy Horse and Sitting Bull. Crazy Horse moves toward the Black Hills, and Sitting Bull retreats to the north.

July 14—The Fort Laramie Treaty is effectively negated by the United States Congress.

August 26—Crook's force, supplemented by elements from Terry's command, moves out on the trail of Crazy Horse. McGillycuddy is in charge of the travois train carrying wounded. Rations run low. Horses begin to die from exhaustion and lack of forage. This four-hundred-mile trek becomes known as Crook's Starvation March.

August 31—The column goes on half rations. The two thousand soldiers begin to eat horses as they die.

September 9—A group of Crazy Horse's people are driven to ground in the Slim Buttes. Lt. Philo Clark leads a successful charge. Chief American Horse and many warriors, women, and children are killed. Several soldiers are killed and many severely wounded are added to the travois train. Rations give out completely. Soldiers are forced to kill their horses for food.

September 13—Crook reaches the Belle Fourche River and is met by supplies from Crook City in the Black Hills. The Starvation March is ended.

October 21—Col. Nelson Miles defeats Sitting Bull at Cedar Creek.

November 8—McGillycuddy leaves Camp Robinson in the company of Pvt. John Holden. He will pick up Fanny in Chicago and deliver Holden to the National Asylum for the Insane in Washington.

November 25—Col. Ranald Mackenzie defeats the last of the hostile Cheyenne under Dull Knife. The raid is conducted in severe winter weather. The survivors flee to Crazy Horse's village, where they are by necessity turned away.

December 16—Crow scouts massacre thirty Miniconjou chiefs and warriors under a flag of truce as they try to surrender. Their people are driven back into the elements and rejoin Crazy Horse's hostile camp.

December 18—Lt. Frank Baldwin, two-time Medal of Honor winner, destroys Sitting Bull's camp on Ash Creek in present-day Montana. Many lives are lost, and many women and children captives lose limbs to frostbite. Sitting Bull flees to Canada.

1877

January 8—Col. Miles attacks Crazy Horse's camp at Wolf Mountain. The Sioux are defeated and driven into the elements with no food or shelter.

May 6—Crazy Horse surrenders to Lt. Philo Clark near Camp Robinson, Nebraska.

September 6—Crazy Horse is bayonetted by Pvt. William Gentles outside the adjutant's office of Fort Robinson. He dies five hours later.

1879

January 29—Valentine Trant McGillycuddy is appointed Indian agent at Red Cloud Agency, later known as the Pine Ridge Indian Reservation.

1886

McGillycuddy is relieved of his duties as agent. He moves to Rapid City, South Dakota, where he is elected mayor and serves as dean of the South Dakota School of Mines.

1890

December 29—A band of renegade Sioux under Big Foot surrenders near Wounded Knee Creek on the Pine Ridge Reservation. The surrender is bungled. Two hundred Sioux and sixty soldiers die, many more are wounded.

December 30—McGillycuddy, after riding all night from Rapid City, sets up emergency medical station for the survivors of the Wounded Knee massacre.

1897

Fanny Hoyt McGillycuddy dies of a stroke in her home in Rapid City.

1898-1912

McGillycuddy serves as the Montana and Pacific Coast medical inspector for Mutual Life Insurance Company.

1915-17

McGillycuddy is reactivated as a military surgeon during the worldwide flu epidemic. He serves in California mining camps and with the Aleut Indians in Alaska.

1939

June 6—Valentine Trant McGillycuddy dies in his final post—house doctor for the Claremont Hotel in Berkeley, California.

1

I never needed much sleep. Even as a boy a handful of hours could sustain me, and now after almost ninety years I seldom close my eyes for more than a few minutes at a time. Being able to doze off during a lull is a blessing. Needing sleep is a gift. You won't believe this, but bone-numbing exhaustion is something you will miss.

Most of my life the gentle rock of a saddle horse over rolling hills could refresh me so completely that at the end of a twenty-mile march I could swing down to the ground and feel wholly rested. Now no one uses horses anymore. They're mostly a novelty. It's fast trains, automobiles, even airplanes, and I ride a lifeless hickory rocking chair into every familiar night.

Beyond the wavy glass of this room's only window the lights of freighters move across black water to and from the ports of San Francisco, Oakland, Berkeley, and the communities to the south. But more and more it is battleships, troop convoys, vessels of destruction. Another great war is about to begin and I'm glad I will likely not have to live through it. I've seen enough of war. Seen enough of what one nation can do to another, enough of what is done in the name of love of land.

Some nights there are fifty ships, some nights only a few. The ships that are moving out to sea show no pattern in their peregrinations, and somehow that is soothing. Those are the ships that interest me the most. I watch them as I lean forward, forgetting to rock, holding my breath until their lights fade into the darkness.

I did not begin this life as an imaginative man, but now the feel of things is easy for me to remember. I go back to rocking and drift toward the men on the ships. I feel their fears and think about their wives and girlfriends left at home. I see the young men on the decks swaying with the tide, I smell the rot of seaweed, taste the salt spray in their faces, and feel the wind's caress in the hair of the hatless ones. I recall the feel of the earth pulling from under them. Though I've not spent much time at sea I have lived on the prairie, within an ocean of another kind. I can feel the wind pushing up waves of tall, lush grass, and I know that such grass is the bedrock of all that struggles to survive on those cruel and beautiful plains.

The hotel where I live and work as the house physician is almost always quiet by midnight, and sometimes I can hear, or think I can hear, the diesel engines clanking in the bottoms of the ships, the strain of movement against the iron hulls, the crackle of ship-to-shore radios. But when I close my eyes, more and more often mixed with those modern sounds are sounds that seem more natural to me, the pleasant monotony of a single deep drumbeat, the keening of distant, wild women, the crackling of sagebrush crushed under worn boots. I hear the squeak of saddle and harness, saber tips against spurs, the willing grunts of good horseflesh. When those sounds come to me I feel I'm moving in time as surely as the sailors are moving on the sea, and I prepare myself for the memories that are now my life.

There was a battle that the Sioux called "Where the Girl Saved Her Brother," and I have thought about it often in the more than sixty years since that June day in 1876. The story came to me through one of the wounded men in Captain Henry's battalion. They had been sent to engage the Sioux who had attacked our pickets as we bivouacked on Rosebud Creek. Henry had chased the Indians into rough country while we in the main force tried to organize. With every charge of his infantry the Sioux fell back. After the fact it was clear that they had been chasing Crazy Horse and he had been leading them into the same trap he had used, ten years before, to kill Capt. William Fetterman and the eighty troopers in his command. Only Henry's alertness kept the command from a similar disaster.

A soldier was brought into my field hospital with a head wound. Head wounds always bleed badly, so his face was covered with a copious quantity of drying blood even though the wound was not fatal. The soldier lay in the midst of twenty other men, most with wounds more severe than his. More casualties were coming in and among the hills above the creek, the battle popped and squealed like a grotesque child's game. This was my first battle and I was at first frozen with terror. But as the work increased I took to it, and soon I was able to push the fighting to the back of my mind. A tourniquet here, morphine there, stitches and dressings. Morphine, morphine, until the stock of drugs was strained and still the sinister popping in the hills sent more suffering men to my improvised clinic.

"The bastards'll overrun us," a dazed man shouted. "There's thousands of them. The bastards'll overrun us."

Others wailed and moaned with the delirious soldier, but the man with the head wound jabbered excitedly about a woman who had ridden into a blaze of carbine fire and pulled a trapped warrior onto the back of her horse. "We had the son-of-a-bitch and a God-damned woman saved him." The man was bitter. "We had the bastard. A God-damned woman." He spoke as if the whole hospital was listening.

At the Rosebud Fight General Crook was in command and had seemed completely in control, but he had failed to scout the ground ahead, and as a result we were surprised by Sioux warriors. I was forced to perform feats of which I had never dreamed I was capable. A recruit with an arm severed just above the elbow stared wildly ahead while I tied the arteries of the bloody stump. "My sweet Jesus," the man whispered. "The savage took my arm."

"Yes," I said, working as fast as I could to stem the bleeding. "Yes, but it came off cleanly."

"No," the man said. "He took my arm. With an ax. Took it, held it over his head, and rode off screaming like a devil."

Later, on a rickety travois dragged behind an

exhausted horse, bouncing over the ridge above the next drainage, that soldier died. By then, in charge of moving fifty-six wounded over the fifty rough miles back to safety, I was more depleted than I had thought possible. I blamed that fatigue for my relief at the soldier's passing. However now, at my advanced age, I am not sure that exhaustion played any part in my reaction to the soldier's death. Now it seems quite reasonable that death would be preferable to living with the vision of another human being stealing your arm, holding it high, and riding away in triumph. That I believe to be cruelty, absolute and complete.

But it has not all been cruelty, far from it. The best of my life happened long ago, when Fanny was still alive. She was my good wife, the only woman I ever truly loved, and she is ever on my mind. But I'm an old man and I have loved many things. That's what I want to talk about; how love of one kind or the other can shape a life.

The seminal event of a life should come when a person is old and can make whatever decision is necessary with knowledge and wisdom. That is not the way it was for me. The turning point of my existence came suddenly on the sixth of September in 1877. The loves that have comforted me since that day were only beginning to prove themselves, so I did not realize that the Great Plains of North America would never be the same.

2

I was born among the Great Lakes of the Upper Midwest, but it seems I was always drawn westward. In my early twenties, my desires to move and to do were insatiable. I was young and wiry, confident to the point of arrogance. I was a doctor even then, but working as a surveyor for the United States government. I was a colt, responding to a hunger I could not name.

One day, in the summer of 1873, I found what I had been hungry for on the plains northwest of Fort Lincoln in what was then the Dakota Territory. We'd been marching twenty-five miles a day under an unusually cloudy sky and made the burgeoning settlement of Bismarck just at dark. Our job was to survey the boundary between the United States and British America, and we had finished the section that is the northern boundary of the state of Minnesota and marched to our new base at Fort Lincoln. We would cross the Missouri River the next morning, and I was aware that when my feet touched the western bank, I would be entering a new land. Beyond the river lay the high plains of North America. Anticipation over what the grasslands might feel like gripped me like a schoolboy considering the satin hair of the girl sitting in front of him.

On the night of our arrival on the Missouri's eastern bank, we warmed and refreshed ourselves at a crude saloon. No one in our party knew much about the

Great Plains and I, for one, clambered for the stories told by a crusty trapper who insinuated himself into our band. He had just come in from the West and was filled with stories of what was in store for us. He promised that we would see buffalo, antelope, elk, grizzly bears. There would be mountains and cold-water rivers filled with trout. He talked of wind and grass, and skies that took up half the world. And he talked in hushed tones of Indians, the Lakota Sioux, who were not to be trifled with.

I was still a drinker then and the wee hours of the morning found me and the trapper alone at a table made of twisted cottonwood planks before a fire that had smoldered to nearly nothing. The saloonkeeper's boots protruded from the end of a bench. His body was hidden from our view by a second table, but his rhythmic breathing assured us that he was still with us at least in body. I was twenty-four years old, a doctor and scientist, but young and inexperienced. I was untested. I had not seen men die of frostbite or arrow wounds. I had not seen battle. I had not seen buffalo or wild Indians. But the old trapper, Gifford, had seen it all, and I sucked his knowledge like a butterfly sucks nectar.

His long hair was braided into plaits that hung halfway to his waist. One eye was bad and peered dully out into the oblique shadows of the saloon. Like all of us, he was scared to death of Indians. The Lakota were the worst, according to Gifford, and if our survey party saw any Indians on the plains west of the Missouri, they would be Lakota. Other tribes trespassed onto Lakota hunting grounds at the cost of their lives. "It's best not to be seen," he said. "Best to keep your ass low and out of sight." He looked me up and down and shook his head. "They get ahold of a scrawny young galoot like you and they'd make jerky of you. Knives," he said, "they love to use their knives."

Gifford seemed like an old man to me then—he must have been all of forty-five—and though I was sure his talk was hyperbole, stimulated by the whiskey I bought for him, my neck bulled in response to a chill that seemed to come from nowhere. "They aren't Christian, you know," he went on. "They don't bury their dead, but lay them out on platforms in the trees. Bones and human hides draped over limbs like the Devil himself flung them up there."

Anatomy had been one of my favorite subjects in medical school, and phrenology of particular interest. "Have you seen those burial sites?" I asked. "Have you seen skeletons and skulls?"

"Seen 'em. I torn one down not a week ago. I scattered bones to the four directions."

"And skulls?"

"A big one and little one wrapped in the same blanket."

It had to be a mother and infant. The thought of measuring those skulls, holding them in my hands and considering the way those people died, excited me. "Where?"

Gifford drew me a map on a brown paper sack with a bit of charcoal from the dead fire. The site was two days northwest of Bismarck, not fifteen miles off the survey crew's line of march. Gifford pushed the paper toward me as if it were smeared with something vile. "That's where it is," he said. "But you're a fool if you go there."

The next day we crossed the Missouri River on a crude ferry held against the current by a guyline and pulled from the western bank by a rope hitched to a team of four mules. All our horses and equipment crossed in one trip. We were squeezed onto the rough platform of logs, and muddy Missouri River water washed over our boots. The force of the river pushed the flatboat downstream, and the guyline strained under the pressure. At the end of the pull rope the mules settled down in their traces and lunged up the eroding bank in fits and starts. The ferry surged across, dipping her nose into the water as a weasel might nose the blood of its prey. At midstream I felt the world shift, as if we had crossed a fault line hidden by the great, roiling river. In another two minutes the ferry slid onto the shore of the Great Plains and lodged tight.

There was a great deal of activity as we unloaded the ferry and readied ourselves to climb out of the river bottom and on to Fort Lincoln. But eventually I got my foot into the stirrup and the horse between my legs. He surged up the bank that the mules had scaled and suddenly I was there—on the Great Plains of America's continent. The world opened wider than I had ever known it and instantly a delicious tension came over me. The feeling was as palpable as the taste of chokecherries or the smell of wood smoke. It seemed to settle on me from the giant sky and I knew from the beginning that it had something to do with distance, the endless grass, and the sweep of eternal wind.

That night, just at sundown, I walked out onto the prairie to smoke a cigar. As the sun slipped below the clouds on the western horizon their undersides were lit in a way that was peculiar to me. I had noticed sunsets before, of course, but for the first time it dawned on me that it was the sun reflecting from the bottoms of the clouds that created the pinks and lavenders. The colors radiated upward and over my head to the opposite horizon. I felt diminutive and was dumbfounded to discover such a simple truth. How could I not have known how a sunset worked? Then it occurred to me that this was the first time that I had viewed a sunset unobstructed. To that instant I had watched my sunsets from the brushy hills and narrow valleys of the Midwest. I understood then that I was indeed in a different world, and that I was now blessed with access to the entire sky.

3

For three days we fussed with details at Fort Lincoln, and all I could think of was getting back on that horse and moving under that immense sky. I found myself staring at the sky over the walls of the fort, glancing out the gates when I found them open, questioning people who had been on the plains through the seasons. This new land seemed as exotic as the moon, clearly a land of movement, and I wanted to be part of it.

When we were finally back in the field we rode with a detachment of soldiers, for our protection, northwest for two days. I kept Gifford's map in my saddlebag and, when our column made camp at the confluence of the Knife River's two branches, I knew that we were as close to Gifford's burial site as we would get. I should have asked the lieutenant in charge of our escort for permission to investigate the burial ground, but I was sure he would refuse. Instead, I determined to fall behind the march the next morning and strike out for the site on my own. I thought it might take me a couple of hours to reach it; I could catch the column again by nightfall.

The insolence of a young man trained in the sciences can be thoroughly exasperating. In later years I found myself in charge of such men and, let me tell you, they complicate the world at large. Now I cringe to think of the chance I took that morning and the danger I brought to the column. But then I was selfish and overjoyed to get out into that swaying grass by myself.

The horse under me was a good one and I let him have his head as we moved along the ridge that overlooked the North Branch of the Knife. It's hard to imagine what it was like for my horse, a forest animal from Wisconsin, to move through miles of unsullied grass that brushed his belly with every step. To a horse the Great Plains must seem an endless, luscious banquet, a land of equine dreams that touches his two dearest desires: his need to eat sweet, fresh grass and his passion for unfettered movement. The horse and I reveled in our freedom and, as the morning wore on, forgot our ties to the column that was moving westward while we moved northeast. Neither my mount nor I considered the danger we might be in.

Gifford's map was inaccurate in one critical area: Its scale was grossly condensed. It was my first encounter with a white man's perception of the plains. Later I realized that distance was nearly always underestimated. Before I reached the burial site the sun was almost directly overhead and beat down with a harshness that was startling after the amenity of the morning. I passed a cool pool of the North Knife formed where an oxbow cut deep into the riparian zone. The pool was barely visible through the cottonwood and willow of the riverbank, and it looked inviting to a white-skinned Irishman sizzling under an unfamiliar sun. But Gifford's burial site was just over the hill and I pushed on, driven by a curiosity that has always been at once a blessing and a curse.

On the small scale Gifford's map was precise. The pair of cottonwoods that had held the scaffold were just as he described them: lonely and growing, oddly, on high ground where you would not expect enough moisture to sustain such trees. The desecration of the site was also as Gifford had described it. The bodies had been torn from the tree limbs, and the blankets and bones scattered. I recognized the femur of an infant and saw that it had been chewed by coyotes or wolves that had beaten me to that wind-washed knoll. Even in the simmering heat a chill flushed through me, and I glanced around to find only waving grass and persistent wind. I am not usually a believer in the supernatural, but I swear the spirits of the dead were there. The air felt thick as I rummaged through the bones in search of the skulls that I knew would be of great interest, not only to me but to the curators of the National Museum as well. I suddenly considered what might happen to me if I were discovered by the contemporary relatives of the corpses I was pawing through; in my eagerness, I pushed on.

At the time I felt very lucky that the skulls of the mother and her child had not been disturbed by scavengers, as some of the other bones had been. When I'd left my comrades that morning I had had the forethought to bring along a burlap sack for transporting the skulls. As I picked them up to drop them in now, I inspected them. They were not fresh. The skin and hair that clung to them was dried hard as a drumhead.

Ordinarily I would have taken more time with my inquiry. I had instruments in my saddlebag for recording the structural dimensions and testing the teeth, but suddenly I wanted to get away from that place. Superstition gnawed at my consciousness as I cinched the sack tight with a length of leather and tied it to my saddle horn. I swung up onto the horse, determined to leave all absurd mysticism there among the remaining bones, and rode back down the hill to pick up the Knife River for my return to the column.

When I reached the river I was already behind my projected schedule: I would be lucky to catch the column by the time they put their cook fires out for the night. Yet I still did not feel pressed for time. Once I had gotten away from the burial site the hot prairie won me over again, and my mood returned to the levity of the morning. The sun pressed hard and sweat rolled down across my face and abdomen. The earth radiated heat up at me and the good scent of sweet horse filled my nostrils.

The pool in the bend of the Knife attracted me even more than it had the first time I'd passed it. Silvery water shimmered through the trees and, like a teenager, I was unable to resist. The reins did not have to touch the horse's neck before he turned toward the coolness among the trees. We wound our way silently through the willow to the river's edge, and I slid off as he lowered his head to drink.

The sound of a horse drinking has always comforted me. There is no hint of a dog's slurping; it is more a mechanical gulping noise, efficient and uniform. The water pulses up the throat as neatly as blood through arteries. As I stripped off my clothes I watched the water of the Knife being taken into my mount and marveled how that liquid, mixed with nothing but the grass we rode through, could fuel him indefinitely.

When the horse looked up his head jerked back, and he snorted and pawed the water. I had to laugh, assuming that the whiteness of my naked body must have startled him. He had not seen anything so skinny since the scarecrow on the farm where he was raised, nothing so white since last winter's snow. There is little more homely than a naked Irishman, and nothing more susceptible to sunburn. I wasted no time slipping into the Knife's welcoming water, but the horse refused to be calmed. His ears pointed straight up and I had to smile. "It's okay, boy. I'm covered up." I ducked under the refreshing water and pushed out toward the center of the pool. Like an otter I sliced to the deepest part of the river then dove vertically. I took a childish glee at flashing my iridescent bottom to the heavens.

I resurfaced thirty feet from the bank. I was smiling and flung my head to push my hair back and out of my eyes. When I was able to focus again, I saw that my horse's ears were still upright. And as I watched a second horse, riderless and decorated with a single feather braided in its mane, trotted to his side. They squealed a greeting to each other just before I dove and, terrified, began swimming underwater toward the cover of the cattails that grew near the bank.

Instinctively I knew that my only chance was to conceal myself in the cattails until I could slip out of the water and make my way either on foot or, with luck, on horseback up and out of that river bottom. My lungs were bursting as I snaked into the cattails but I did not let myself pop my head out and gasp for air. As quietly as possible I pushed up through the surface tension only as far as my nostrils and took a long slow breath through my nose. The green, growing, meaty leaves of the cattails with their accompanying bottle-brush spikes hid me well, and I resolved to remain hidden until I was sure that no one would see me move from the water to my horse. I let my chin come out into the air and became aware of my own breathing. I tried to quiet myself and slowly pivoted to take in as much of the riverbank as possible without giving away my position.

I expected to find a war party of Sioux stopped at this shady place to escape the midday sun. But there was nothing on the bank to my left. I swiveled farther and studied the two horses. They had made friends and stood tail to nose, snoozing and brushing away the other's flies with their tails. Neither showed any sign there were humans about. For an instant I imagined the horse was a stray, the nearest Sioux miles away. When I swiveled to my right, I found that the nearest Sioux was much closer.

At first he was indistinguishable from the cattails, and though he was only a few feet away I had to squint to be sure of what I was seeing. Even slick-wet his hair was much lighter than I had anticipated. His eyes, too, were not the coal black I had been taught to expect. He was a young man, a few years older than I, and he crouched silently in the water as I did, hoping that I had not seen him. Our eyes locked and for a long sickening second I imagined he would spring at me with his knife drawn. The feeling sank into my stomach and I thought I might vomit. Then I realized that he could no more draw a knife than I could. We were both naked, attracted to this prairie oasis for exactly the same reasons and accepting its coolness in the same way.

It is hard to say how long we remained frozen in that terrified stare, but at some point a red-winged blackbird came and claimed his territory by perching on the cattail not a foot above my head. I couldn't see him but knew he was a male by his loud *check, check, tee-err.* I can't believe he had any idea that two humans were contemplating combat in the lower reaches of his domain but, if he did, his response was appropriate. He gave another *check, check* and lifted his tail. I, of course, couldn't see what was happening, although my Sioux counterpart did and a small, involuntary smile spoiled his sinister glare just as I felt the fecal matter hit my forehead. As involuntary as his smirk, my hand came up and splashed the whitewash away. The blackbird bolted for the sky with a squawk and my Indian friend burst into a full-fledged grin. I noticed a small stone tied with a thong behind his ear as bubbles irrupted where his lips tried to hide in the water. In an instant we were both laughing loud enough to frighten the horses into a few nervous snorts.

At this point the Sioux stood up and pointed at me.

"Zintkala tunkhee," he said with a laugh. I knew no Lakota then and this man knew no English, but I understood his meaning perfectly. I pointed back at him.

"Birdshit, yourself," I said.

He laughed again and dove long and lean out toward the center of the pool. Though his rear was not nearly as white as mine, I was surprised to see that it was not the golden brown of his body. He wore a second stone tied under his left arm but nothing else. He was smaller than I and, though sinewy, not nearly so bony. There was no pinched chest or knobby elbows. He was sleek and hard, lithe and perfectly formed and for an instant I was embarrassed to let my body arch into the air where it could be seen. But the center of the pool invited me, and so I sailed first through the air and then through the water to where the Indian treaded water.

We swam around each other, not in a confrontational way; more as if we were members of a water ballet who were unaware that they were not alone. We stayed in motion yet at the same time we lounged: now on our sides taking long luxurious strokes, now on our backs spouting water like freshwater leviathans. Eventually we made our way to shore and sat in the shallows listening to the sounds of the river-bank. The sun was hot and while my face and hands were long since browned by exposure, I felt my shoulders beginning to burn. I needed shade, but I was too self-conscious to stand up and reveal myself to the

Indian. I thought perhaps we had regressed back into another standoff until, when an unfamiliar *ca-ca-ca* issued from the underbrush, the Indian stood without hesitation and slipped from the water as easily as a mink.

His entire body was exposed to me then and I tried not to stare. Every muscle in his legs and abdomen was defined and rippled as he snuck up the bank toward the *ca-ca-ca* that continued to purr in the thicket. His body was hairless—none on his chest, arms, or legs. His uncircumcised penis, shriveled from the cool water, did not reside in a nest of hair but protruded from a bald and shining pubic area. He picked up a few river pebbles as he moved into the undergrowth, and his ease with his nakedness gave me heart. When I came out of the water to follow him, I tried not to think of the nest of wiry orange hair that cursed my loins.

We crept through the bushes with the Indian occasionally holding up his hand to stop me while we waited for another *ca-ca-ca.* My guide stared hard in front of us before each step. Finally, at the edge of the riparian zone, just where the bluestem began, I saw his eyes narrow and, following them, spotted a family of sharp-tailed grouse in the grass just as the first stone neatly took off the first head. The second stone missed, but the third hit another bird hard enough to break its wing. At that point the remaining grouse took to the air. They left behind the dead bird and a cripple that was caught and dispatched in an instant. My

Indian was overjoyed with his conquest, and I must say that I too was excited. We danced around bare to the world and held the grouse high.

I clapped the Indian on the back. "Well done! Well done!"

"Lila oyul wa'ste," he said and licked his lips. He rubbed his belly and laughed.

I pulled on my coarse wool uniform and the Indian slid into his buckskins as a green ash fire burned down to coals. Then we ate the birds, roasted over red embers, with all the clean, cool water we could drink. My first communion in my adopted land.

4

At the back of my mind I knew the lieutenant in charge of our military escort must have detected my absence by now and could easily be frantic. But still it was difficult to pull myself away from the little camp where the Indian and I lay digesting our meal. We could not speak, but we managed to communicate all that was important. A cloud bank was developing in the west and the air had already begun to cool.

When I rose and went to my horse the Indian rose, too. He stood behind me as I tightened the cinch and slipped the bit back into the horse's mouth. I turned and offered my hand but he did not seem to know what the gesture meant. I had to reach out and take his hand from his side and shake it. That made him smile and I smiled back before turning, guiding my stirrup to my left boot, and swinging up onto the horse. The Indian had moved alongside the horse and stood looking up at me. To my horror his hand rested on the burlap sack containing the skulls. Just then a cold wind rattled the cottonwood leaves and swept down on us. I wanted to push his hand away; instead I reined the horse away roughly. The Indian didn't take it as rudeness. He laughed and slapped the horse's rump as we lunged from the trees and up the riverbank.

When I reached the tableland at the top of the bank, I was struck by another blast of cold air. The temperature had dropped twenty degrees since our midday dip and, in the west, huge billowing thunderheads had already formed. The day was turning sour before my eyes, but I pointed my horse southward of the building clouds and started off in pursuit of my survey crew.

Ten minutes later the rain began. At first a few huge cold drops, then wind and more rain. The sky was blue behind me but purple above. The west was black and mushrooming with a hint of green at the edges, where the clouds seemed to sheer off in ribbons and go with the wind. I pulled my hat low and leaned into the gusts as they drove volleys of rain over the yielding grass. Everything was wet: the saddle, the horse, the burlap sack holding the skulls. Before we had gone a mile I was as wet as I had been swimming with the Indian. Only now I was cold, shivering even before the hail began.

In a few hours the prairie had turned from an Eden to a wind-lashed, freezing hell. I was blinded by the fury of the storm. The hailstones grew larger and harder as the temperature continued to drop. The horse squealed as the hail hit him, and I knew that we needed cover quickly. The shelter of the river was too far behind, however, and there were no other trees in sight. In fact I wasn't sure where I was until the land to my right began to climb in a familiar way. The hill that led to the burial ground rose to the north. We needed to go southwest but the scaffold trees were only a quarter mile away and, though it was the wrong direction, it seemed our only chance. I reined the horse right, touched him with the spurs, and, as he sprang into a lope, felt the sack of skulls beat twice against my thigh.

The hail was building up in windrows and my horse slipped on his way to the top of the hill. We were both bruised and trembling from the cold as we found the partial shelter of the cottonwoods. Most of the leaves and some of the branches had already been beaten away, and we leaned miserably against the gnarled trunk as I prayed for the storm to stop.

My prayers were impotent. The wind increased and the hail came at me from all directions. There was thunder and sizzling lightning. The cottonwoods would give me no shelter, so I slid down and pressed against the poor horse. As I did so my face smacked up against the skulls and I felt a surge of superstition. I jumped away from the skulls but the hail drove me back. My face smashed hard between the infant and its mother and finally I could stand it no longer. I tore the sack open and, taking a skull in either hand, climbed the side of the horse until I stood on the saddle with the wind and hail lashing me. I was able to reach the first crotch in the cottonwood, and I wedged the skulls there like the eggs of a ghastly bird.

Now, I don't expect you to believe this—God knows I did not believe it was anything but coincidence for years—but minutes after I rid myself of those skulls the wind began to subside. The hail turned back to rain and finally tapered off to nothing. By the time my horse and I had hobbled down that slippery hill, the sun was beginning to show in the west and the temperature was again on the rise. It was an initiation of sorts, to a climate that renders you powerless, punishes you at will, yet nourishes you by supplying what you need in doses small enough to make you grateful.

5

Four years later, on the morning of September 6, 1877, I was twenty-eight years old. Much had changed since I first saw the Great Plains. I had lived through the Great Sioux War. I had ridden with General Crook on his ill-fated Starvation March. I had seen the dark underbelly of the grasslands. Yet in many ways I was still a boy and it's possible that the powerful emotion that came over me when I stepped out into the vast prairie on that fateful morning was not a result of my inexperience but a naïveté inherited from my parents. I am a McGillycuddy, from the city of Detroit. Because I was born on Valentine's Day in 1849, they chose to name me Valentine. The name has been hard to deal with. It is sure to elicit cockeyed looks from hotel clerks and ticket agents, but even harder to deal with is the legacy of a Protestant Irish upbringing: We are all great sufferers, guilty from birth, and hold impossible expectations of ourselves. We are also fools for beauty. When I think of the Great Plains that surrounded me that September day, my throat still wants to choke down and my eyes want to close gently enough to allow me to feel one eyelid touch the other.

Sunsets and music have always threatened to make me cry. Sometimes I laugh too easily, and my temper still needs to be watched at all times. If self-control had not been emphasized by my Presbyterian parents I might have been a fighter. Though I have always been tall, thin, and lacking in brute power, a day has seldom passed that I haven't thought of punching someone in the nose. I still swear too much and on mornings like the one I'm remembering, I could feel the roll of whiskey in my mouth. It had been three years since I had had my last drink, but the longing for the sting of spirits at the edge of my tongue had never left me.

Contract surgeons like myself were private doctors, but we wore government-issued trousers, white shirts, and officers' coats. In fact there was very little difference between us and regular army. Standing on the porch of the first rough house in a row of eight reserved for officers, I suppose I looked just like any

Ennis Public Library
501 W. Ennis Ave.

lieutenant at six-thirty in the morning. My suspenders hung at my sides; my collar was still unbuttoned. Reveille had sounded only a few minutes before, and soldiers were beginning to move from the barracks at either end of the parade ground. It was Camp Robinson, Nebraska, a cluster of crude buildings between distant ridges and sandstone buttes. To the south cedar trees ran up the drainages of the bluffs and across their tops. The effect of the trees was to frame the rock outcroppings in dark, luxuriant green and to make Camp Robinson, an outpost of civilization, seem puny and insignificant.

Our quarters were really little more than a log cabin. The floors were hard-packed earth, and the glass in the two windows was cloudy and filled with imperfections, but the walls were plastered and the building was good enough to keep the rain and wind out. I felt lucky to have it. If not for General Crook taking a special interest I would have been billeted across the parade ground with the junior officers, and there would have been no possibility of bringing my new bride to the post. It had all come together, and now that Fanny was there I couldn't wish for anything more.

Fanny had rubbed the earthen floor until it shone like polished hardwood. She had hung curtains and painted the door and window frames. Our cabin was very different than the palatial childhood home I lured her away from, but she had made it as comfortable as was possible with the limited resources available.

There were a dozen other officers' wives at Camp Robinson, and Fanny had immediately found a place in the tiny society that was struggling for survival. She rode horses almost daily with some of the other wives. She was in great demand at all post parties, played a hundred different card games, had helped form a literary club, volunteered at the hospital, and was a favorite among my superiors. Still, at the back of my mind was the question of how long she could remain happy on those plains. Against her parents' wishes she had married a military contract surgeon and, though she had never said it, I wondered if she looked at this time at Camp Robinson as a temporary lark. How could she not expect that we were only deferring our life in a medical center like Detroit, Washington, or Chicago, where culture was healthy and strong?

But I wasn't thinking of my new marriage on that morning. There was a tension in the cool, dry air; I remember the feel of it easing into my lungs. The quarters of the commanding officer, Col. L. P. Bradley, stood not twenty feet to the west. The shadow of our cabin sliced across the whitewashed wall of the colonel's larger house. The contrast of brightness announced the coming of the sun, and I turned to watch the molten disk push above the cedar-laced ridge a mile to the east. The night had been chilly—near freezing—but this sun promised that the day would again be warm and dry. More enlisted men were wandering from the barracks on the east and west sides of the parade ground. A sentry walked back and forth in front of each barracks and, across the parade ground, another marched between the adjutant's office and the guardhouse. Far to the south horses milled inside a huge corral and an officer swung up onto a fine gray that sidestepped under his weight, tossing its head.

The familiar crew of Sioux and Cheyenne camp loafers was just waking up. There were a few tattered tepees and other shelters around the edge of the camp, and several of the most notorious of that sorry bunch were simply wrapped in blankets on the ground. One small fire trailed a thread of smoke straight into the still air. It was tended by an old woman I had seen several times at the hospital. She was a drinker and suffered from syphilis. Among the idlers she was not unusual. Her spirit was gone, her self-esteem nonexistent. During my first examination I had found long, jagged scars on the woman's thighs. They were self-inflicted and signified that the woman had once had a husband who died in battle. The missing digits on her hands meant she had lost children, too. The woman had refused to speak, so there was no way to know if her losses had occurred in an action in which I had played a part.

In addition to the usual riffraff hanging around the camp there was a small group of Indians at the northeast corner of the parade ground. There were four of them, all with horses. Two remained mounted and watched the activity of the camp with aloofness. These were not men looking for handouts or whiskey.

They were princely fellows, warriors of the northern bands who had come in earlier in the summer. Their dress was not as elegant as it had been in battle. Now the moccasins were worn, the leather faded and the quillwork frayed. The men were well worn, too. They had earned the respect of both the white soldiers and the reservation Indians. They stood on the periphery of the camp, watching, no doubt feeling some of the same sensations that ran through my blood like electricity.

I could hear the sizzle of pork from the iron skillet just inside the cabin. Fanny was a hard worker and rose every morning with me though she would not have had to. She took great pride in caring for our little home and, I suppose, for me. Though I'd been fending for myself for years, I enjoyed the attention.

There was no time to walk to the hospital to check on my patients before breakfast, but I did have a few minutes to enjoy the morning. I stepped off the porch and felt in my breast pocket for a cigar. There was one left but no match. I tasted the cigar with my tongue and was reminded again of whiskey. It was impossible not to wonder for the millionth time if I would ever stop missing the taste and feel of it.

Another officer stepped from his quarters two doors down. It was Lt. Philo Clark. He was handsome and bright, with sharp eyes and wavy brown hair. He was of average height, but quite fit, and walked with a self-assured gait. A white Stetson was his trademark. The Indian scouts, for whom Clark was the commanding officer, called him White Hat. He was widely regarded as the most promising young officer in the army, clearly bound for high commands, and something of a prodigy when it came to Indians. He could speak several of the plains Indian languages and use their sign language as well as the Indians themselves. My own modest ability to communicate with the Sioux and Cheyenne was partially due to many nights sitting around a campfire with Philo. As a result of these talents, and many others, he had earned a special place on General Crook's staff despite his youth. He reported directly to the general and was privy to high-level discussions and decisions that belied his rank.

Philo and I shared the same constitution, and the crisp morning air was something we both seemed to need. In addition, we were campaign mates and got along well. When he looked my way, I took the unlit cigar from my mouth and held it up. He was just reaching for one of his own and waved me over.

"Doctor," Philo said, "you seem like a man in need of some fire."

"I am, sir," I said. "But please don't think me Cro-Magnon."

He struck the match on the porch rail of his house and held it up. "Hardly," he said. "The volume of your brain chamber makes that highly unlikely."

I rolled the cigar in the flame and pulled slowly until the tobacco flared. "Too much volume or too little?"

Philo smiled and applied the match to his own cigar. Once it was lit we leaned back against the porch and looked out over the parade ground to where the group of infantrymen had finally formed up and a sergeant, with a head so large that it stood out even at the distance of a hundred yards, paced in front of them. We usually had no trouble finding subjects of conversation. We'd served together under Crook on the Yellowstone Campaign and shared the sort of danger and hardship that made conversation between men easy. On this morning, however, after our initial banter, nothing more came to either of us. The preceding two days had been trying for Philo. He was central to the drama that had been playing itself out for months—no, playing itself out for generations.

The difficulty centered around the war chief Crazy Horse who, along with his band of over eleven hundred people and nearly twenty-five hundred horses, had come into the Red Cloud Agency four months before. They were the last of the Sioux to surrender, and hope had been high that the Sioux War was finally completely over. Philo had been the one to accept Crazy Horse's surrender and when they came in, I had ridden out to treat the young chief's ailing wife, Black Shawl. After the massacre of Custer, Crazy Horse's reputation had blossomed, as had Custer's. At the time of his surrender Crazy Horse was perhaps the most feared and hated of all the Sioux. We were anxious to get a look at him.

We met the tattered Indian column seven miles north of Camp Robinson, and it was clear that they had suffered unimaginable hardship through two years of war and an exceptionally hard winter with little food or shelter. The faces of the women and children were gaunt from hunger. The warriors stood tall on their thin horses and I scanned their faces, trying to guess which one was Crazy Horse. We all expected him to move forward, perhaps rush forward at a gallop as a show of power. But no Indian moved. I looked hard at those defeated warriors and saw the ghostlike signs of malnutrition, the missing limbs from battle and frostbite. They had dressed for the occasion in what was left of their finest: leather shirts and leggings, beads, feathers, paint on sunken cheeks, an occasional headdress of eagle feathers that hung to the ground. It was from the ranks of the headdressed Indians that we expected Crazy Horse to come. Still no one moved. I let my eyes rove over the warriors again and was shocked to find a face that was familiar. The light eyes stared back at me as if he, too, was trying to recall where he had seen my face. Philo sat his horse beside me and I felt him growing uneasy at not knowing whom he was to accept the surrender from. He called for Red Cloud, a cousin of Crazy Horse, to identify the leader. I could not take my eyes off the man who looked so familiar. He was one of the plainer warriors, smaller than most, no headdress or flashy streaks of paint, and he looked at me with the same recognition with which I looked at him.

It was not until Philo and Red Cloud rode forward that I realized that I had indeed seen the warrior before, several years before the war, on the banks of the North Branch of the Knife River. He had aged; now he was probably in his middle thirties, but he looked older. He wore a simple buckskin shirt and a single eagle feather in his hair. His clothes and pony carried no decoration, a sure sign of his poverty within the tribe, and every soldier in the column was stunned when Red Cloud led Philo to this simple man. There were dozens of warriors who better fit the image in most of our minds, but this man, the one I had shared a swimming hole with four years before, was the war chief, Crazy Horse.

Initially, he seemed unimposing. Yet he had a presence that drew all eyes to him. He looked straight at me that day and our gazes lingered; neither of us let on that we had once met. With recognition of Crazy Horse came the realization that I had misunderstood the nature of the man's power. It was not in his sinewy arms and legs but in his force of character, exhibited in the way he moved. He dismounted in one motion and seemingly without effort, covered the distance between the armies that had opposed each other for years of bitter conflict and offered Philo his left hand. "Friend," he said in simple, soft-spoken Lakota, "I shake with this hand because my heart is on this side; I want this peace to last forever."

There was a quiet and unique dignity to the man. His face lacked the typical high cheekbones of the Sioux. It was melancholy, and there was in it a humble resignation to fate. But something in the pale eyes made it clear that this surrender was for his starving people and, if there had been only himself to consider, Crazy Horse would have fought on forever.

Philo had brought ten wagons of rations and a hundred head of cattle to feed the surrendering column, and in typical Indian fashion the men refused to eat until the women and children were fed. A warrior died later that night but not from malnutrition. He died from gorging himself when he finally permitted himself to eat. I would have liked to open the man's abdomen to relieve the pressure that finally killed him. Though I had seen it done once in a hospital back east, operations like that were unheard of on the plains then and my superior, Doctor Munn, flatly forbade it.

When the procession finally came into Camp Robinson, thousands of Indians from the nearby Red Cloud Agency, who had given up long before, turned out to hail Crazy Horse. Although the ponies and guns had been taken away, there was nothing we could do about those burning eyes of Crazy Horse. The procession strung out for two miles and, when the vanguard neared the crowd that lined the way, the defeated warriors began to chant the most mournful song I have ever heard. The melody touched my heart. When the warrior's voices were joined, first by the women and children of Crazy Horse, then the agency Indians who had turned out to honor them, I was forced to bite my cheek to keep it from trembling. I was afraid to let my eyes shift from straight ahead, so I was never sure which of the officers who rode alongside me muttered, "By God, this is no surrender. It's a bloody triumphal march."

6

Now, summer was turning to fall; Philo and I leaned against the porch without speaking for some time. I'm sure we were both thinking about our promises made that day to Crazy Horse. I looked at his face but his features were stony and blank. The ability to reveal nothing in his expression was one of the skills that made Lt. Philo Clark so good at the politics of military life. It gave him an advantage when commanding the Indian scouts and ensured that he had a very bright future. But destiny is heedless of talent. Philo went on to write a marvelous study of Indian sign language. He was on a rapid promotional path but never became a general as we had all thought he would. Instead, he died of some obscure condition of the brain at the age of thirty-nine. There may well be some odd irony in the fact that I've outlived him by nearly fifty years.

Mobilizing one group of Indians against another was one of General Crook's most successful tactics, and so it was one of Philo's main jobs. It was easy to encourage old rivalries and blood feuds among the indigenous peoples, but actually directing the ancient animosities and jealousies was another matter. It was a sign of great confidence that Crook had put Philo in charge of so important a tactical command. Philo was also General Crook's aide-de-camp, so highly trusted that when he'd left Camp Robinson two days earlier, Crook had left him in charge of arresting Crazy Horse.

There were no official charges against Crazy Horse—which would have been needed to arrest a white man—just a vague accusation that his presence was unsettling the reservation Indians.

I let my eyes rest on my friend's face. Philo felt the pressure and turned with a sad smile. "Something is going to happen today," he said. "He's too inflammatory. Half the reservation loves him and half hates him. They all envy him." Philo narrowed his eyes. "I bumbled the arrest yesterday. He did just what Jesse Lee told me not to let him do. He ran for the Spotted Tail Agency and Lee arrested him last night. A rider came in with the news early this morning."

"Christ almighty," I said.

Lieutenant Lee was regular army but was also the agent at the Spotted Tail Agency thirty miles to the northeast. He and his wife, Lucy, were friends of Fanny and mine. Lee, too, was a confident man, and I knew he would never let Philo forget that his plan to arrest Crazy Horse had failed. It made sense that Crazy Horse would flee to the Spotted Tail Agency, because old Chief Spotted Tail was his uncle by marriage. Jesse no doubt had explained all this to Philo, and now he'd use it to rub salt in the wound of his failure.

Philo puffed on his cigar and looked out over the parade ground. A few more northern Indians had appeared from nowhere. They sat their ponies lackadaisically but we knew that the posture of the men was more a sign of complete ease on their horses than of sloppiness. They were clearly warriors who had suffered with Crazy Horse during that terrible winter in the north. "I'd already made one mistake," Philo said. "I didn't want to make another."

He was referring to the advice he'd given Crook. Since Crazy Horse's surrender in the spring there had been rumors of him going back on the warpath. I was sure these rumors were mostly the dreams of a defeated people. There was also great jealousy of Crazy Horse's popularity by Red Cloud's people, the result of which was a reservation-wide unrest. But when another rumor spread that Crazy Horse intended to kill General Crook, Philo had advised Crook to stay away from Crazy Horse's camp. Crook gave the order for Crazy Horse to be arrested. "His presence made the situation too volatile," Philo said.

"You couldn't take the chance," I said, though in my heart I knew Crazy Horse had never plotted to kill Crook.

"With all the summer talk about him breaking away to go buffalo hunting, to make war on the Crows, to join Sitting Bull in Canada—that threat to kill the general, real or not, sealed his fate."

"Is Jesse bringing him here?"

"Yes. They're probably getting ready to leave now."

Philo concentrated on the far side of the parade ground. He watched a group of five warriors as they loped in from the east. A quarter mile out they picked up speed and when they reached the parade ground, they circled at a run. The warriors whooped and, because they had been disarmed when they surrendered, waved sticks in the air. These were more of the old hostile warriors, and several agency Indians chided them as they made two more rounds of the parade ground. A few of Philo's scouts, who were well armed, walked into the open and defied the riders. "They sense it," Philo said.

I now saw the deep strain on his face, though perhaps it was only visible to a friend. "You've done a good job, Philo."

"It's a difficult situation." He spoke as much to himself as to me. "I know you agree that the man is due our respect. He's remarkably brave. Trouble is, he's a pillar of strength for good or evil."

The truth of what Philo said affected me then and affects me more now. I looked out past the growing activity of the parade ground to the prairie beyond and wondered how in the world I'd arrived at that place and at that time. I'd done my medical training at the Marine Hospital in Detroit. I did well and, as a point of fact, was one of the medical school's youngest lecturers. By a trick of fate, at the age of twenty-one I found myself the surgeon on a crew of engineers surveying the Great Lakes. The feeling that engulfed me in our open boat on those giant, frigid ponds has never left me. The vastness surrounding the boat and the sense of a great unknown under it all was profound but tame compared to knowing that, beyond the pine-fringed rimrock that sheltered and dwarfed Camp Robinson, there was wild wind driving waves of grass to the horizons. I could feel myself and all the camp floating, drifting without an anchor on that endless sea.

"Doctor?" It was Fanny. She always called me Doctor. "And Lieutenant Clark. What a lovely morning." She curtsied and Philo tipped his white hat. "Your breakfast is ready," she said to me. "Your egg is nearly done."

She was lovely. Her charm distracted me from my darkening thoughts. After she'd nodded to Philo her eyes turned onto me, and the watery depth of them sent a tremor of passion through my body. It seems silly now but that wave of desire unnerved me. I was ignorant enough to worry that her power to excite me might be purposeful. Back then I wanted to believe that she was a demure, simple young lady. Now I thank God that she was not. Now I wish I'd given in to the urge, put myself between her and Philo, and run a clandestine hand up under her dress.

She smiled as if she were reading the passion in my mind and turned back toward the cabin. "Good day," Philo said.

"It certainly is," Fanny said. She took another look at the golden bluffs before she walked back to our cabin, and the way her eyes refocused on the distance ignited me again.

I took a moment to gather myself and asked, "Would you care to join us, Philo?" I put my cigar out on the side of my black boot heel, touched the burnt end to be sure it was out, and slid it back into my shirt pocket.

"No," Philo said. "I think I'll wander over to the adjutant's office and see if there's any word from Lee. But thank you." He was preoccupied and pushed away from the porch with both hands behind his back. "Come to midday mess with us, Mac. About twelve-thirty. There should be more news by then."

"I shall," I said.

Philo straightened his hat. "They may have left by now," he said without looking at me. He was watching two more warriors riding straight and slow from the south. It was the opposite direction from the Spotted Tail Agency, yet somehow they had gotten word that Crazy Horse would be coming in under arrest. They wanted to be there when it happened.

Philo seemed unable to move. He watched the Indians and squinted his eyes in thought. "They'll be arriving before long," I said. "Jesse will see to it that it comes off without a hitch." I reached out to assure Philo with a touch on the arm. "Things will work out for the best," I said. "They always do."

Then Philo turned and smiled. "You've got an extraordinary attitude, Mac. I wish I shared it with you." He nodded and started off across the parade ground toward the adjutant's office. A man in a dream.

Philo was understandably distracted. His good name and career were riding on the outcome of Crazy Horse's arrest. It seemed ill advised to me even then because I, no doubt more than any other white man, knew Crazy Horse's mind. The day after his surrender I rode out to his camp—a mile and a half from the fort—with my assistant, Johnny Provost, who was half Sioux and spoke fluent Lakota.

The Lakota women had erected the camp during the night, and by the time Johnny and I arrived it was already in decent order. We attracted a great deal of attention as we passed among the tepees. The warriors stood and stared, some defiant and some with sad smiles on their faces. The women hid from us and the children chattered like nervous squirrels, but they followed in the wake of our horses. We were quite a procession, and by the time we reached Crazy Horse's tepee the whole camp was alerted to our presence. Crazy Horse came out to meet us. Johnny dutifully introduced me to the chief as Doctor McGillycuddy, the medicine man. Crazy Horse extended his hand and I smiled, recalling his first response to my own outstretched hand years ago, when he had not known what to make of the gesture. He rolled the unfamiliar word around in his mouth. "Magillicutti."

I took the hand and shook it. "Crazy Horse."

He nodded and I knew that he remembered our first meeting. There was a slight smile but then he shook his head. *"Mita wicu ki."*

"He wants you to look at his wife," Johnny said.

Crazy Horse's hand was still in mine and our eyes were still locked. I took the opportunity to look at him closely. The smooth youthfulness of his skin had given way to wrinkles around the eyes, but there remained a quiet strength that was undeniable. "Of course," I said. I moved ahead and into the tepee.

The tepee was cold. They had not bothered to build a fire even though the nighttime temperatures were still dipping toward freezing. Black Shawl sat on a buffalo robe lacing a moccasin. When she saw me, she jumped to her feet. Treating a Sioux was often difficult; because they feared white men, they did not want to seem vulnerable or weak.

I reached out and touched her forehead in search of an elevated temperature. She did not shy from my hand. I found her to be near normal. I took her hand and led her past Crazy Horse and Johnny out into the light of day. I looked into her eyes and put my ear against her chest. There was a great deal of congestion—most likely consumption, a condition not uncommon among the Lakota.

"Johnny," I said. "Fetch my bag." I looked again into Black Shawl's eyes, trying to see if she was suffering more than she let on. "Let's give her sulfate and add some quinine. She might also have a touch of malaria."

It took a minute for someone to bring water, but Black Shawl took her medicine like a trooper. "Now tell her to rest." I turned to Crazy Horse. "You have to let her rest."

"Asnikiyl kiya yo," Johnny said.

Crazy Horse nodded. He was no longer a savage war chief. He had become a worried husband. *"Han,"* he said and pushed her toward the tepee. Then Black Shawl, who had been absolutely quiet, surprised us.

"Thank you," she said, then disappeared into the tent.

Crazy Horse looked at us with pride. He smiled and reached out his hand again. "Magillicutti," he said. *"Kuna nita wicu ki glo u hoo."* He smiled and nodded and I looked to Johnny.

"He says come back sometime."

I nodded that I understood, and Crazy Horse nodded, too. "I will," I said.

I returned the next day to find Black Shawl much worse. She had no doubt been running on adrenaline all through their terrible fugitive winter. But now in the relative comfort of the Agency, her system was letting down. I stayed with her and Crazy Horse for the worst of it, fearing for her life. Days later, when the fever broke and she began to come around, Crazy Horse and I were bonded over our vigil.

I visited his camp every chance I got for those few months between his surrender and the fateful day that Philo and I leaned dumb against that porch rail.

I had talked with Crazy Horse for hundreds of hours about the topography of the plains, our mutual love of horses, the wild grass and animals that were so important to us both. I had seen his humility and his untiring attention to the needs of his people. I knew of his love for children. I had surveyed his land from corner to corner. I had been the first white man to stand on top of the tallest peak in his sacred Black Hills, an unwitting facilitator of the gold mining to come.

Even though his presence might be a threat to the civil order of the reservation, that threat could not be removed by arresting him. In fact Crook's decision to arrest him was mostly a show of authority. I thought Crazy Horse would be scolded for not kowtowing and be released within hours. I was naive not to know that something more Machiavellian was afoot.

7

Where food was concerned, there was very little variety at Camp Robinson. My breakfast was almost always the same: one egg, because they were in very short supply, a mound of fried side pork, a stack of pancakes, and a glass of buttermilk. I could have done without the buttermilk, but Fanny insisted that I drink it. She said it would keep my skin healthy, for heaven's sake. I did what I was told, concluding that it was her Michigan upbringing that had made her believe so strongly in the cosmetic powers of buttermilk. There was, of course, no scientific evidence for Fanny's claims. On the other hand, there was the empirical evidence of her own famously smooth, rosy complexion. Who could say for sure?

I stole a glance at her as I sat down at the table. She was a stout woman, every bit as heavy as I was, but unlike me she was stately. She had great powers to focus on a given task and that morning, in typical fashion, she concentrated on cutting her pork into bite-sized pieces. It gave me a chance to stare, uninhibited, at her. Her hair had a reddish cast though it was much darker than mine, without the sun-bleached orange of an Irish heritage. Her eyes were light, with the ability to change colors with her garments, and her mouth was forever curled up at the edges as if ready to burst into a smile.

When she rode with the other military wives she kept every inch of skin hidden from the savage prairie sun. She looked a little like an Arab sheik riding sidesaddle, but I was not alone in thinking her beautiful even then. In fact I had been the one who advised her to protect herself from the sun at all times. I'd witnessed incredible examples of what the Great Plains' sun could do; even now I recall the anguish of men burnt as if by fire after losing their hats in a battle. Wounded men came in suffering more from sunburn than from the arrows stuck in their flesh and bones. One particularly unfortunate man had been tortured by the Sioux—fingers cut off, stripped naked, beaten, and left to die. Three days after coming under my care he did indeed die. Not from the torture, but from the sun blisters that covered most of his body. They broke, leaked fluid, became infected, and finally brought the soldier's life to an agonizing end.

All that came to my mind as I regarded the beauty of Fanny's skin. "Doctor? What are you thinking?"

"Nothing." I laughed at myself and took a huge forkful of pancake.

"Is it the trouble with Crazy Horse?"

"No, no. That's played itself out. It's ancient history now."

"Oh?" Fanny was surprised. "Was there violence? They haven't harmed him, have they?"

"No. Jesse Lee has him in custody."

"Then he's safe. Good, I never believed what they said about him. And poor Black Shawl." She shook her head. Fanny had accompanied me many summer evenings and we had spent hours with Crazy Horse and his wife. "He's a good man," Fanny said. "You know I never believed he killed Custer."

I had to smile at her often-expressed sentiment. "Oh, he killed Custer all right."

"But you like him. You seem to prefer his company to most of the officers at this camp." I nodded and took another mouthful of pancake. She had no idea that Crazy Horse and I had met once before the war. "Poor Private Holden would agree, don't you think?"

The thought of John Holden caused my chewing to pause. "Mr. Holden was quite insane," I said, as pompous as a preacher. "He believed all sorts of wild things."

Fanny clucked her tongue and shook her head. She had traveled with me from Michigan to Washington in the company of Pvt. John Holden, a survivor of what had come to be known as Crook's Starvation March. We delivered him to an insane asylum in the capital, a tremendous opportunity to see Washington at the army's expense though a sad and difficult task. I tried to keep them apart so Fanny would be spared the man's ravings but it was impossible to remain diligent on a trip of four days. I had told her that Holden's babbling was imagined. Most of it was in fact true. The things he raved about had driven him mad. I know because I was on Crook's Starvation March, too.

"And what is so grim that you have knit that handsome brow, Doctor McGillycuddy?"

"Oh, I was just thinking about our trip to Washington. How grand it was." I knew Fanny liked to talk about Washington. We had been wined and dined by both military men and esteemed members of the medical community. We were even invited to dinner at the surgeon general's home.

"I don't remember it as grim," she said. "I remember it as grand indeed." As if she had been reading my mind she added, "The evening at Doctor Woodworth's mansion was my favorite."

"Yes, I know. You liked the crystal, the silver, the number of servants"—I was laughing now—"the feathers in Mrs. Otis's boa, the smoked salmon, the smell of Doctor Henry's pipe."

"The lights on the Capitol steps, the carriage you rented from the hotel." She was standing, reaching to clear the dishes. "The way you looked in your dress uniform, your wit, the way those old office-bound doctors envied you." She surprised me by kissing me quickly on the top of my head. I had some hair then, but it had been thinning at an amazing and depressing rate since I'd joined the army. I felt her breast touch my shoulder and when I pulled away, shc laughed. "It's time for you to do your rounds, Doctor."

"It is indeed," I said as I stood up. "I'll take my noon meal with Philo and his mates."

"Oh you will, will you?" Fanny teased.

She moved so close that her face blurred in my vision. Then I laughed, reached out, and pulled her in. She kissed my neck and I can still almost feel the heat of it.

"Yes, I will," I said. I closed my eyes as a wash of what Holden suffered rushed over me. For an instant I couldn't let her go and held her tighter until she put the dish she had been carrying down on the table behind me. Then she touched the back of my head with a gentleness that was much wiser than her years.

Finally my grip eased and I pulled away far enough to look into her eyes. "We'll go back to Washington one day." I said it because I knew she would like to hear it. But there was the burn of a lie in my throat because for all its hostility, I had come to love that gnarled, windblown land too much to ever leave.

She nodded. "I can't help seeing you the way you were that day coming out of the operating theater. You looked so professional and serious in your long white coat. You looked so learned."

She stepped back and I pulled my suspenders up and over my shoulders. "I was only an observer," I said as Fanny held my coat. "No more than another student."

"Oh, silly." She brushed the back of the coat. "You've seen more than all those teachers and students put together."

When I faced her, she brushed the front of the coat. "I've seen a great deal of battlefield surgery," I said, nervously rolling the ends of my mustache, "but nothing like that. My God, Fanny, they opened a man's belly. They looked inside and sewed him up again!"

"You can do anything those old fogies can do." She kissed me on the cheek. "You're destined for greatness, Doctor Valentine T. McGillycuddy. I've known it since I met you."

My smile came involuntarily. But I was late and pulled my watch from the small pocket inside the coat from nervous habit. It was seven o'clock; I turned on my heels and walked to the door. Through the cloudy glass I saw that the number of Indians around the parade ground had grown further. The northerns were on the east side and the reservation Indians on the west. I hesitated before opening the door. "And what have you planned for today?" I asked as lightly as I could.

"Mrs. Munn and I want to ride up to the spring on the south ridge for a picnic. Doctor Munn is ill and she's a little lonely. Could you come along?"

I shook my head without looking at her. "No, not today. In fact, why don't you postpone your outing until tomorrow?" I gave that a moment to soak in. "It might be best if you stayed indoors today. If you wait a day, I'll go with you." Then I looked at her. "Would you do that for me, Fanny?"

She felt my urgency and though there was a question in her eyes, she nodded. "Certainly," she said. "It would be a hundred times better with you along anyway."

8

The walk to the hospital took me past the west infantry barracks. Fifteen or twenty reservation Sioux squatted in a circle playing a game of chance in which they threw bones into the dust at the center of the ring. I never understood just what they saw in the bones to make them laugh and chide each other but, like everyone on the frontier, these Sioux loved to gamble. Standing over the circle for a moment I laughed with the warriors when the bones revealed that a young man of eighteen had lost his knife to an older warrior. These men were all of Red Cloud's band and army scouts under Philo's command. They were allowed to have weapons and were paid a private's salary, making them wealthy by tribal standards. Most of them would be leaving soon to fight the Nez Perce with General Crook, and that gave them even more prestige than their salaries.

The sentry who had been marching back and forth in front of the barracks made a wider swing and looked longingly at the gamblers. I tipped my hat to the private and the man nodded back, "Mornin' to ya, Doctor."

The man was a stranger, though not the accent. "County Tyrone?" I asked.

"Aye, sir. Via New York and lately of a dozen God-forsaken western posts. But Irish, sir. Pretty much like you." This was a code for communicating that he knew that I was not Catholic and that I'd been raised in an environment even more rigid than he had known. The soldier was not young, perhaps in his late forties, and his ruddy complexion suggested all manner of rough living.

"And you're supposed to be guarding this post?" I asked.

"Aye. For another hour, then on to post three. Then post one." He pointed with his bayonet toward the adjutant's office and guard house. "They rotates us 'round." He stared with blank, gray eyes and I considered that half the fighting contingent of the frontier army was made up of men just like this, disadvantaged Irishmen who knew no other way to survive.

"You'd best get on with it," I said. Men who didn't know me sometimes tried to take advantage of the fact that I was a surgeon. I saw to it that they treated me like the officer I was. The man nodded sullenly and turned back to his duty; I watched him hike his rifle to his shoulder and continue his slouching march in front of the west barracks. If it weren't for a little education and the difference in religion, that could have been me in later life. Hell, it could have been me despite those differences. I wondered if Fanny and her family thought I might end up pacing back and forth in front of some desolate army barracks, a simple military Mick.

The usual collection of children waited for me around the hospital's porch. Most of the names were known to me: High Dog, Mounts Thrice, Bear, Good

Voice Flute. They were a collection of scalawags not unlike the gang I had run with on the streets of Racine, Wisconsin, and later, when Father moved for a job, in Detroit. Of course these children's fathers did not come to this place pursuing jobs. These families were forced to live here, and I marveled at how carefree the children appeared under such circumstances. Children are incredibly durable, and those young Sioux laughed and joked like all children. Their good humor insinuated itself into the routine of the hospital and made it a more pleasant place to work.

Johnny Provost was waiting at the door. The children descended on me and Johnny tried to shoo them away with the tails of his nearly white coat. "Go on, now. Let the doctor pass. *Iya yo.*" He held the children out and let me squeeze into the crude waiting room behind him. He closed the door and pulled it hard to be sure it was latched. "Morning, sir." With his thumb he motioned toward the children. One was jumping at the window like a puppy. "They're agitated, sir, with all this talk about the northerns going back on the warpath. They've been pestering me all morning to play the electric dollar game. They have a new fish who's been talked into making a try for the coin."

The electric dollar game involved an ancient hand-cranked generator, left over from some quack rheumatism therapy, a bucket of water, and a silver dollar tossed in as "fish bait."

"Excellent," I said. "It's always good fun. After rounds we'll give him a go at it."

“Yes,” Johnny said. “Rounds.” He picked up a tattered clipboard and a lead pencil from a rough bench in the hallway. “Just the three old patients and a Corporal Pressler who was kicked by a mule yesterday. Doctor Munn admitted him, figured it was a femur fracture.” Johnny shrugged. “Don’t think the doctor’ll be in today. Told me to tell you to have a look at him.”

I stared at Johnny, waiting. He shrugged again, then put his thumb in his mouth and tipped his fist up. He rolled his eyes. “I’d say he’ll be under the weather all day.”

We were walking down the hall to the one and only ward, a large room at the end of the hospital with a dozen beds. The floorboards we walked on were unplaned pine planks, cut from the surrounding hills, that creaked as we passed. The cracks between the boards were more than a quarter inch wide and, in the winter, frigid air came up; the floors could get cold enough to freeze any liquid spilled on them. But that morning, with the temperature rising fast outside, the air coming up from the dark crawl space was refreshing.

The hospital was one of the largest buildings on the post, though still just nine rooms. Doctor Munn had a small office next to the ward. Across the hall was a staff room, where I had a desk and lurked on my hours off like a pack rat. There was a room set up for surgery. The kitchen was at the end of the hall, and the sounds of Private Kempler swearing at the dishes he was washing spilled out into the hallway. “Carrington and Murphy had good nights," Johnny said. He adjusted his glasses and looked at his clipboard. "They both got tincture of opium and camphor and their bowels seem to have tightened up. Color's better, must have been bad water."

"And Simmons?" We stopped at the door to the ward and Johnny shook his head discreetly.

"Not so good, sir."

I pushed into the open room and was met by greetings from the men on the ward. It is a bad idea to become too familiar with patients, so I just nodded and walked to the first bed along the left wall. An older soldier lay with the sheet down to his waist. His chest was covered with coarse black hair, and a jagged scar followed the line of his right collarbone. "Mr. Carrington," I said, "I understand you're doing a little better."

Carrington smiled. His face was leathery and tough. His teeth were bad; he was missing several along the right side of his mouth. "Some better," he said. "My bum's pretty sore."

"I should think so," I said as I looked over Johnny's notes. Then I turned to the next bed. "And you, Murphy? You feeling better?"

Murphy was younger yet just as hard a case. He nodded but, like all the cowards and goldbricks I've met in my life, wouldn't meet my eyes. "Not good enough to go back on duty."

"I'll be the judge of that, Private. You two were on the woodcutting detail together?" The privates nodded. "Did you drink out of Hat Creek?"

"It's hot as hell out there, sir," Murphy snapped without looking up.

"Of course it is, Private. I'm not suggesting that you go without water." I turned to Johnny. "I believe the beef herd is on Hat Creek. Is it not?"

"It is, sir," Carrington said.

"Make a note, Corporal." I turned back to Carrington. "And did you drink from the creek below the herd?"

Carrington shrugged. "What of it, sir?"

"Your condition could be caused by tiny creatures that can be carried inside animals other than yourselves."

"I ain't no animal," Murphy muttered.

"Quite probably the creek brought those tiny creatures to you from the cattle."

Carrington smiled as if he were being put on. "Now, Doctor, you don't think we'd drink water full of tiny creatures." He laughed and Murphy snickered along with him.

"These creatures are too small to be seen."

"Oh?" Murphy glanced up. "If they're so small, how do you know they're there?"

They laughed again but I ignored them and turned to Johnny. "Corporal, I think Privates Carrington and Murphy are ready to return to duty. Inform their company commander and remind him about the regulations on potable drinking water." I started toward the next bed as Murphy began to mutter.

"I ain't up to it," he said under his breath. But I was ready for him and spun around to cut him short. Both men froze in their beds. They were apparently aware of my reputation for temper and low tolerance for nonsense.

You are fit for duty, soldier. Understood?"

"Yes, sir."

My lab coat had bunched at my waist, and I straightened it while the fury drained from me. I turned slowly and walked to the next bed. "Morning, Simmons. How are the fingers?" I laid my hand on the man's forehead and from the corner of my eye saw Johnny silently motioning for Murphy and Carrington to get up and get dressed. I smiled and winked at Simmons, who looked confused but finally smiled back.

He was not a well man, though. "I'm burning up, sir," he said. "Don't know what's wrong with me. It's just a scratch."

"Well, it's more than a scratch. You were bitten by a viper. These things can be very serious." I unwrapped Simmons's hand and uncovered the wound in a way that kept it concealed from the patient. The thumb was black and weeping, nearly as big as Simmons's wrist. The index and middle fingers were swollen, too. All the digits were beginning to split.

"It's better, isn't it? Feels better. I should probably be getting back to my company, too."

"I don't think so, Mr. Simmons." I rewrapped the hand, tied the dressing tight, stood up, and put my hand back on Simmons's head. Carrington and Murphy were dressed and lingering near the door. "I'm afraid that thumb needs to come off."

"No." Simmons's face distorted and Carrington and Murphy disappeared.

"Yes," I said. "Maybe a finger, too."

"I need my fingers, sir."

"The poison was too much. If we don't operate, your life will be in danger."

"But I need my fingers," Simmons said softly.

"We'll leave you some fingers, soldier. You'll get along fine." I turned to Johnny. "Corporal, please prepare Mr. Simmons while I look at that femur."

"Yes, sir."

Moving to the other side of the room, I saw a frightened young soldier. It was Corporal Pressler, the victim of a mule kick.

The corporal was in pain but managed a grin. "Are the northerns going back out, sir?"

"I shouldn't think so, Corporal."

"But Crazy Horse run, didn't he?"

"I've heard that he's in custody."

"Ain't that going to stir them up?"

"You don't need to worry about that."

"The hell. You think these hospital walls would keep them out if they took a mind to get inside?"

"Let's worry about your leg. I'm told you got too close to the business end of a mule."

"That I did, sir."

I pulled the sheet aside to look at the leg. The man's body odor was stirred by the action of the sheet and it was impossible not to wince. "When was the last time you took a bath, soldier?"

"You mean the whole works?"

"The whole works."

"The regulations say hands and face once a day."

"And the whole body once a week."

"I never heard that."

"It's a fact. And I assure you that you'll have a bath today." Because of the odor I had to hold my head back to get a look at the leg. The thigh was swollen terribly, and the imprint of a mule shoe was clear in a yellowing black bruise. I lifted the sheet farther and saw that the foot was splayed out to the side.

"Can you move your toes? Try."

Pressler strained but nothing happened. The effort made him grimace. "Them mules is tough once you get 'em mad. I swear, I'll never call one a name again."

"That might be a good resolution." I replaced the sheet. "We'll deal with you this afternoon. After you've had that bath. Are you in pain, soldier?"

"It hurts."

"Sit tight. I'll be right back." I left the ward and walked down the hall to the dispensary. From a cabinet I took a syringe, a bottle of pure water, and a vial of morphine sulfate powder. The procedure was to mix a measure of the powder with one cubic centimeter of water, then extract the liquid with the syringe. I tapped the glass with the nail of my middle finger to clear the bubbles.

It took only a few minutes for the pain to begin melting out of Pressler's face. His fear was subsiding, too, but I patted him on the shoulder because I knew the pain was not finished. "We'll work on you this afternoon."

Simmons had been moved to the operating room but his voice could still be heard. The chloroform had begun to take effect and he babbled about serpents and the Garden of Eden. Another few minutes were needed for the drug to take full effect; I waited at the open window of the ward and saw that the throng of children had grown. When they saw me, they began to plead for a chance to play the electric dollar game. I nodded to them through the glass and looked out across the parade ground. A sentry paced back and forth in front of the guardhouse and beyond, a half-dozen mounted Sioux waffled in the heat waves beginning to rise with the dust. The day was warming rapidly and, even though the hospital walls afforded a sort of insulation, the tension from the surrounding hills could still be felt.

"Ready for you, sir." It was Johnny.

I lingered at the window and rubbed my hands together. Looking down at them I thought about what they had done in their twenty-eight years and wondered what they might be called on to do in the future. Now, of course, I know what the events of that day finally forced them to do, but that morning I was shaken by my duty as a doctor to take a thumb and perhaps fingers off another man. When I looked up, a puffy white cloud was building vertically above the butte to the east. It might well develop into a thunderstorm by nightfall. I took another moment to watch it form from within itself, then I pushed away from the window and followed Johnny down the wooden hallway toward the operating room.

9

By the time the operation was complete Simmons had only two fingers on his right hand. It would have been wonderful to save all the fingers but the infection had gone too far, and even then I knew it was better to take more than was absolutely necessary and not risk having to operate a second time. Johnny had made a cryptic comment about the value of fingers as I began to take off the second one: "God's flyswatters," he'd said. Just before Simmons had gone out he'd told Johnny he'd rather die than lose his fingers. By making the comment that he did, Johnny hoped I would take the risk and leave as many fingers as possible. It was Johnny's Indian side raising its hoary head above his understanding of science. I responded by explaining, for the hundredth time, our duty to do whatever possible to preserve life. When I invoked the Hippocratic oath, Johnny's eyes dipped like a chastised schoolboy's.

I was perhaps too optimistic about Johnny's grasp of philosophic oaths. He never seemed like anything but a reverent, kindly, and considerate white man to me. But in that assessment I was naive. Unlike his brother, Charlie, the Indian in his blood was latent. Charlie was the kind of man who used his blood to get him out of honest work. In addition, he was dishonest to the point of the criminal.

In the five years that Johnny had served me, first in the field then as my hospital steward, I'd made the error of thinking that his mind worked like mine. Now I shudder to imagine what the Indian part of his mind was thinking. If I had it to do over again, instead of giving him the responsibility of being my interpreter and assistant I would have sent him off to be educated. With his experience he might have done well at Carlisle or perhaps Dartmouth. Instead, I continued to surround him with the worst elements of his own ignorant and, as it turned out, deadly culture.

He had an inordinate fear of the habits of his mother's people. Some people have a dread of burning to death; others can't stand the thought of drowning. Johnny's deepest fear, which he'd confided to me late one night the year before after we had spent twenty hours treating victims of the Rosebud Fight, was to die from arrow wounds. He'd seen hundreds of men with multiple arrow wounds. The Sioux could shoot arrows faster than the troopers could fire their rifles. Some nights Johnny dreamed of the sound of arrows coming fast at him. A succession of hisses, few deadly enough to kill but every one sufficient to disable him so that the second, and third, and fourth hisses could deliver their stings.

In most patients multiple arrows were stuck in the back or buttocks, maybe a tomahawk gash on the head or shoulders. Sometimes bullet wounds were delivered so close that the skin was burnt from the powder. A few soldiers whom Johnny and I worked on were scalped or partially scalped. And in every case the terror of the close combat was still on their faces. That horror transferred immediately to Johnny's face, and he was barely able to proceed. The sight of wounded coming in bristling with arrows petrified him. At those times I accentuated my calmness and gently badgered him until he got a grip on his hysteria and was able to give me the help I needed.

When the wounded began coming in I, fighting my own demons, would deliberately remove my coat, hang it over a camp stool, roll up the sleeves of my white shirt, remove my tie, and don the cleanest apron available. I would point to where I wanted the stretcher bearers to lay the first patient. I tried to project a scientific mien—stepping back, considering the best way to carry out our duty. If I tugged on my mustache it was to conceal my fear from Johnny until the decision was made. When I turned to Johnny, I had to have an order for him. Had I shown any sign of uncertainty I think he might have broken and run.

No matter how the feathered, broken, and filthy arrow shafts terrified him, Johnny always responded to my orders. He depended on me to quickly wrestle a solution from any situation. I had to determine if the arrowhead was made of steel or flint by inspecting the entry wound. By touching the shaft I was often able to tell if it was lodged in bone or flesh.

Bone created the gravest problem. Arrowheads cling to bone as if they have teeth. Pulling on the shaft usually resulted in the shaft coming loose and leaving the deadly head deep inside the traumatized wound. To avoid the need for blind operations into such wounds, I fashioned wire tools that would hook around the shafts and thread down into the festering wound, then around the head. When I asked Johnny to gently pull on these homemade implements, the arrowheads almost always came away with the shafts intact.

I tremble to think what the pile of arrows extracted from soldiers after each battle meant to Johnny. Sometimes after hours of arrow surgery, with the battle cracking all day in the distance, he had to sit alone for an hour to restore his nerve. Only when his hands stopped shaking could he go to the duty he liked the best, comforting the wounded. And when he did come back into the tent he would find me, faking steadiness and calm, reviewing the procedures we had performed that day.

Later I found out that my efforts to influence Johnny's actions by my own created a deadly shield for him. As it turned out, his Indian side was never as far from the surface as I thought. When I was not able to protect with my example, he was not strong enough to resist.

Years later the Pine Ridge Reservation was plagued by a series of livestock thefts that threatened the fragile tranquility of the Sioux and Cheyenne who were residents there. The culprit was Johnny's alter ego and brother, Charlie Provost. Stealing horses and cattle was a very serious offense, and Charlie had been lectured about his errant ways before. Criminal action would certainly have led to Charlie's imprisonment, but under the circumstances, and with Johnny interpreting because Charlie had never fully learned English, he was given one more chance. Through his brother, Charlie was chewed on for the best part of an hour. He heard about responsibility, honesty, and duty to community. The lecture affected him deeply; Charlie withdrew tighter and tighter into his blanket until, when the chastising was finished, he sat recalcitrant with downcast eyes and refused to even speak. When he was given leave he walked directly to the blacksmith's shop, where he borrowed a pistol, then stepped behind the corral and summarily blew his brains out. I heard the shot and ran to the site but there was nothing that could be done.

To be honest, I did not consider Charlie a great loss. When the news reached Johnny, though, something snapped inside. A crowd had no sooner gathered around the sight of his brother's suicide than a second shot rang out. I instantly feared that Johnny had taken his own life for his part in his brother's death. But that was a white analysis. The truth was so preposterous that I'm only now beginning to understand.

Instead of Johnny Provost an innocent bystander, Clementi Bernard, lay with his head in a pool of blood behind a reservation building. Johnny leaned against the back wall with a pistol in his hand. When I eased the gun away from him he looked into my eyes and said, "I'm sorry, sir. My brain whirled."

Even his manner of speech had changed. When he had heard his brother was dead, he had not acted in repentance as I had feared but in reverence for the beliefs of his mother's people. "Charlie could not be allowed to travel into the next world alone," he said. "Now he travels with Clementi."

I stared at my trusted aide of five years in wonderment. I had no idea that such beliefs were in him. "My brain whirled," he said again.

He stood trial in Deadwood and at least partially because I pleaded extenuating circumstances, he was found guilty of the lesser charge of manslaughter. I was pleased when he was given a light sentence of five years in the Detroit Correctional Institution. But in the end my efforts on Johnny's behalf were all for naught. He died in prison before his term could be served, another victim of the terrible collision of cultures.

The taking of Simmons's fingers left me sad, so Johnny got the job of dressing the wound and bringing the patient around. As I washed the blood from my hands, my mind wandered back to what was happening somewhere on the road between the Spotted Tail Agency and Camp Robinson. Crazy Horse was likely on his way, in the custody of Jesse Lee and Spotted Tail's Brules. It was also possible that he had made a desperate run for the North Country. I had then, and have now, mixed feelings about which of those two possibilities would be best.

Working the blood out from under my fingernails, I thought about Philo's mess. It was a group of officers of mixed ages; the participants varied according to who was in the field. General Crook was on his way to Camp Brown to organize the massing of troops to fight Chief Joseph and the Nez Perce. He had taken several of the officers with him and more would follow, but Lieutenants Delaney and Schuyler would be there, along with Major Randall, Captain Bourke, and Colonel Mason. Red Cloud, the old devil himself, was a frequent participant. There were times in our history when I would have declined an offer to sup with Red Cloud but then I had nothing against the old warrior, and besides, there would be news from Spotted Tail.

Stepping from the laboratory and into the hall, I saw the door and suddenly longed to be outside and alone. But there at the window were the children. I had forgotten my promise of the electric dollar game. It would have been easy to simply push past them, but the game would only take a few minutes and besides, it was great fun. In the laboratory I found a wooden bucket and filled it with water. The old generator that some entrepreneurial bandit had sold as a rheumatism cure had been reduced by the years to a bundle of wires, gears, and magnets. It had been manufactured by the Peabody Company in Toledo, Ohio, and as I tucked it under my arm I noticed that it had been patented. I was shaking my head, wondering how a patent for such a device would read, when I pushed open the door and walked into the mass of squealing children.

They crowded around and I had to raise my voice in a growl. Acting like a bear always made Indian children stand back in momentary fear; I used the phenomenon to give me time to place the bucket in the center of the hospital's porch. Two cylinders were wired to the generator. I dropped one into the bucket of water and stood tall with my hands outstretched for order. It was like wading in a sea of thigh-high, half-naked hellions. You could usually hold them back by spreading your fingers if your hands were big and clawlike, but that day one boy shot in and touched the bucket as if he were counting coup on a Crow warrior. "Enough!" I shouted. The children stood erect at the sound of my voice, which only a few could understand. "Now, who is our fish?" I asked. There were blank faces all around. I tried it in Lakota. *"Hogan?"*

The blank faces turned to smiles. The son of Sharp Nose pushed another boy forward and said something to the effect of, "Willow Bear says he can get the dollar from the water."

Willow Bear was a large boy whose face suggested some Cheyenne blood. He stared at me—a rare act for any Indian, but particularly unusual for a child. It wasn't a defiant stare, more awe than challenge. He must have been fresh in from the north, a bit nervous about being so near a white man. "So you think you can get the dollar?" I took a silver dollar from my front pocket, flipped it into the air, and caught it neatly.

Willow Bear gazed at the dollar with interest but was clearly uneasy, and I'm not sure he knew what it was. "Your medicine is strong," the boy said in Lakota. It occurred to me that part of the awe in Willow Bear's face had to do with my reputation as what he would have called a medicine man.

"Perhaps your medicine is stronger today," I said. "Hold this." Willow Bear took the second cylinder. Three boys were already fighting to see who would get to turn the generator's crank. The biggest boy won out, and I gave him the sign to begin. Willow Bear began to sing a thin, strained medicine song and seemed surprised that he felt nothing from the cylinder held in his left hand. As was the tradition, in my best Irish tenor I began the first verse of "Pat Malloy" as a counter to the medicine song. When the crank was turning at top speed and both songs were in full swing, I dropped the dollar into the bucket. Willow Bear closed his eyes and, though he sang even louder, his voice revealed his trepidation. The music continued to rise until we were both singing at the top of our lungs. Then Willow Bear opened his eyes wide, plunged his free hand into the water, and ended up sitting on his bottom, ten feet away.

The children exploded in laughter and I plunged my hand into the water to retrieve my dollar before it disappeared. Johnny had come out onto the porch and was laughing along with a couple of Sioux women.

Willow Bear was, at first, terrified, but as he came to realize that he was not hurt and that if he didn't regain his dignity things would get even worse, he stood up, dusted himself off, and joined the laughter. Johnny, ever ready to help me, picked up the machine and began coiling the wires. As I stepped off the porch in the direction of Lieutenant Clark's mess, I came very close to Willow Bear. The boy did not look up but muttered as I passed. *"Peyata suta yuke lo,"* he said.

I looked to Johnny. "There is stronger medicine," he said. There was little use responding to the boy. I have always known there is stronger medicine than mine. For any man to think otherwise is a dangerous act of hubris.

10

The first face I met as I stepped into Philo's house was that of Red Cloud. He sat at the head of the table with his big hands flat in front of him. His features were bold, the nose large, the cheekbones high, the mouth full and inscrutable. Black hair with a few streaks of wispy gray hung in vague waves to his shoulders. Here was the only Indian ever to win a war with the United States. He was already a shrewd politician who had traveled to the East Coast and seen the cities of the whites and won the second, perhaps more important, war—of public opinion. The whites in the eastern cities loved him and he at least pretended to love them and their ways.

"Red Cloud." I nodded first to the chief then to Philo, Captain Bourke, and Lieutenant Schuyler. The others, if there were to be any, had not arrived yet. In the kitchen the cooks, Phillips and Boswell, were busy at their craft.

"Sit down, Mac," said Schuyler. "I was just telling these three gentlemen how this situation reminds me of a problem I ran into in Russia." It was clear that Schuyler was drunk. "Colder than Billy Hell up there, you know, and the people are horsemen. Natural-born cavalry. Everybody knows horses up there."

"But Walt, what's the cold of Siberia or those people's equestrian proficiency have to do with this situation?" It was Captain Bourke. "This is a situation of a renegade with popular appeal."

"Exactly," Schuyler said. He hesitated and took a swallow of whiskey to gain enough time to formulate a response. He was saved by a knock on the door. Lieutenant Delaney stepped in and everyone acknowledged him with a gesture. But Schuyler still had the floor and had thought of something to say. "In Russia there was a Cossack bandit, Boris or Nikita or some such name, and they couldn't get him caught. He was like this damned Crazy Horse, forever making threats."

"But did he ever threaten to kill a general?" Bourke asked. "Did he ever say he was going to war with the government? 'Go north and fight until not a white man is left.' "

"I thought that damned Grouard admitted he mistranslated," said Delaney as he sat down and pulled a pitcher of water from the center of the table. "I heard he said, 'Fight until not a Nez Perce is left.' "

A few eyes glanced at Philo. Grouard was in his employ, and Philo had acted on his information. "That's neither here or there," Bourke said. "The fact is, he's an upstart. He's been stirring up trouble since he came in. He's a pretender to Red Cloud's throne."

Everyone looked to Red Cloud. After an adequate pause the old chief spoke. "He has threatened the safety of the people," he said in a mix of English and Lakota. Everyone waited, but Red Cloud would say no more.

The quiet of the room was broken by Phillips coming from the kitchen with a platter of beef and potatoes. "Now, the greens is still coming but you can start on this cow meat." He set the platter down in the center of the table. "Everybody got their tools? There's water in that jug and milk over there. Can I freshen anyone's whiskey?" Schuyler held up his glass.

"Thing is this," Schuyler said after he'd handed the glass to Phillips. "Fellows like this Crazy Horse are a threat to us all. A threat to law and order. The chief said it. He meant Crazy Horse is a threat to Indian people but it goes for us, too." The meat and potatoes had reached Schuyler and he paused to scrape some onto his plate. No one filled the void with conversation, so Schuyler went on. "Quick, efficient police action is what's needed."

Philo had not said a word and sat staring distractedly at his plate. It was hard to say how he was taking Schuyler's drunken banter, but I was afraid the man might go on to insult Philo directly. "He's not exactly your average criminal," I offered.

"Certainly not," Schuyler said. "He's a good military man, but he's got that faraway look in his eyes. You, Doctor, of all people, have seen the look. Like he's thinking of something not in this world."

"They say he's a sort of mystic," Delaney said. "Revered by some of the Sioux." He glanced at Red Cloud, whose face was still expressionless.

"It's more like he's got them under a spell," Bourke chimed in. "He's like a Broadway actor." There was some nodding from men with their mouths full of potatoes.

"But I don't think he's acting." The words came out of my mouth before I had a chance to think the comment through.

"How do you mean, Doctor?" Bourke said.

I lifted a forkful to my mouth while I tried to figure out what I'd meant. As in the case of Schuyler, I was saved by another man coming through the door. It was Major Randall, and I took the opportunity to change the subject. "Ah," I said, "the leader of the Crows."

Randall laughed heartily and made room for himself at the table. "What we got here?" he asked as he took the platter from Red Cloud.

"Raw buffalo," the chief said with a wry smile. He was referring to Randall's experience of the winter before. The major had led a band of 250 Crow allies over the Big Horn Mountains in a horrendous blizzard. They had been saved only when they found a small herd of buffalo that had taken refuge in a stand of sagebrush. They killed the buffalo and ate them raw because no fire would remain lit. They had saved their limbs from debilitating frostbite by thrusting them into the animals' body cavities.

"Don't know if I can eat it," Randall said, "without my feet being in a nice warm place."

There was more laughter and I found myself thinking about black, frozen toes. I'd seen hundreds and had taken many of them off. Then I thought about the fingers of Simmons, then the fingers of children and beastly cold. I saw great puddles of slushy blood, the edges frozen solid. A winter blast cut my face and forced me to shake off the image. When I remembered that I was at Philo's table, a mincemeat pie was going around and the host was making excuses for the fact that it was not holding together as it was served. "Boswell"—Philo spoke loud enough for the cook to hear—"is an excellent cook. But pies are not his forte."

"I believe it was Oliver Wendell Holmes," Bourke began, "who once wrote an essay to demonstrate that the isothermal line of perpetual pumpkin pie was the line of highest civilization and culture."

"That would make this outfit uncivilized and uncultured," Randall said as he flopped a runny piece of pie on his plate. Boswell was standing at the door with a deflated posture.

"Quite true," Bourke said. "But the converse of Holmes's proposition is also true: Pie, of any kind, cannot be made except under the most aesthetic surroundings." He smiled at Boswell. "Amid the chilling restraints of this savagery and barbarism, pie is simply an impossibility." That caused a smile to appear on Boswell's face.

"Go ahead, Captain," he said, "have another piece. You want a ladle?"

That brought laughter around the table and the meal to an end. Schuyler finished his whiskey and left with Randall. The others followed them out, but Philo caught my eye and I knew he wanted a word.

When we were alone, Philo exhaled and shook his head. "This whole thing stinks," he said.

He was speaking in some way of Crazy Horse but I wasn't sure just how. I waited, honored that Philo was using me to let off some steam. "I'm a strong believer in the military, Mac. You know that."

"I do."

"I understand about command and how it only works if orders are followed to the letter." Philo went silent, thinking about something complicated and private.

"You're worried about what might happen if Crazy Horse rides into this camp."

"Oh, he will be riding in," Philo said. "Bradley got word that they left first thing this morning."

"And what will the friendlies do when he arrives?"

"God only knows, but I think we can hold a lid on things."

“They seem quite restless.”

“You could say that,” Philo said. “An Oglala named No Water rode two horses to death yesterday. Trying to kill Crazy Horse before he got to Spotted Tail.”

“Christ almighty.”

Philo got up and closed the door to the kitchen. “They were at the White River ford at ten o’clock,” he said. “Lee sent a messenger ahead.”

“Who’s with them?”

“I’m afraid a considerable contingent from both sides, but the principals are Lee, Crazy Horse, Spotted Tail, and Touch the Clouds.”

“Touch the Clouds?”

“You know of him. Chief of the Miniconjous. Tall. They say seven feet. He’s been with Crazy Horse since the beginning. I guess old Spotted Tail read his nephew the riot act when he showed up uninvited. There was some fear of a general uprising. I think Touch the Clouds is coming along to see that no harm comes to his old comrade.”

“Did Jesse think the situation was in hand?”

“Oh, Jesse. He promised Crazy Horse the world if he’d come in.”

“Seems like Crazy Horse is always being promised things that can’t be delivered.” There had been a broken promise of a separate reservation for Crazy Horse’s people. I had probably spoken too hastily. Now I cringe at my insensitivity: Philo was surely involved with that hollow promise.

But I didn’t need to worry. Philo had not heard

because he was deep in thought, staring at the tabletop and shaking his head slowly. "There's a lot of politics to consider," he said. "That old chief who just left here has to be considered. What would that sort of preferential treatment look like to him?"

Philo was right. The situation was massively complicated. He was troubled by something more than Red Cloud's feelings, though. I tried to see what was worrying him, but when he looked back at me there was no sign of anything deeper than a mere complication in normal duties.

"I need to get back to the hospital. I've got a soldier with a fractured femur," I said. "Ugly son-of-a-bitch." I rose and smiled. "The leg, not the soldier."

That got a laugh out of Philo just as Boswell knocked on the door. "Beg your pardon, sir. Could we clear the dishes?"

"Certainly." Philo gave me a familiar salute. "We're finished here."

11

More Indians were gathered in the warm stillness of the parade ground as I stepped off the porch of Philo's house. They lounged in the sun like catamounts or stared from the shade of the buildings like mule deer from chokecherry thickets. Now there were some Cheyenne and Arapaho. These tribes had traditionally been allies of Crazy Horse but there was no way to tell how they would react to his arrest. As I dug the morning's half-smoked cigar from my breast pocket, I made a rough calculation of the number of Indians around the camp. Perhaps a couple of hundred. Certainly, I thought, Bradley was considering dispersing them.

Fanny was standing on our porch as I started across the parade ground. She waved and came down the steps. I stopped and watched her as she ran to my side. I had not yet come to admit how a man needs a woman, how she can be both a guide and a place of refuge. I should have known it from the way I ached for Fanny when we were separated, but I hadn't come to grips with any of that. As a young man I was such a fool. While she came across the parade ground toward me I refused to let myself think about her body moving under her cotton dress. Now I take time to recall every curve of that body, imagine how every muscle flexed as she walked, but then I distracted myself by snapping a match into flame with a thumbnail. The cigar was lit by the time she reached me and I concentrated on my puffing, as if there was no other thought in the world.

"May I walk with you, Doctor?" She fluttered her eyelashes theatrically.

It was all I could do to keep from taking her in my arms. But I didn't. Instead, I mumbled something like, "Delighted," and resumed walking.

"It's beautiful out today. And you made me stay inside." I only grunted. "It's boring just sitting in the house."

"I'm sure, but as you can see emotions are high." I swung a hand to indicate the camp.

"Emotions are always high," she said with a smile. There were tiny droplets of perspiration on her forehead and I resisted the temptation to wipe them away with a finger. We passed a pair of junior officers, who tipped their hats.

"You have such respect," Fanny said when the officers had passed.

Only, I thought, because they don't know the real Valentine McGillycuddy. "It's for my humanitarian work in the field of hemorrhoids," I said.

"Valentine!"

The way she said *Valentine* always made me chuckle. "I'm sorry, sweetheart. A case of momentary insanity."

"Momentary?" Fanny smiled.

There was a group of Indians at the main entrance to the hospital, so we skirted the building and came to the back door. Johnny met us. "There are some people who want to see you, sir."

"That bunch at the front?"

"Yes, sir, a Cheyenne holy man or some such nonsense."

"I see. Could you escort Mrs. McGillycuddy home?"

Johnny grinned boyishly. "Of course, sir. Be my pleasure."

I leaned down and kissed Fanny on the forehead and she whispered in my ear, "I'm looking forward to this evening, Doctor."

It was difficult not to smile. "Don't tarry, Corporal. We've got a nasty leg to set."

"Yes, sir. He's all cleaned up and ready to go, sir." Johnny shepherded Fanny toward the door. "I'll come straight back, sir.

When I stepped out onto the front porch, the crowd of Indians had grown. A half-dozen warriors stood behind the same band of children that had been there that morning. Behind them were ten or twelve women. They giggled and chided the men in Lakota. Willow Bear, the latest inductee into the electric dollar club, stepped forward. His shyness had diminished. I understood him to say something like, "High Wolf is here to test your medicine."

A tall, burly Cheyenne stepped in front of the boy. Like many of his tribe he was handsome and held himself in a way that suggested that he was aware of his appearance. He wore his hair in long, tight braids that hung down over a naked, hairless chest. There were tiny blue feathers braided into the hair; I recognized them as being from a kingfisher, the most delightful bird on a prairie filled with delightful birds. Fringed leather straps encircled High Wolf's wrists, and a medicinc bag hung from his neck. This man had a reputation. He was a warrior and a medicine man, known for his courage and his arrogance. *"Winyn wan apiya yapi takuni'sni,"* High Wolf said. To heal a woman means nothing.

He was referring to my success with Black Shawl's tuberculosis. The contempt in his voice had to do with the fact that Black Shawl was Crazy Horse's wife and that while the Cheyenne were generally allies of the Oglalas, there had been a falling-out. I met the medicine man's stare and, though it might have appeared that I was fencing with High Wolf, I was actually only scrutinizing the man. Here, I thought, was a man who had fought shoulder to shoulder with Crazy Horse on the Little Big Horn, now filled with contempt. "To heal a woman is not nothing," I said.

High Wolf couldn't have understood me but he laughed, and my face grew instantly hot with the insult. I held my tongue and waited to hear what he wanted. He pointed to Willow Bear, rubbed his fingers together to indicate money, then pointed to himself.

He wanted to play the electric dollar game. I'm sure a smile spread across my face. "Is that so?" I said. "It would be a pleasure to oblige you."

High Wolf gestured again toward Willow Bear and said something about his power being much stronger.

"Well, my good friend," I said with poorly concealed glee, "we'll have to see about that." I scurried into the hospital and returned in a moment with the generator and the wooden bucket of water. A murmur ran through the crowd when they saw the strange machine with the red and black wires. The women chattered and poked High Wolf with their fingers. High Wolf paid no attention to them but instead stared with intensity at the machine, which could have been a sign of trepidation but was more likely an attempt at psychological intimidation.

"Here's the game, High Wolf." I fished a dollar from my pocket and dropped it into the water along with one of the wired cylinders. "You take this in one hand"—I held up the other cylinder—"and grab the dollar with the other."

High Wolf's eyes traveled from one component to the other. He nodded, then turned to the side. He took a small stone from the medicine bag that hung from his neck, fell to his knees, and plucked two blades of grass from the earth. He rolled them in his hands, then put them in his mouth with the stone. He began humming his medicine song and looked at the sun, which was now into its downward slide. The song increased in volume and High Wolf turned to face the four cardinal directions. The crowd began to join in with his singing. When he stepped up and took the innocent-looking cylinder in his left hand, I pushed the children aside and began to crank the machine myself. I turned the handle with all my might and began to whistle "Pat Malloy."

The medicine song grew in volume as High Wolf raised his muscular right hand. The whole crowd swayed and swelled with life and rhythm. I was cranking like a man possessed when suddenly High Wolf's arm came down with tremendous force on the edge of the wooden bucket. The stays burst and the slats smashed under the blow. Water exploded in all directions and the song ceased.

High Wolf screamed from the enormous jolt of electricity that kicked his arm upward. But the shock was instantaneous and when it ceased, the dollar lay high and dry in the remains of the bucket. High Wolf reached into the wreckage and picked it up. There was a moment of silence as the medicine man held the dollar up for all to see. When he moved it to within inches of my nose, the crowd roared with approval.

Then he jerked the cylinder in his left hand and snapped the wires leading to the generator. He laughed, dropping the cylinder into the mess. Instinctively, I began moving toward the medicine man, but I made myself stop. It was just a silly game. Let him keep his dollar. Let his prestige increase. It didn't matter.

High Wolf and his band of admirers moved away from the hospital porch and I watched them as the dust of the parade ground puffed up under their bare and moccasined feet. With some difficulty I raised my eyes and concentrated on the line between the browning prairie and the blue sky. Through a corridor of grass between the eastern buttes rode another group of warriors. They were being drawn to the camp. They, too, sensed the importance of the day.

I picked up the pieces of the generator and stepped back into the hospital. Johnny had been watching from the window. "The bloody savage ruined our fun," he said.

"He did, indeed." I dumped the generator into Johnny's arms. "Put that away. Perhaps it can be fixed." Then I brushed at some of the water that had splashed on my coat. When my hand hit my watch, I instinctively took it out and looked at the time—nearly two o'clock. "I'll be needing your help with Corporal Pressler," I said.

12

Pressler was squeaky clean for the first time in who knew how long. His hair was slicked back and his face freshly shaved, complete with two nasty nicks on his chin. He tried to smile when I came in but it was obvious that the painkiller was wearing off; and his face contorted instead.

"Are we ready to get that leg straightened out?" I asked.

"Ready as we'll ever be." He grimaced. "Maybe not quite. I was thinking a little nip of something beside water might be nice.

Just then Johnny came into the room with a tray full of equipment. In addition to leather straps, clamps, and splinting material there was a hypodermic syringe, a vial of morphine sulfate powder, and a bottle of red-eye whiskey. "It seems that Corporal Provost has anticipated your request."

Johnny smiled with pleasure as he poured Pressler a tall glass. He handed it to the patient and held his head up so he could drink. "There you go," he said. "That'll smooth things out for us all."

The amber liquid slid from the glass, and I found myself concentrating on the film left on the concave surface as the level fell. The smell of that microscopic layer of spirits is in some ways more powerful even than a full glass.

We watched Pressler finish his whiskey before carrying on with our work. "Corporal, could you call Mr. Kempler from the kitchen while I administer something to reinforce that whiskey?"

When Johnny went to get Kempler, I injected five milligrams of morphine into Pressler's arm. While we waited, I stole a glance at the tray holding the bottle of whiskey. I didn't dare let my eyes linger. When I turned back to Pressler, I swear I could feel heat against the side of my face, as if the bottle were generating its own energy.

Pressler's eyes went glassy just as the two men returned from the kitchen. Johnny, who had helped set many legs, went to work strapping the patient to the bed. Kempler looked on with some uneasiness. He was a meaty man and nervously wiped his hands on the apron he still wore. I pulled Pressler's sheet back to expose the leg, and Kempler squinted his eyes with empathy. "Corporal Provost, are we prepared with the chloroform if it's needed?"

"Why no, sir, we're only setting a leg."

"I'm aware of what we are doing, Corporal." I looked at Pressler's eyes. His agitation was diminishing; the pain was seeping away as the drug spread through his body. "But this is not a normal broken leg. I'd guess that femur is in at least three pieces. If we can't get it straight by normal means, we may have to operate."

"Operate on a broken leg, sir?"

"Yes, Corporal. I observed such an operation in Washington, D.C. The chloroform?" I gave Johnny a look that told him he had asked enough questions.

"Yes, sir. It's just here. Only take a moment." He brought a vial of liquid and a cloth mask out of a small wooden box.

To Kempler I said, "I want you to take a good grip on the private's foot. One hand over the top of the arch and one under the heel. Put a boot against the bed and pull straight when I tell you to. Don't jerk. Just a firm, constant pressure."

Some of the color had drained from Kempler's face. "Take ahold, trooper," Pressler said. He was feeling bravado that both Johnny and I knew would be short lived.

"Corporal Provost, if you're ready, please lie across the private's chest." Johnny did as he was told and I nodded to Kempler, who swallowed hard and put one big boot against the bed. "As the patient said," I whispered, "take ahold."

The bones shifted and ground under my hands. "Lean a little farther back, Mr. Kempler. Now rotate gently to your left. More." I massaged the pieces toward a normal position but one was floating and twisted inside the muscle, which was now rock hard. Pressler whimpered. "Steady, soldier. Try to relax your leg." I motioned for Kempler to rotate more.

A high-pitched moan issued from Pressler. "There now," Johnny said. "There, there."

I put my hands under the swollen leg and tried to lift the floating section of bone into alignment. Pressler sobbed and I asked for another inch of rotation. The leg was sweating in my hands; Kempler's color was completely gone. "Buck up," I said to everyone. "A little more, Kempler. Soldier! Relax this leg!"

But the loose piece of bone would not budge. "All right," I finally said, "ease off gently. Are you still with us, Private?"

There was no response. "The poor boy's passed out, sir," Johnny said as he stood up.

"And you, Kempler?"

"That's a son-of-a-bitch, sir."

"It is that." I sat back down on the stool beside the bed. Legs like that sometimes healed if they were simply splinted as they were, but at best they would always be crooked. Pressler would be a cripple, in pain most of his life, and useless to his family. To splint a crooked leg is little better than taking it off. But there was another option. At the time it was a bit of a long shot, I'll admit, but one of the operations I'd seen in Washington had to do with straightening bones through surgery, actually going inside and physically manipulating the bones into place. Doctor Munn would have had an apoplectic fit if he knew I was even contemplating such a procedure. But Munn was an old-fashioned doctor, a leftover from the War of Secession. And besides, on that fine autumn day he was drunk.

"Corporal Provost, anesthetize the patient, please."

Johnny's eyes widened but he went to work. I stood up to wash my hands in the basin against the wall. "Mr. Kempler, thank you for your service. You may return to your duties. But stay close; we may call on your brawn again."

Pressler began to moan softly and move his head from side to side. Johnny looked down at him with the chloroform mask in his hand and the expression of an older brother or even a mother. When he looked up, his eyes were too sad for the situation. "You shouldn't worry, Corporal," I said. "This procedure might not do Pressler any good, but it shouldn't kill him, either. It might make him a whole man."

That seemed to assuage Johnny's fears, and when I asked him to begin dripping the chloroform he did so with some relief. In moments the sweet, pungent odor was leaking into the room from under the mask held tightly against Pressler's face. His moaning was muted, and soon he stopped swinging his head from side to side. Johnny continued to administer the anesthesia while I prepared to make the incision.

When I touched Pressler's thigh, a feeling came over me that was familiar. I took a moment to try to recall where I'd first felt it. It was the sensation that had enveloped me in that open boat, the first day of my wandering from the hospital in Detroit. I'd felt it many times since—my first battle, my first look at the Rocky Mountains, even my wedding night. But I'd felt it most strongly when I'd first cast my eyes on the grasslands that the Sioux called home. It was the taste of adventure, the unknown, unimaginable possibility.

The literature on this sort of operation, though sparse, made sense. After the muscle was cut, the bone could be manipulated into place with common surgical tools. Once things were lined up, the incision could be closed and the break treated like a simple fracture. The wound would have to be watched for infection. But lacerations were common in battle and around the camp. Johnny and I had managed hundreds of gashes that were more severe. Still, it was a procedure that might have been done only a dozen times west of the Mississippi. This was virgin territory and I took the excitement of it in like a drug.

The skin was stretched tight over the swollen leg and cracked like a ripe watermelon as the scalpel moved diagonally above the knee. The flesh rolled up and outward in the scalpel's wake, and Johnny mopped the blood. When we got down to white bone, it was easy to see why the femur had resisted clicking back into alignment: A section the size of a rifle cartridge had twisted longitudinally and wedged between the two main pieces. When I reached in with forceps and extracted the chip, the bone settled into line. There was no way to replace the chip, but the bones seemed tight. Pressler was young; there was no reason the fractures wouldn't heal.

Johnny made a low whistle. "Slick as gooseshit, sir."

"I should take that as a compliment?"

"The highest order, sir. If we can keep him clean, he'll heal up fine."

Peering into the wound, it seemed so easy. Like so many things: It was simple, if you had the courage to do it. I began to stitch the muscle. "Are we ready with the splint?"

"Right here, sir." Johnny was still applying chloroform but held up the splint kit. "You performed a bit of magic, sir. I wish that Cheyenne holy man would have been here to see it.

I went on stitching, moving from the muscle to the skin, cinching things up tight, and swabbing away the blood with soapy water. Ten minutes later the splint was in place and Johnny had stopped applying chloroform. When Pressler started to come around, he was sick. "Go on," Johnny said as he directed the private's head into a bucket. "Puke your guts out." He stroked the back of Pressler's head as he would a child's.

When I stood up, I felt at once elated and exhausted. "You've got control of things, Corporal."

"Absolutely, sir." Johnny's small, soft hands continued to pet Pressler's head. He even let a curl of hair wind around one finger. I was touched. "I've never seen anything like it, sir," Johnny said.

"Nonsense, it will be a common procedure in no time. But thank you, Corporal. You did a fine job yourself."

Johnny beamed, and I smiled back as I moved to the basin to wash the blood from my hands. From that position I could see out the window. Time had slipped away. Now the shadows of the buildings and the cottonwoods of the camp stretched across the parade ground and snaked over hummocks that had been invisible only an hour before. There was an unnatural haze over it all and, at first, I thought it might be dirt on the glass. But the dirt was in the air. Dust. Particles of earth hung in the stagnant atmosphere, the product of horse hooves, boots, and bare feet. Disoriented, I moved closer to the window and was shocked to find the parade ground crowded with Indians. Hundreds of warriors. No, thousands of warriors. Women and children clustered behind them. And soldiers, perhaps three-quarters of the camp's complement, assembled in loose ranks.

Only the sentries seemed to move. Back and forth in front of their posts, slowly, as if only they had duty here. The camp was suspended in a dusty fog and when the others did move, they moved as one, pulsing this way and that, swelling and contracting. I was seized by a sense of destiny moving in on our puny camp. I didn't bother to dry my hands, and there was no sense trying to explain to Johnny why I bolted from the door and down the hall.

When I stepped from the hospital, the scene came alive. The reds and blues of the blankets swirled in my eyes; the dust entered my nostrils and brought the scent of horses and rawhide. The sounds of the women trilling softly, the clank of cavalry, and the muted whistle of a red-tailed hawk, aloof and high above the cottonwoods, came directly into my consciousness. When I looked to our quarters, I saw Fanny standing on the porch and very near her, emerging from between our home and Colonel Bradley's, at the head of a long line of horsemen, rode Crazy Horse, the captured war chief of the Oglala.

13

My first thought was for Fanny's safety. There was an incongruity in the way she leaned over the porch rail. She looked happy, interested, as if this were a Fourth of July parade. But the fighting men who filed past were wild and more exotic than anything the world would see again. I wanted to go to her, wanted to be there, standing between her and the serpentine string of feathered warriors and painted ponies. But a throng of people stood between me and my wife; she was impossibly out of reach.

I moved twenty feet out onto the dry parade ground, to where Crazy Horse could be seen riding south between Jesse Lee and Spotted Tail. Behind them came hundreds of Sioux, Crazy Horse's Oglalas, Spotted Tail's Brules, the Miniconjous of Touch the Clouds. But all eyes were focused on Crazy Horse. He and his small, hard, spotted pony moved seamlessly, more like a gentle satyr than a man on horseback.

There was dignity in his posture but melancholy in his face, and those eyes of his commanded the attention of all the gathered tribes. Chief Spotted Tail rode beside him with gravity, his head erect, the hands that held the reins poised above the saddle horn. He did not look from side to side but seemed fixed on the horizon. Jesse Lee wore his black campaign hat and held his face more rigid than I had ever seen it. I wanted to extinguish that seriousness on all their faces and idiotically raised my hand as if to wave to them. There was no way any of the men could have picked me from the mass of people; still, I felt they knew I was there, and I pushed through the Indians in an effort to intercept the column.

Red Cloud's Oglalas chided the northern warriors. The Miniconjous rode solemnly, following Crazy Horse the way they had followed him through years of suffering. A big, ugly-mean Oglala to my right threw a stone that hit a mounted warrior in the shoulder. But the warrior didn't flinch. There was potential for riot, a chance of war and bedlam breaking to the surface. Far to the east was a cluster of warriors, several with full headdresses; in the center stood Red Cloud himself, looking on iron faced, as if he were watching a play whose outcome he already knew.

To the east of the adjutant's office three companies of infantry had been mustered. The fourth had been assembled beside the guardhouse. There were only a few yards between the two buildings, and a dozen mounted troopers filled that gap. The adjutant, acting for Colonel Bradley, stood at the door to his office. It was Maj. Fred Calhoun, the brother of Jimmi Calhoun who had ridden with Custer and been terribly dismembered at the Little Big Horn just a year before. Calhoun watched the procession for only a moment before retiring into his office.

Desperate to be there when the column stopped, I pushed ahead and was twenty feet from the guard-house when Lee and Crazy Horse pulled their horses up and dismounted. The crowd had been murmuring but suddenly went still. The parade ground was eerie with silence when one of Crazy Horse's lifelong friends stepped up beside him and stood close. Lee signaled that he should remain near Crazy Horse as a guard. They all started their walk to the adjutant's office.

A Red Cloud warrior broke the silence. "You are supposed to be a brave man." He laughed. "Everyone can see you are a coward." Quicker than the eye could register, Crazy Horse lunged for the man. But the guard grabbed him in his powerful hands. He held Crazy Horse tight, whispered into his face, and, as if his friend's voice had charmed him, Crazy Horse regained his composure and followed Lee to Major Calhoun's office.

"I'll get an audience with Colonel Bradley," Lee said. He left the group of warriors and pushed his way toward the general's quarters. Crazy Horse stood with his arms folded across his chest and waited. The piercing sound of an eagle-bone whistle split the silence. Then another whistle, and another, and another, until the camp was one pulsing whine of Sioux breath through the leg bones of dead eagles.

The sound did not abate until Lee returned. I was close and could see that he was furious. He looked right at me and swore. "The bastard won't listen."

Then he turned to Crazy Horse. "The adjutant has his orders. He wants you to go in *there.*" He pointed to the guardhouse.

To Crazy Horse, one log building was very much like any other. He let himself be led in front of the mounted soldiers. Voices in the crowd rustled like birds in brush. A lone woman began a high, sad song. When Crazy Horse passed me, our eyes met and the chief's flashed with recognition. But neither of us said a word. Now Crazy Horse looked more like a tired old man than the youthful Adonis I had met four years before.

He had no idea what lay in store for him inside the guardhouse. But I knew. I had cared for men who had lost their health in that rat hole. They were chained in cubicles with no ventilation except for a tiny square of sky above their heads. They were never brought out or unchained and lived in their own waste. It was a terrible place for any man, but for a man like Crazy Horse it would be unendurable.

The officer of the day was Captain Kennington. He was a young, stout, red-faced man, and when he opened the door an incredible stench belched out behind him. Even standing twenty feet away, I winced. Crazy Horse stiffened but, still not sure what was happening, let himself be led inside. The door closed and silence fell again on the crowd. No one moved or spoke. The breeze refused to stir the cottonwood leaves. There was only the woman singing in the distance and the pale sky stretching to the horizon.

Then there came the sound of a scuffle behind the door. The sentry I had talked to that morning was now pacing in front of the guardhouse, and he tensed up at the sound of the officer of the day swearing. The building seemed to swell; the seconds stretched like the traces of a workhorse.

The explosion of the door was accompanied by Crazy Horse's scream. It was a primal sound, the noise of an animal, but not pitiful: reckless, and wild. He came through the door swinging a knife with two frightened soldiers on his back. They clung to him, terrified to be so close but not brave enough to let go. Then two more soldiers were dragged into the melee and Captain Kennington made several futile thrusts with his sword. An Indian raised his rifle to shoot Crazy Horse but it was batted away in the struggle. Then another Indian seized the arm that held the knife and was sliced as if by magic. Blood gushed from the Indian's wrist; he ignored his wound and got control of Crazy Horse's arms as Kennington began to shout. "Stab the son-of-a-bitch! Stab the son-of-a-bitch! Kill him! Kill him!"

Crazy Horse went down as the crowd converged. I was swept along and was close enough to touch the sentry when he jabbed hard with the bayonet. Then the struggling stopped and the soldiers pulled back. Crazy Horse was still held to the ground, hard hands pushing his face into the dirt. But everyone stood back as I fell to my knees beside the chief. He lay still and when I slid a hand under his side, it came away crimson with blood. Then Crazy Horse turned his head slowly and looked up at me. His voice was shockingly soft. "McGillycuddy," he said. "Tell them to let me go. They have hurt me enough."

14

The crowd pressed in as I knelt over Crazy Horse and suddenly I was dizzy with claustrophobia. I struggled to my feet like a man coming up from the bottom of the ocean. My shout, directed at Captain Kennington, had the texture of a gasp. "Keep them back," I said. "We need air here." The captain, who was now frightened and white, directed his men to form a line and push the gawkers away with their rifles. Being taller than most, I could see over the closest heads that the parade ground had become a scene of turmoil. There was more dust than before, and a wave of emotion radiated out as word passed that Crazy Horse had been stabbed. Some were terrified, already running for the hills that surrounded the camp, some were elated, and many were racked with grief. Open battle could break out at any moment but I tried not to think about the military situation. I, after all, have always been a doctor.

When the Indians in the immediate vicinity were pushed back, I breathed again and gathered myself to speak calmly. "Now Captain, have this man taken to the hospital."

Kennington was as young as I but a hard man whose

blood was still high from the struggle. His wide blue eyes were at once terrified and angry. He snorted like a bee-stung bull. "I've got orders to put him in the guardhouse and I follow my orders, sir."

Kennington was not thinking clearly. "If you put him in the guardhouse," I said, "there will be a slaughter." I waved my arm toward the throng of agitated Indians who pressed in on us.

The infantry was trying to disperse the crowd, and already the Sioux were forming into two opposing camps. There was shouting from Red Cloud's agency Indians; the outnumbered Crazy Horse people drew into a tight circle as confirmation of what had happened made its way to the most distant onlookers. Weapons came out from under blankets and the sound of hammers being pulled to the ready could be heard. Some of the women began to keen.

Struggling for composure, I made myself heard. "This man is seriously injured, Captain. He cannot go into the guardhouse."

"He's a damned savage," Kennington hissed. "And I don't take no orders from a contract surgeon."

Kennington's granite blue eyes were unblinking and though I wanted to strike him, I knew the man was right. He had his orders. They had to be changed. "I'm going to see Major Calhoun. Move that man at your own peril." I thrust a finger at Kennington's nose. "Your own peril."

The guards were holding the people back; the path was clear halfway to the adjutant's office. Outside our protective ring the cavalry was moving across the grain of humanity to help disperse the factions. Still there was an instant of fear as I came to the point where the guards held back the circling Indians. I had no way of knowing what would happen when I left that ring of soldiers. The adjutant's office was only a few yards away but I hesitated, suddenly deeply aware of the wildness beyond the perimeter of armed men. In addition to the exotic sounds of inscrutable language and the swirl of vivid color, a feral smell wafted across the parade ground that both repelled and attracted me. Then Jesse Lee was beside me. "I'm with you, Mac."

We gathered ourselves, pushed through the guards and into the roiling sea of feathers and flesh, raven black hair, and piercing eyes. We were buffeted but not assaulted. After walking twenty feet we stepped into the second protective circle of infantry surrounding the adjutant's office. Calhoun met us at the door. He looked past us and into the parade ground. It was pandemonium. "Son-of-a-bitch," he hissed, then let his eyes shift like an animal's down to us. "Inside," he said.

The walls of the adjutant's office were heavy pine logs, but the excited shouts and mournful wails came right through. "What the hell went wrong?"

"Crazy Horse has been stabbed," I said. "He's lying in the dirt. He needs to be taken to the hospital immediately."

Calhoun was a good soldier and managed to remain

calm. His eyes stayed fixed as he tried to sort things out in his mind. I had a moment to study his features. He resembled his brother, Jimmi, and it was impossible not to recall the reports of the mutilation of Jimmi's face. His nose had been cut off, sticks forced into the bare holes where his ears had been, and all his teeth broken out.

"He has to go in the guardhouse," Calhoun said, but as if someone else were saying it. All I could think about was Jimmi Calhoun at the Little Big Horn. Certainly this brother knew what the Sioux had done to his own flesh and blood. Could he be thinking of revenge?

"That's quite beside the point now," Lee was saying. "There's a battle about to erupt. If you put him in the guardhouse this camp will explode."

Through the adjutant's office walls came the savage smell of the parade ground. It seeped through the logs. I recognized it as similar to the smell of a storm on the wind, of animal tracks and entrails. It was the smell of the silent battlefield on the Little Big Horn. Jimmi Calhoun's eyes had been gouged out and replaced with his own testicles. Now Jimmi's brother turned his own eyes on me, and I had to shake my head to see that they were dark brown and normal. "How bad is the bastard?"

"I can't say until I examine him. But if you put him in that guardhouse he'll die. A lot of people could die."

"Maybe that's what should happen," Calhoun said.

"Maybe we should finish it right here. This day." For a terrible moment it seemed that Calhoun had made his decision.

"Don't be foolish," Lee said. "You can change Bradley's order. The situation demands it. Do it right now. Let the doctor take him to the hospital."

Calhoun took a moment to study us. His eyes shifted from one to the other. "Can't do it," he said. "But you can bring him in here. I'll vacate." He shrugged. "That's the best I can offer."

Lee looked at me and we both knew it was all we were going to get. I began to nod first. "It will have to do."

While we were inside the infantry had fallen out and joined their two protective perimeters. Flanked by the cavalry, they had formed a larger circle around the guardhouse and the adjutant's office. Crazy Horse lay behind the line, surrounded by a dozen soldiers and friendly Indians. Somehow Johnny had made it through and had rolled Crazy Horse over onto his back. He sat on the ground cradling the warrior's head. I pushed several Indians out of my way to get to them.

"Bless you, Corporal," I said to Johnny. "Help me get him into the adjutant's office."

"Here," Johnny said to the bystanders. "Lend a hand here."

Indians took Crazy Horse's legs and Johnny and I took his shoulders. "Easy," I demanded. With Jesse Lee in the lead and pushing people aside, we moved toward the log building.

By the time we entered, Calhoun had moved out to oversee the calming of the parade ground. The excited tenor of the crowd had modified to a wail that sounded too sick to be truly dangerous. We laid Crazy Horse on the hard wooden floor, and I sent Johnny to the hospital for my bag. Then something came over me and I began pushing people from the room. I turned Captain Kennington and Jesse Lee toward the door, then pushed several Indians out behind them. Emotion welled up inside me; I felt I might burst into tears. I became more physical than was necessary and advanced on the remaining gawkers with my head down, intent on clearing the room before Johnny returned with the medical bag. If someone resisted, I pushed hard and they yielded. But when I laid hands on the last man, a shirtless Indian, it was as if I'd found a granite statue among mortals.

Blindly, I had been pushing people at chest level, turning them and propelling them out the door with a good shove on their shoulder blades. Now my hands found a rippled abdomen where the chest should have been. The abdomen didn't move and, when I looked up, my eyes were only at chest level. Elevating my glare, I found the calmly defiant eyes of the biggest Indian I had ever seen. There was no doubt that this was Touch the Clouds.

There was only one more tentative shove left in me. It was clear that Touch the Clouds intended to stay, and I was exhausted. My hands rested on Touch the

Clouds' chest and I looked up into the chief's long, smooth face.

15

Touch the Clouds' eyes threatened to pull me into his consciousness, but I forced myself to turn to my new patient. Crazy Horse was on his back, his eyes open, staring, and filled with pain. His teeth ground together and an involuntary moan issued from somewhere inside. "Blankets," I said, pointing to a pile of gray wool government issues on a shelf. I searched my mind for the word in Lakota but before I found it Touch the Clouds had scooped up the entire stack.

The blankets were rough and dusty—unused, no doubt, since late last spring. But we made a bed of them and moved Crazy Horse onto it. The last blanket was rolled into a pillow for Crazy Horse's head and when the chief was as comfortable as possible, I laid a hand on his chest to feel the strength of his heart. I had barely determined that the heart was still pumping strongly when Johnny came through the heavy plank door with my medical bag in hand. Behind him Jesse Lee slipped in and stood silently along the wall near the place where Touch the Clouds had settled and sat cross-legged and motionless on the floor.

"The whole camp's in an uproar," Johnny said as he handed the bag over. "Like Hell's about to jump the fence." He spoke matter-of-factly and reached out to touch Crazy Horse's brow.

Lee read my mind with a glance. "I've already seen after Fanny," he said. "Bradley's stationed a squad of riflemen around the officers' quarters."

"Thank God." I nodded and opened my bag.

The first thing I did was mix a dose of morphine and administer an injection to Crazy Horse's upper arm. It was the standard procedure for a seriously wounded man, and by the time Johnny had removed Crazy Horse's leather shirt the sound of his grinding teeth had begun to diminish. A small white stone with a hole in its center hung from a buckskin thong under Crazy Horse's left arm. It would be in the way of dressing the wound but when Johnny reached to remove it, Touch the Clouds let out a grunt and lunged forward. Lee caught the huge Indian before he got to poor, alarmed Johnny. "That stone is part of his medicine," Lee said. "It has to stay."

My eyes focused on the stone. I had of course seen it before, yet only then did it occur to me that the talisman might be magic. When I looked at Touch the Clouds, who had settled back into a sitting position but appeared ready to move if he had to, I could see in his eyes that it was no mere pebble. "Leave it," I said. "We could use the help."

We rolled Crazy Horse onto his side and looked carefully into his wound. It was no more than two and a half inches long and was located the width of my hand above the hipbone on the left side. The bleeding had slowed dramatically; only a watery pink liquid leaked from the gash. The wound needed to be probed, cleansed with soapy water, then swabbed with iodine. Johnny built a fire in the stove and set a pot of water to boil. In the lull before the water boiled, Lee motioned for me to follow him outside so we could talk without being overheard.

The parade ground was nearly empty. The entire area had been cleared of Indians, though the different factions had moved only to the edges of the camp. Warriors howled and rode horses back and forth in front of their contingents at breakneck speed. Both Lee and I knew that the braves were wearing their war ponies down so that, if a battle began, they could fight on the superior strength of a second wind. It was mostly bravado; still, the situation was volatile and unpredictable. The sun had begun to set golden, and the shadows of the soldiers standing guard along the west side of the camp stretched across the bronze parade ground and into distorted ghoulish shapes. The shadows tapered to images of ten-foot bayonets in the trampled dirt.

Lee chewed on an unlit cigar and paced in front of the building. He glanced out to where a few tepees stood on a rise a hundred yards beyond the camp's perimeter. A fire was beginning to blaze between the tepees. A chant issued from the general turmoil. "How bad is he?" Lee asked.

"I can't tell you. Serious."

"Will he die?"

"Perhaps. But he's uncommonly strong. He has that going for him."

Lee bit down hard on the cigar and drove his right fist down on the doorjamb as he turned. "Christ," he said. "It's my fault. I talked him into coming to this shit hole. I promised he'd get a fair hearing."

"I imagine Bradley already had his orders."

"Yes. And I believe those orders came from a lieutenant!"

Lee was referring to Philo Clark. "He's acting for General Crook," I offered. "Crazy Horse is his responsibility."

"He may have been given that responsibility by Crook but not by God. Clark is responsible for that man's death."

"He's not dead yet. And besides, it was a mistake. Philo didn't plan any of this."

Lee fumbled with a match but didn't try to light the cigar. He rolled the match between his fingers and chewed on the cigar violently. "What makes you so sure it wasn't orchestrated?"

"It was a brawl."

"That doesn't mean the intent of this whole arrest wasn't to get Crazy Horse out of the way."

"You may be right about that much," I said.

"You know everyone in this damned sordid affair has spies, from Philo to Red Cloud to Crook. Well, I've got a few informants, too, and I'm going to find out just what's going on. I don't like it when I'm forced to break my word. I don't like it when I endanger innocent people. Lucy's over there with Fanny right now." He pointed to our cabin. "They're being guarded, scared to death, and I hold Philo responsible. I hold him responsible for anything that might happen."

My conversation with Philo earlier in the day came clearly to my mind. "I don't think he wants Crazy Horse to die," I said.

Lee bit a big piece of cigar off and spit it into the dirt. "Let's hope he lives," he said.

16

The water was just coming to a boil when I stepped back into the adjutant's office after my discussion with Jesse Lee. The evening was too warm to have a fire in the stove and as a result, the air was stifling. Johnny was busy spreading out dressings on the table near where Crazy Horse lay on the floor, so I jerked a window open. The air was refreshing but made the wails of the encamped Sioux seem very close. Touch the Clouds sat on the floor on the other side of the room with his long legs crossed and his arms folded in his lap. Perspiration glistened on his bare, hairless chest. His expression was blank, but his physical presence was so imposing that I felt uneasy. Somehow the scrutiny of this warrior was not unlike my memory of old Doctor McGraw during my training at the Marine Hospital in Detroit.

One of the differences was that McGraw was usually drunk. If the truth were known it was probably McGraw who taught me, through example, to love whiskey. Of course I was prime for the addiction. I'd like to blame it on an adolescent reaction to the strictness of my father, who always believed the worst of his son but demanded the best.

Old Doctor McGraw would lean against the wall in one of the wards while I stitched the lacerations or set the bones of sailors who had spent the night brawling in the city. He never drank on the wards but always had a bottle in his desk drawer. By three o'clock in the afternoon his face would be swollen red and he would hesitate before each sentence. But he was a good doctor and a good teacher. He taught me to deal with the rampant syphilis of the port town and the not infrequent cases of yellow fever and malaria. Unlike my father, McGraw encouraged me to use my temper when it was the only way to deal with an enraged sailor in need of doctoring. "Bludgeon them if you have to," he'd say. "They'll submit if it's coming from a doctor." In the years after the Civil War Detroit was a big, boisterous, and brutal city—the perfect place to learn the art of medicine. And McGraw was the perfect mentor. He was a man of science, classically trained, a believer in progress, manifest destiny, and civilization.

So how did his prize student end up here in this pagan place, with the evening breeze bringing a savage song that raised the hair on the back of his neck? In some complicated way McGraw was at the heart of it. "The exploration of the human spirit," he used to say, "involves pushing to the limit religion, politics, science, the physical, and even our darker passions. We all go to the limit, but the best of us almost always come back to the concept of civilization."

There was nearly no heat around Crazy Horse's wound. It was oddly cool, as if nothing violent had occurred. McGraw would have asked what that coolness might mean. With the intent of teaching, he would have asked what could be done if it suddenly turned hot. We would have talked about whatever answer I might give for days, analyzing it, altering it, thinking it through again. But there was no time for that sort of luxury on the day Crazy Horse was bayonetted. McGraw was fifteen hundred miles away and could not help his student do what was needed. I had missed my old mentor before but there, kneeling on the floor of the adjutant's office on September 6, 1877, I longed to feel and smell his whiskey breath over my shoulder. From the beginning he had figured me for an exceptional student with a tremendous future. When I was eighteen, he gave me his rounds to perform. I graduated at nineteen, and McGraw saw to it that I was offered a job on the faculty in my twentieth year. I was young enough to believe that I had found my niche in the world. But in a matter of months from the date of my faculty appointment I, too, began keeping a bottle in my own desk drawer.

A single shaft of setting sunlight had moved across the floor and now bisected Crazy Horse's body. As I washed my hands in the hot water on the stove I asked

Johnny to open another window and cool the room down more. We both tried to ignore the stoic Miniconjous chief sitting in what had become shadow. The feeling I got from Touch the Clouds was so much like the feeling I recalled from those years in Detroit that memories of lectures, work in the Detroit police department ambulance corps, and moonlighting at the Dearborn insane asylum flooded my mind. It was not until I asked Johnny to gently roll Crazy Horse onto his side that I understood why those memories clambered to be revisited.

It had been drunken old Doctor McGraw, watching me work and knowing that my own energy was turning me into a younger version of himself, who finally sent me on the path that had led to this moment in this place. Were it not for McGraw taking me aside one late, alcohol-soaked night and confiding the torment of his life, I would never have seen the Great Plains, never felt the power of a nomadic life, and never had the chance to use my skills to try to heal the last war chief of the Oglala Nation.

"Just hold him like that, Corporal. Where I can get a good look with the light from the window."

Johnny's small hands were surprisingly strong and steady. They didn't hesitate when Crazy Horse moaned and turned his head quickly, catlike, to look into my face. When he saw it was me, he relaxed. "That's it, easy," I said. "We need to see what there is to see."

Without being asked Johnny took one hand off the

shoulder he was holding and pushed the bowl of warm soapy water to where I could reach it easily. With a damp swab I washed the nearly dried blood from around the wound then, taking up another swab with a pair of forceps, began to probe the wound itself. I held it open with my left hand and dabbed the soapy swab as deep as I dared. Crazy Horse's muscles tightened and his teeth ground together, but he did not cry out or jerk away. I could feel the eyes of Touch the Clouds, not quite passive, at the back of my head.

McGraw had offered me a drink in the office late that night and taken a full three inches in his own glass. Both of us were exhausted after an enormous day. "Get out," McGraw said.

I was confused and my expression must have showed it. "Sir?"

"You're too young to work the way you're working. You'll want to marry that little Hoyt girl soon. You've probably already been dreaming about rolling her around in the hay."

I was surprised and stammered. Somehow McGraw knew that I had been walking out of my way to and from work in hopes of catching a glimpse of Fanny Hoyt on the front porch of her parents' house. Just the mention of her name embarrassed me, and though I had not yet been bold enough to speak to her, I felt McGraw could see into my soul. I hastened to leave the subject of Fanny Hoyt. "Work won't kill me. I'll endure."

"Certainly you'll endure. But that isn't good

enough. You should leave a mark, a road sign on the journey of civilization with your name on it."

In medicine?"

"Certainly. But you can't do that at this Marine Hospital. You need real knowledge to leave a mark. You need a life with breadth. It can't happen if you don't gain some experiences outside your field."

"I'm thriving here."

"Nonsense. Look at you. You're skinny enough when you're healthy, but now you look as sick as one of your God-damned patients. The bags under your eyes make your nose look like a fucking packhorse." McGraw was drunker than usual. He seldom resorted to profanity, though neither of us were strangers to strong talk. "Get out, Valentine," McGraw said. "This life isn't good for you."

Again I stammered. "I don't know what you mean."

"Bullshit. You're working twelve, fourteen hours a day. It's literally driving you to drink. My God, lad, what are you hiding from? Give yourself a chance to see what you're made of." He shook his head. "You want to end up like me?" he whispered.

"I've always admired you."

"Well you've got damned poor taste." He reached out and took my wrist in one hand, pulling his watch from his vest with the other. He counted the beats of my heart. When he was done, he threw the hand away. "About as regular as a lumberjack's payday." McGraw sipped his whiskey thoughtfully, then looked up. "You know I think a lot of you and because I do,

I'm asking you to get out of here. Get outdoors. Expand your horizons so you can help mankind. Take a look at the uncivilized parts of the planet before you settle down to medicine. You need to know the enemy."

I wanted to respond but McGraw went on. "You've studied some engineering. There's a grand adventure about to take place. A geodetic survey of Lake Michigan is about to begin. I put your name in to be an assistant engineer and recorder, and I don't expect any back talk." It was the first step of my westward migration.

It was impossible to tell how deep the wound was or what organs might be involved. It could be that the bayonet had missed or not reached anything vital. It could also have pierced the liver, kidney, or gut. If that was the case, the wound would likely be fatal. But at that point there was no way to know. It would be a long night of waiting. My probing hadn't let me know what to do but had, at least, cleansed the gash to a depth of nearly two inches. That was as deep as I dared go, though I had not reached the bottom of the wound. By the contractions of Crazy Horses's back muscles, I knew the pain had been immense; the last thing I wanted to do was further agonize my patient. I took a second swab in the forceps, dipped it in the narrow tray of iodine, and went back into the wound. Again, Crazy Horse refused to feel the pain. When the swab came out, blood flowed behind it. Johnny applied pressure with a fistful of gauze.

The bleeding never stopped, but when it slowed we dressed the wound. With Johnny's help I eased Crazy Horse onto his back. Before Johnny returned to his duties at the hospital he lit a lamp and prepared another syringe of morphine. He laid it on the adjutant's desk beside the extra dressing material that he knew I would need later. "Is there anything else, sir?"

I sat on a chair in the lamplight with my elbows on my knees and my hands clasped in front. Across the room, still on the floor, sat Touch the Clouds. Between us, with his eyes open and staring at the ceiling, lay Chief Crazy Horse. "Would you check on Mrs. McGillycuddy?"

"Certainly."

"Ask her to prepare a meal for me." I raised my eyes from Crazy Horse to Touch the Clouds. "For us," I corrected. "And perhaps some small portion of broth for our patient."

"It's as good as done, sir." Johnny laid his hand on the doorknob but stopped when I spoke again.

"And Corporal? If the tactical situation changes, see that we're notified."

"Absolutely, sir." He opened the door. Along with the cooling autumn air came an increase in the distant sound of the mournful, eerie chant.

17

When Johnny returned, he told me that there were two sentries in front of our cabin who had looked suspiciously at him as he approached from the shadows. They were nervous, and that made Johnny nervous. He thought there was a chance they might shoot him but, when they recognized him, they relaxed and allowed him to proceed to the porch without challenge. "It isn't right," he told me, "for soldiers to guard a man's wife."

When Johnny had arrived Jesse Lee was there pacing the floor, angry and as nervous as the guards. Lucy and Fanny had looked on from the wooden bench that served as our couch. Jesse was attempting to calm the ladies. "The situation is in hand. There's great confusion but that's working toward a sort of military stability. There's nothing to worry about." I can almost hear Jesse saying that, as much to reassure himself as the ladies.

The first thing out of Fanny's mouth was a question about my welfare. "Is the doctor all right?" she whispered.

"Yes, ma'am, he's fine," Johnny had said.

Jesse came up behind Fanny and asked what the situation was at the adjutant's office.

Johnny said a strange look came over Jesse's face and Fanny laughed out loud when he said, "The doctor would like some supper."

"Is everything stable?" Lee asked. "Is the patient stable?"

"Yes, sir. Doing as well as can be expected. Doctor was just wondering about food for him and them two Indians."

Fanny and Lucy had already begun a meal and told Johnny it would be on its way soon. Then Jesse Lee took Johnny by the arm and led him outside. Fanny came to the porch and I'm sure she was miffed to be excluded from the conversation. Johnny and Lee stood near the guards, at a distance that made it impossible for Fanny to hear what they were saying. She would have realized they were talking about the military situation. Though she knew little about the army she was always perturbed to be left out like a child.

They had discussed, Johnny said, the relative strengths of Red Cloud's people and Crazy Horse's, and where the Cheyennes and Miniconjous might fit into the situation. Then one of the guards raised the butt of his rifle off the ground and called into the night. "Say. Stop right there. Halt!" There was some confusion and the guard would have shouldered the rifle if the Indian boy had been slower. But he slipped between the guards so quickly that neither had time to stop him. He was upon Jesse and Johnny before they knew what was happening.

Fanny, still standing on the porch, came quickly down to their sides when she heard the boy pleading for Johnny's help.

"Wasicu wakan," the boy said as the guards closed in and took him by the arms.

"I'm not the doctor," Johnny said. It was Willow Bear and he was looking for me.

"Wasicu wakan," the boy said again. *"Tunke hoksi yuka kte lo."*

Fanny demanded to know what the boy was saying. "Apparently the boy's sister is having some trouble," Jesse Lee said. "He mistook Corporal Provost for Mac."

The guards still held the boy tightly and Fanny stepped up close. "Tell me what's wrong," she said.

"Winyan ki kikiya un." He pointed toward a group of tepees just visible on the other side of the camp.

"Those lodges are Cheyenne," one of the guards said.

"The boy's sister is having a baby," Johnny said. "Sometimes they get excited if things don't happen right away. They have midwives and their own medicine men."

Fanny considered Johnny and what he had said. Then she studied Willow Bear. "How long has it been?"

"Tohanyan hwo?" Johnny asked.

"Hinhanni tahon."

"Since morning."

Johnny told me that when the boy faced the distant campfire it was reflected in his face, and when Fanny knelt down the boy's eyes shone with their own fire. "Tell him to go to his sister," Fanny said.

Johnny translated and the boy looked at Fanny. "I'll talk to the doctor." Fanny stood up. "Go on now. Go to your sister."

18

It was after Johnny came and went that Fanny learned Crazy Horse had not wanted to surrender. The Lees told her the story of how he had suspected treachery and how Jesse had, without intent, delivered him to just that. Like any rational person, Fanny never truly understood why the army ran things the way it did.

I always marveled at our women. Their men lived in a harsh world; we knew several military wives who found that world too repulsive to bear. But most of the women, and particularly Fanny, seemed to cope well with the reality of our situation. Though some of the individual acts of cruelty troubled her deeply, there was a great deal about the lives of the men at the camp that seemed to fascinate her. She told me once that in an elemental way, they were different from the men she had known growing up in Detroit. They were vital and self-possessed like none of those privileged boys could ever be. Sometimes even her sense of propriety couldn't keep her from laughing at the boys her father had encouraged to court her.

Rolling her eyes, she told me of endless hours spent sitting on the porch of her family home with James Martin, whose family was preeminent in the Michigan hardware business. The Hoyts would have been thrilled to have James as a son-in-law. He would have made a wonderful husband for any girl. But thank God, Fanny said no. I knew the man, of course, and I have to admit I was intimidated. He was well educated, pleasant, and attractive in a fashionable way. He was from a family far superior in most people's minds (including my own) to my Irish immigrant clan. But when I questioned Fanny on the subject some years later, she laughed and said that from the time she was thirteen she had wanted a man for more than fashion or lineage.

One cold February night, years after the day I am telling you about, when the coal furnace in our Rapid City house was clunking and ticking to keep up with the frigid Dakota wind, she confided that for years she had struggled with guilt from fantasies about men. They were sensual fantasies, the kind she could never tell another soul. By the time she was old enough to entertain suitors like James Martin, she had grown to accept such thoughts as part of her nature. It took her fifteen years of marriage to be able to admit her desires and passions to me. Though we both knew that such things had to be secrets from society, she never again denied them to herself and never denied them to me. Secrets and confessions are all part of a life well lived.

When she sat on the porch with James Martin she was only marking time, waiting for something to happen. She had no clear idea what she was waiting for until the afternoon I walked past the tall white house with the broad porch where she sat entertaining her suitor. Poor James waved me over and introduced her as his fiancée. She admitted having noticed me walking past before. As she took my hand her piercing gaze cut right into me; had I been a little wiser her secrets would have been known to me instantly. Her hand was warm and strong, her voice low but playful. "Doctor McGillycuddy," she said. "It is nice to finally meet you, and James is joking about me being his fiancée."

I was a bit dumbfounded—or was I simply dumb? My self-perceived inferiority expressed itself as a kind of shyness. Still, James extracted from me my plan to join the Great Lakes Survey. Fanny was, or pretended to be, fascinated by the fact that I was to be both a surveyor and a surgeon and travel the entire Great Lakes system, perhaps the Great Plains. She asked if I thought I'd enjoy sleeping under the stars. After thinking for a moment I said yes, I thought I would. Since I'd spent so few nights under the stars at that point in my life, my answer was a bit of a wild guess, something to keep the conversation going. But in this long, long life of mine I have seldom made a prediction that was more correct.

Fanny liked my answer. "You're a rugged, outdoor man then?"

I looked her in the eye for the first time. "No," I said, "but I might well become one."

Somehow James Martin had been left out of the conversation, and he never got back in. Our courtship was begun by his introduction and carried on by mail during that first survey adventure on the Great Lakes. I'm afraid James was bewitched by Fanny. There would later come a time when she used him shamelessly as a way to see me.

19

Once my senses were attuned to it, the song of the Sioux encamped around Camp Robinson seemed comfortable and right. It filled what would have been a sterile adjutant's office. The voices were mostly women's. Because they were so distant and high pitched, I found myself bowing my head and straining to make out the words.

When I raised my head from Crazy Horse's prone body, my eyes fell on the rigid form of Touch the Clouds. He was staring back. A familiar chill made me stiffen. It was not exactly fear, not merely fascination, and not wholly unwelcome. It was the same chill I had first felt on the train from Omaha, Nebraska, to Cheyenne, Wyoming Territory, in the spring of 1876, months before the massacre of Custer at the Little Big Horn.

Only the hills of Ireland, as my parents described them, could have been greener than the prairie rolling past the train windows. Hundreds of miles of grass, on both sides of the train, to the distant, treeless horizon. I'd spent the year before sitting in an office, drawing maps of the plains from my survey notes. I had found the surveyor's life to my liking; after the Great Lakes survey I'd signed up to help survey the northern plains. But surveying had a drawback: The maps needed to be made, and that meant office work in Washington, D.C. When the telegram came from General Crook, it was like a reprieve from prison. "Can McGillycuddy's services be secured for the field? If so, send him at once."

The great expedition against the Sioux, the Yellowstone Campaign, was finally beginning. Crook was in command of the southern pincer that would move north to meet Generals Gibbon, Terry, and Custer, all converging on the Sioux who were summering somewhere near the confluence of the Yellowstone and Big Horn Rivers. I had met Crook only once, briefly, a year before, on the survey for which I was then drawing the maps. I had no reason to believe I had impressed the general; certainly he had his choice of hundreds of military surgeons. To be honest, I was stunned that he had asked specifically for me. It was true that I had recently helped map most of the war zone, but Crook had requested my services as a surgeon.

The train I traveled in to Cheyenne was dedicated mostly to the military en route to the front of a war that had been simmering for years. Now that miners were pushing into the Black Hills, in blatant violation of the treaty of 1868, and thousands of reservation Indians had joined their recalcitrant cousins in the north, hostilities would certainly boil over and flood the entire northern plains. The country I had come to love more than any other might well be changed forever. I felt a need to witness the change.

The sleepy pioneer town of Cheyenne in the Wyoming Territory had become a bustling depot for materiel being loaded onto wagons and hauled to Fort Laramie, where it would be transported on to Crook. The general, with a thousand troops and hundreds of Indian allies, was camped somewhere farther north, near the site of the annihilation of Capt. William Fetterman and his entire command ten years before. The Fetterman Fight had been termed a massacre; the newspaper accounts of it marked the first time I ever heard the name Crazy Horse. Then Crazy Horse had been only a lieutenant for Red Cloud, but it was rumored that he planned the strategy that lured Fetterman out of Fort Phil Kearny and into the ambush that killed him and eighty other soldiers. It was primarily this action that had won the war for Red Cloud.

In Cheyenne the preparations for war distracted me, but once I'd hitched a ride on a freight wagon for Fort Laramie and had breathed in the sage smell on the prairie breeze I was oddly overwhelmed by a sense of well-being.

Fort Laramie was a fountain of rumors; I discounted them. The hostiles were camped hundreds of miles north but, in the civilian population, fear ran high. The soldiers, on the other hand, were itching for a fight, a chance to even the score on these upstart Indians who refused to follow Red Cloud onto the reservation. Against the advice of the enlisted men I'd met, I joined a mail carrier just setting off for Fort Fetterman.

I have always loved good horses. To watch them move is soothing. To move with them is a sensation too sublime for common expression. The mail carrier had a small remuda of ten horses and told me to choose whichever one I liked. I roped a big bay gelding with a thin blaze between his eyes and white front feet. The horse's name was Buford. He carried his head high and had a way of flipping those white feet out as if he were in a parade. No matter how far we traveled in a given day Buford's head never went down; his ears always stayed pricked and alert. The next morning he was always easy to catch. He carried me the two hundred miles to Fort Fetterman without a misstep. But when we arrived, the army had moved somewhere north from Fetterman. Their exact location was unknown.

Crook's orders were for me to report to his camp "at once," so I approached the mail carrier about buying Buford. Good horses like him were hard to find on the frontier, however, and the man flatly refused my offer. But the next morning, while I was saying my goodbye to Buford by putting my head against the horse's and whispering a thank-you, the man recanted. "Christ," he said, "a man likes a horse well enough to kiss it, I reckon I shouldn't stand in the way."

I slipped the thirty dollars into the man's breast pocket and led Buford away. We joined a group of freight wagons that were chasing Crook. They were headed toward a valley I remembered from my surveying days as one of the most pleasant I'd ever seen—the valley of Rosebud Creek.

Buford carried me another two hundred miles, and now I remember that trip as a journey back into paradise. Quiet engulfed us, distance stretched to new limits, and even as it was happening I told myself the pleasure I received from the strong horse, the long vistas, and the fresh wind was indulgent. But I didn't really believe it. Everything seemed so real, so alive. It was spring and the days were warm. The earth was exploding with grass and flowers. The nights were cold, just right for sleeping, and I was more than happy to roll my blanket out onto the ground and lie on my back, watching the sky and listening to the bullwhackers drinking and telling stories around the fire. I had left my new wife back in Washington and with a war about to begin, I felt guilty for enjoying myself. It seemed absolutely impossible that hardship could be ahead, yet I knew it was true. The closer we got to Crook's camp, the more the men talked of Indians. When they spoke Crazy Horse's name, they whispered.

Months at a desk in Washington had dulled my senses but in these last few days I had relearned how to feel, smell, and hear the subtleties of the plains. I was home.

Fanny, wise woman that she was, had known that I'd had enough of crowded urban life and encouraged me to join Crook's command. She would go back to Michigan to wait for me. When I'd boarded the train in Washington, she kissed me full on the mouth in front of everyone on the platform. Her fingernails dug into the back of my neck and her hot breath was in my ear. When I looked I found that she was crying. "I'll walk out to Otter Point every Sunday," she whispered.

The thought of Fanny revisiting the site of our first intimacy, on the shore of Lake Huron, still thrills me. How absolutely surprised I'd been to see poor duped James Martin's two-horse gig picking its way to the survey crew's camp at the mouth of the Detroit River. I was pleased when James and three friends disembarked with picnic baskets, but my heart sped up when Fanny appeared from among them.

We'd spent the whole day together, walking the shoreline, telling each other what had been happening in our lives. James paced near the fire but Fanny paid him no mind. Near nightfall, after James had pleaded to start back to Detroit, Fanny led me out to Otter Point, a mere quarter mile from the camp. When we came to the large flat rock that marks the point, Fanny moved close enough that her perfume made my head light. The sun was setting, its last rays warm and soft. She stood looking up at me and I leaned toward her lips.

I tried to bring myself to ask her for a kiss but as soon as the thought was in my mind my hands were along the sides of her face. I brought her close and kissed her too hard and too long. When I pulled back she was smiling.

I was frightened by my passion. "Oh God," I said.

"I'm sorry." But Fanny held a finger to my lips and it was all I could do to keep from kissing them, too.

"No," she said. "I wanted you to kiss me."

"But it was wrong. I'm so sorry."

Fanny laughed. "You're joking," she said.

Lord, how I wanted to explain away my ardor. But James Martin had found us. "Well, I'm not joking," he said. "We have to leave for the city immediately. It is getting dark."

"Yes," I said. "Yes, you must be going." James reached for her arm; she let him take it and lead her toward the waiting gig. But her eyes continued boring into me. She smiled over her shoulder until they were out of sight. Though my fascination with the Great Plains compelled me to take other surveying jobs, Fanny and I were married within eighteen months.

20

I can see Crazy Horse now as clearly as I ever saw him. His features were as much Caucasian as Sioux but, of course, no one ever mentions that. If anyone in this day and age were asked, they would say that Crazy Horse was the essence of Indian. The essence of Indian is a dynamic and fashionable thing. It is also a slippery concept. Is a sedentary full-blood more Indian than a nomadic half-breed? Is a Christian Oglala more Indian than a pantheistic Norwegian?

That day in the adjutant's office it dawned on me that the two chiefs who shared the space with me would have been watching from the distant bluffs the year before as the supply train I had attached myself to wound its way into Crook's camp. That camp was on the Tongue River, where the land is rough and sprinkled with the white and pink of wild roses. In the early stages of the war it still seemed as safe and holy as my parents' home in the center of Detroit. The bluffs to the west were five miles away, so the area of the camp was an easy place to defend. Though the soldiers were nervous, no one expected an attack. Crook had chosen a safe place to wait for his Indian allies. He would not move without support of his Crow, Shoshone, and Pawnee soldiers. It was their chance to even ancient scores, with the help of an army of whites easily as ruthless as the hated Sioux.

When I was first ushered into Crook's tent, I found the general engaged in a lively game of whist. That was the day I met Captain Bourke, Lieutenant Schuyler, and Lieutenant Clark for the first time. The four men were hunkered over a small field table and howled as each trick was played out. The air in this command tent was quite different from that in the camp in general. It eased my mind to see that the general himself seemed cool and confident. When his grizzled face looked up from a hand he had just lost, his gaze fell on me and his wise eyes studied me as if I were from another world. He made me feel even younger than I was.

Crook's brow knit and the silver head began to nod. "McGillycuddy," he said. "You travel fast." Then he smiled. "And you have a grand sense of timing."

The other men laughed because they knew the Sioux were near. Then a silent order was given, and Bourke and Schuyler took their leave. Philo Clark remained, and Crook offered me a chair. Ever since the telegram had found me in Washington, I had wondered why I'd been chosen. Now, I thought, he's going to tell me.

"There is going to be a battle," Crook began. "We had a little mix-up getting in contact with our Crow scouts but that's worked out now and they're due in here soon. After that it could happen anytime. You'll be attached to the Second Cavalry." He watched me for a reaction. When there was none, he nodded. "It's good to have you here," Crook said. He winked an eye. "Lieutenant Clark will show you to your unit."

That was it. I was being dismissed. I rose with the general and offered a stiff salute. "Follow me, Doctor." It was Philo, already outside the tent flap.

We walked through the camp of a thousand men and nineteen hundred horses. There was excitement, but the activity was ordered and focused. I followed Philo, listening politely as he explained the layout of the camp and how it would move when the Crow arrived. We talked of the campaign and the topography of the land. Philo asked pertinent questions about my work as a surveyor. But it was hard to concentrate on what was being said. There was still the great unanswered question of why I had been called from Washington. Finally, after meeting the officers of the Second, I called Philo aside. We had taken to each other immediately and, though it was not then my nature to be so forward, I hazarded a direct question. "Why did he want me?"

Philo knew exactly what I was asking and smiled before making a reply. "It's hard to say what he sees in people," Philo said. "He's studied your maps. Perhaps he saw something in the way you rendered this land that he recognized." We had stopped under an ash tree that sustained itself from roots deep enough to reach the water of the Tongue. "He loves this place, you know. Sometimes I think he regrets having to bring war to it." Philo removed his white hat and mopped his forehead. "Could it be that he thinks you have the same passion but are in a position to heal the damage he is obligated to create?"

Philo's candor and perception were surprising. "I do have a great admiration for these plains," I said.

Philo nodded as if he expected as much and replaced his hat. "General Crook has a gift. He knows the landscape and he knows all the players. He must have thought you'd do your duty well."

"Yes, of course," I said. "But what *is* my duty?"

Again Philo smiled. "You're a man of science," he said. "I guess you'll know your duty when you see it."

21

Philo was always lithe in his movements. He slipped through the door of the adjutant's office gently and moved directly to Crazy Horse. The chief's eyes were open but glassy with morphine. Philo smiled; Crazy Horse smiled thinly back. "I know you'll be brave," Philo said.

Crazy Horse understood him and nodded his head almost imperceptibly. Then, with what to most whites would have seemed a gross lack of sensitivity—but there was perfectly acceptable—Philo asked me, "Is he going to live?"

"I don't know," I said truthfully. "It depends on what happened inside. We're going to have to wait and see."

Philo and Crazy Horse stared at each other. "What are you waiting to see?" Philo asked.

"If the blade missed his internal organs he'll probably live."

"And if it didn't?"

"He'll die."

"It would be bad if he died." Philo's voice was low and sincere. As soldiers, he and Crazy Horse had a complicated relationship. I was not surprised in the least when Philo knelt and stretched his hand out toward Crazy Horse's head.

The move brought Touch the Clouds forward and caused Philo to stay his hand. He spoke three words in perfect Lakota—*"He mita kola"*—and Touch the Clouds settled back into his sitting position.

Crazy Horse turned his head slightly and spoke Philo's name slowly. "White Hat," he said. Philo nodded and touched the chief's head as he would any fallen comrade's.

"And if a vital organ is involved, there is nothing to be done?"

I hesitated, because I had recently read a scientific paper that dealt with the repair of internal organs. It was mostly hypothetical, certainly impractical for a frontier camp. Still the paper, written by a Frenchman, had fascinated me so much that I had reread it to Fanny. I remember how she lay in bed beside me, her breasts heavy and so very feminine in her nightgown. Even now, with the lights of another warship appearing around the Cape of San Francisco, I recall the heat of the oil lamp burning on the bed stand and the intense way she inclined her head as I read.

"Correct," I told Philo. "If an organ is pierced, there is nothing that can be done."

Philo shook his head and pursed his lips as if he had just been given a bitter pill. "When will you know?" He stroked Crazy Horse's head lightly.

"If it's a liver, kidney, or gut, his heart will begin to weaken. We should know soon."

Philo rose to his feet. "I've wired General Crook at Camp Brown and Sheridan in Chicago. No answer from either of them yet, but I'm sure they will be very disappointed if he dies."

We faced each other and, as if by silent agreement, stepped to the far side of the room. "I'll do my best," I said. "You know that." Then a wave of bitterness swept through me. "But do you think they will really care?"

Philo nodded his head in the half-light of the lamp. "Oh yes. It's something we've talked about in detail."

He rubbed his bristly chin. “It’s something I wouldn’t expect you to understand, Mac.”

“Come now, Philo. I might surprise you.”

He smiled, amused by my temper. “You often do.” Then he motioned me to follow him outside.

We left the door open a crack and stood close in the starlight. At the periphery of the parade ground campfires had come alive. Horses still snorted, and their hooves pounded in the darkness. Somewhere women wailed.

“There has been a great deal of discussion on what to do about Crazy Horse,” he said. “By rights he could be considered a prisoner of war. But he’s no ordinary prisoner.”

“He’s not a prisoner at all, in fact,” I said. “He’s an Indian settled on the reservation according to treaty.”

“The line is blurry in his case, Mac. But at any rate, he’s no ordinary anything. No man in our lifetime, with the exception of Lincoln, has possessed Crazy Horse’s power to rally his people. He’s a symbol, Mac. Your patient is a symbol of all this.” He moved his arm to indicate everything that surrounded us. His influence is immeasurable and dangerous.”

“Wouldn’t it be easier if he died?”

“The orders are to keep him alive.”

“Well, you’re putting a great deal of pressure on me, but orders or no orders I treat them all the same. I try to keep everyone alive. It’s my job.”

We stood silently. From one of the campfires a low, steady drumbeat began. It filled our consciousness for a long moment. "In a way," Philo said, "yours is a simple job, isn't it, Mac? The big decisions are already made."

I agreed with Philo but by the day's end I would not be so sure. "It's best," I said, "that doctors are spared the burden of creating history. History is best left to men like you, Philo."

Again we stood silently and listened as a shrill voice joined the drum from across the camp. The combination of sounds penetrated my skin. The trill sank to my bones, and the feel of it made me question if I was still a doctor like the one I had just described to Philo. I was certainly different from the young man Doctor McGraw had sent West to gain experience. The change in me, accented just then by the deep sensation from the drum and chant, was like a dirty secret. I shook it out of my head and heart. My mind went completely blank and I tried to start over.

"Fanny?"

"I spoke with her," Philo said. "She's fine. Plans to bring you some supper soon."

"Is it safe, then?"

"For now."

"Is that where the deep concern comes from? You think if Crazy Horse dies there will be an uprising?"

Philo squinted one eye in thought. "No," he said, "the way things stand now, I don't think Crazy Horse's people are that strong. I'm more concerned with the future." He gave me a casual salute. "Do your best, Mac."

"Of course," I said without returning the salute. Philo walked into the night and I turned my face to the sky. The blackness was shotgunned with white holes. I let myself float with the loss of depth perception. I wanted to linger because I knew that when I stepped back through the door, there would be the claustrophobia of being inside. Since I first took work out-of-doors, walls and roofs have conspired to give me a nagging sensation of drowning. Even now I sometimes have to excuse myself, throw open a window, and stick my head and shoulders outside for the air. The urge comes over me at odd times, in a restaurant, in a barber's chair, when I'm examining a guest at the hotel. Occasionally people on the street will look up and point, wondering what has come over the strange white-headed old man emerging from the third-story window.

Eventually I returned to my patient and placed my hand again on his chest. It was a very strong heart but I thought I detected a weakening, some lack of resilience in the muscle that pushed the blood to Crazy Horse's extremities. Touch the Clouds's eyes bored into me as I concentrated on the thready heartbeat under my hand. I did not look up. It was hard to be sure about the heart, so I eased Crazy Horse onto one hip and pulled out the cotton pad that had been under his back. It came away bloody but not excessively so. I replaced it with clean cotton from the desk where Johnny had stacked a supply. The dressing would have to be changed soon, but not yet. I rolled Crazy Horse back to where he seemed most comfortable and sat back on my haunches. My medical bag was on the desk, and I pulled it to the floor and opened it. From a glass bottle I poured a measure of alcohol and ferric chloride into a spoon. Crazy Horse's dull eyes watched the spoon come close and then moved to my face. "This will make your blood stronger," I said. "Open your lips."

The chief's lips parted and he swallowed the solution. "Thank you, McGillycuddy," Crazy Horse said.

"You're welcome," I replied. "Now rest."

He spoke in Lakota simple enough for me understand. "I am not tired," he said. "I am like you."

I slowed my English for him. We had learned to communicate by using a little English, a little Lakota, and a little sign. We had worked on communication for the months since he had surrendered. "Oh," I said, "I get tired."

"You did not sleep for two days," Crazy Horse said. He was referring to when I had treated his wife during the worst episode of her consumption.

"I had good conversation to keep me awake." We smiled at each other, remembering how we had instantly renewed the friendship that had begun between us in the cool waters of the Knife River. After he had surrendered to Philo we sat together in the light from Crazy Horse's tepee fire and talked, through interpreters at first, of the land that had been the subject of the war. We recalled the way it was before.

"You remembered the face of Mother Earth like an

Indian," he said with the shadow of pain on his face.

"It was my job. I drew Her on paper."

"But you knew Crow Creek. You knew that the ducks build their nests in trees there. You told me how the water runs to the sea and how it comes back through the sky."

"I'm a scientist," I said.

"Yes, a man who feels nothing and believes there is an answer for all questions."

That made me laugh. "Is that what I said?"

Crazy Horse's thin lips trembled at the corners, then turned up slightly. "No," he said. "I say that." Then the smile turned to a grimace.

"You shouldn't talk. You should rest."

"I only like to talk to children," Crazy Horse said. "But I like to talk to you."

"Be still," I told him. I laid a hand on Crazy Horse's head and held it there until the eyes closed. "Sleep," I said. I kept my hand on his head; soon the tension slid from the face, and in another minute the breathing went steady and slow.

Crazy Horse's camp was an hour's ride from Camp Robinson. Fanny and I rode out as often as we could. Those long days spent in the surrendered hostile encampment with Crazy Horse were some of the most pleasant of my life. The incidence of dysentery and malaria at Camp Robinson was low, and most of the wounds dealt to heads and limbs during the war had either claimed their victims or improved to the point where my services in the hospital were needed only occasionally. Fanny and I had time and we chose to spend it caring for Black Shawl, a shy, quiet woman, as she fought the tuberculosis that had disabled her. Fanny guessed her to be older than Crazy Horse. She was not particularly pretty, yet she was gracious even in her troubled state. Each day when we appeared, she tried to get up from her buffalo robe and offer us food and water. Fanny, of course, would not allow it. She would gently push Black Shawl back against the coarse buffalo hair and set about trying to master the sick woman's Lakota kitchen. Crazy Horse smiled to watch her wrestling the hot rocks from the fire and into the animal skin filled with water. Eventually she learned to manage, and the water got hot enough to boil beef.

The four of us came to enjoy each other. Both Crazy Horse and Black Shawl remained hospitable after Black Shawl's recovery. They visited us at Camp Robinson, too, but we enjoyed the freedom of the Oglala camp more than the confines of our tiny wooden box. All that summer, up until the sizzling, jealous rumors boiled over, Fanny and I took every opportunity to sit by Crazy Horse's fire. I treated many Indians in Crazy Horse's camp for a variety of ailments. But most of my professional time was spent with Black Shawl. She was timid and, despite her age, was girlish in her reaction to whites. She avoided all but the simplest conversation with Fanny and so, even though Fanny knew the woman had a great deal to say, their talk was limited to children, cooking, the making of clothes. Crazy Horse and I, on the other hand, pumped each other continually for information. Science was so foreign to him that he sometimes took on the role of my student. Weather and stars were left to me to explain. When it came to the animals of the prairie, however, Crazy Horse did the teaching.

One day when the sun was high and its rays came through the thin prairie air without the slightest reduction in power, I lethargically mentioned that I found the predators that followed the buffalo herds frightful. "Especially the wolves," I said. As was often the case when Johnny Provost accompanied me to the camp, he was there in my service. He was as subdued by the day as I and translated in a low sleepy tone. But the heat did not seem to affect Crazy Horse, who snorted with amusement.

Such a chortle never fails to pique my combative nature. "You find my observation comical?" I asked. There was no need for translation. Crazy Horse replied with a wave of his hand.

"They are no more frightful than you or I," Johnny dutifully translated the comment. He became a nearly unnoticed conduit for our conversation.

"That may be so," I said. "But we're particularly despicable creatures."

Crazy Horse laughed. "Speak for yourself, Doctor."

"Surely you've seen wolves turn on their own for the joy of violence," I said.

Crazy Horse shook his head. "Never," he said.

"Well, they certainly do. I watched a buffalo hunter

shoot a big dog out of a herd of young bulls. It was wounded and the others turned on it as if it were an alien species."

Crazy Horse shrugged. "Why did he shoot it? They are not good to eat."

"Well," I said, "I'm not sure why it was shot but the rest of the pack turned on the cripple and tore it to shreds." I punctuated my point with a finger extended skyward. As Johnny repeated my meaning in Lakota he squinted an eye and nodded. "Can you explain that, Chief?" I added.

Crazy Horse sat cross-legged rubbing a long piece of wood with a stone. It had begun as a tree branch; now the shape of an arch was coming out of the wood. It would become a bow for one of the boys of the tribe. He thought about my question, watching the curls of wood peel away behind the stone. Everyone around the fire waited for his response. A few more curls of wood and Crazy Horse looked up and spoke to Johnny, who nodded but hesitated before he spoke. "The healthy wolves," he said, "killed the sick one for their own sake."

I wasn't quite sure what he meant, but I meant to take the offensive. "Exactly," I said. "They are simply bloodthirsty and satisfy their craving whenever the spirit moves them."

Crazy Horse went on smoothing the child's bow. "No," he said. He spoke again to Johnny, slowly, and the translation came even more slowly and with great effort to make it as close to Crazy Horse's meaning as was possible. "They did not want to kill their brother," Johnny said. He thought for an instant. "But if one wolf loses his dignity, all wolves lose their dignity. They did what they had to do only to remain wolves."

Crazy Horse nodded as if he were assuring us that that was his meaning. There was silence around the circle; the words had time to find a place in my mind. They have stuck there ever since.

Another time he said, "The wolves are to be admired. When I ride a horse, I try to be like a wolf. Smooth and fast. If I think it just right, I pass from man to wolf and finally become a bird. Moving over the land becomes effortless."

Lakota is not a pretty language; it is guttural and full of hard consonants. Despite that, the sound of Crazy Horse's voice could become dreamy and poetic. "If I couldn't fly like that," he said, "I couldn't live."

When I looked down at Crazy Horse on the floor of the adjutant's office I could find no wildness in the suffering face. The war chief did not look as if he could fly. He did not look free in the least.

Had the Crows who finally joined Crook during the Yellowstone Campaign to help hunt down Crazy Horse seen him in this state, they would have rejoiced. When those archenemies of the Sioux came riding into Crook's camp, the officers, soldiers, and teamsters congregated around them. The Crows were fierce and haughty, proud of the esteem given them by the troops, but in no time fell into the routine of the camp. They turned out to be less severe people than they looked. In fact once they were comfortable, they were more like teenagers out to prove themselves than Godless heathens. They laughed and joked in broken English and sign language. When the word *Sioux* or the name of Crazy Horse came up, however, their eyes narrowed and their chins elevated. It was hate at its most instinctive level. But it was impossible to know if it was driven by contempt, fear, or envy.

Shortly after the Crows joined us Crook held officers' call in front of his tent. He looked into every face. The long-awaited move into action was at hand. We would march at least twenty miles per day. Everyone should be ready to move after the noon meal. We would try for fifteen miles the first afternoon; slackers would be in danger of attack, capture, and torture at the hands of the Sioux.

Just as the conference came to a close the Crows began pointing to the south and shouting. A line of horsemen, brilliantly attired, was riding at whirlwind speed, with lances and rifles held high. "Shoshone," the Crows shouted. It was Chief Washakie, fierce and vibrant, along with eighty-six of his best warriors. The Shoshone crossed the creek in columns of two, like a company of regular cavalry. They carried two American flags; each lance was ribboned and snapped color into the breeze. They were all well armed and wore warbonnets and scarlet mantles. These Indians were well disciplined, awe inspiring, dangerous. I thought about the action to come; it would be the first combat of my life, and I was glad these Shoshones were allies. It gave me some comfort but I wondered what the Sioux must be like to inspire such excitement.

As the column organized, my new friend Philo Clark spoke with Old Crow, the war chief of the Crows. I marveled at Philo's ease in speaking the Crow tongue. The two men were obviously well acquainted, and it stood to reason that Philo had been instrumental in gaining Old Crow's allegiance.

When all was ready, the war chief stood before the officers and assembled Indians. He commanded, and got, everyone's attention—standing silently, his gray eyes unblinking, until all was quiet. I settled in, expecting to hear a long, self-indulgent speech translated by one of the half-breed Frenchmen. What I heard that day was instead a speech of such fierceness that it startled me.

"These are our lands by inheritance," Old Crow began. He moved his arm to indicate the country all around. "The Great Spirit gave them to our fathers, but the Sioux stole them from us. They hunt upon our mountains. They fish our streams. They have stolen our horses. They have murdered our women, our children."

Old Crow spoke with a strong voice. His hair flashed streaks of gray when his head turned in the sunlight, and the color accentuated the electricity in his face. "The scalps of white men and Crows hang thick in the lodges of the Sioux. Our war is with the Sioux and only them. We want back our land. We want their horses for our young men. We want their women for our slaves, to work for us as our women have had to work for them." The intensity of this warrior's words silenced even the boldest troopers. "The Sioux have trampled upon our hearts," he said. "We will spit upon their scalps."

A cheer went up but it was hollow, and I was suddenly truly frightened. Something was happening that was completely unfamiliar to me. In the lull that followed the feeble cheer I looked into the eyes of the officers and Indians who surrounded me. They were stony and deep; I felt I had missed something very important. The situation had moved beyond me, beyond the land that had adopted me, and was entering a different dimension. For the first time since I'd come to the high plains, I felt alien and out of place.

The column of soldiers and warriors was pageant-like with color and action, pomp and ceremony. Until Old Crow spoke I had looked on all of it like a big parade. But after the chief's speech, as the lean, light column began to move north from Little Goose Creek, I saw that this was like nothing I had ever been a part of. We moved through the same land I had moved through for many days, but we moved with a sort of energy I had never felt. Somewhere ahead of us was a village of tens of thousands of hostile Sioux. There would be a fight and I suffered a twinge of shame to think that my blood was as high as any man's.

22

I was sitting in the darkened adjutant's office wondering what I might do for my stricken friend when there came a rap on the door, and a soldier's voice. "Mrs. McGillycuddy to see the doctor."

I started to stand, then paused long enough to feel Crazy Horse's head one more time. The chief's eyes came open at the touch of my hand. I asked him if it was all right if Fanny came into the room. To my surprise and delight, Crazy Horse smiled. "I would like to see your wife again," he said.

I nodded as I rose to my feet. "And see her you shall," I said.

The corporal who was escorting Fanny carried in one hand a tray draped with a towel, in the other a Springfield carbine. Fanny moved past the soldier and into my arms. She was not frightened, only concerned for me. The light from the lamp shone on her smooth face and reflected from her wide eyes. "Are you all right?" she asked.

"I am. And you?"

She nodded, looking hard into my face, then seemed satisfied enough with my condition to pull away. Her eyes roamed the room and found, first Touch the Clouds frozen in a sitting position against the back wall, then Crazy Horse lying on his bed of blankets. He was staring at her. She did not avoid his eyes—she seemed drawn to them. "Does he understand us?"

"Some. He is under the influence of morphine. The wound is severe.

"The rumors are that he is grave."

"Indeed. Have you heard from Doctor Munn?"

"No." Fanny continued to look at Crazy Horse. "But I spoke with Mrs. Munn. The doctor is still ill."

"I imagine he's gone to bed with a second bottle of medicine."

Fanny pulled her gaze from Crazy Horse. "Valentine," she said, "Doctor Munn would be no good in this situation anyway. You know how he feels about the Sioux."

I certainly did know. My own care of Indians had always bothered Munn.

"You don't need him, do you?" she asked. There was a surprisingly hard edge to her eyes. Her expectations were high and I chose not to answer her question. She looked back to Crazy Horse.

"Lieutenant Lee asked me to advise you that Crazy Horse's people are highly agitated." The corporal was speaking to me. "Apparently some of Red Cloud's bunch are joining with them."

Defection, I thought. "Is there danger of a general uprising?"

"I couldn't say, sir. Things are confused. They tell me that Red Cloud will hold his people together."

"I imagine he will," I said. "It's his great talent."

"I've brought him some broth," Fanny said. "Could he drink it?"

"I don't see why not. It might do him some good."

This seemed to free Fanny of whatever had caused the hard edge in her expression. "Wonderful. And I've brought supper for you and . . ." She nodded toward the back wall.

"Touch the Clouds," I said. "A chief. A comrade, likely a boyhood friend."

Fanny was affected by the idea of these two men as boyhood friends and smiled sweetly. Then she moved very close. "Does the tall one speak?" she whispered.

"No," I said.

"Well," Fanny said as she reached for the tray, still in the corporal's hand. "I'll wager he eats." She uncovered the meal: beef roast, boiled potatoes, the last of the camp's sweet corn. The first plate came to me, the second to Touch the Clouds. When the chief accepted the plate, it looked like a saucer on his knee. Fanny stepped back with wonder on her face as Touch the Clouds began to eat the steaming food with one of his enormous hands.

Then she took the broth to Crazy Horse. The corporal who had escorted her across the parade ground was uncomfortable when she bent down to spoon the broth into Crazy Horse's mouth. He started to move forward to help her; I stopped him with an outstretched hand and motioned for him to wait outside. The soldier was gone before Fanny lifted the perspiring head onto her lap and trickled the first spoonful of broth between the dry lips. Crazy Horse did not look at the broth but kept his eyes on Fanny. He did his best to swallow, though it was clear that the morphine was doing little good. His teeth remained clenched.

I sat in a chair and tried to eat my own supper. "He seems to be suffering greatly," Fanny said.

I left my food and settled on the floor beside her. The morphine had definitely worn off. Before I prepared another syringe, I felt the heart again and found it weaker. The bayonet had surely severed an internal organ.

It was difficult not to reveal disappointment to Fanny. I drew morphine into the glass of the syringe. I could feel her watching as I injected it into Crazy Horse's arm. "His dressing should be changed," I said, then went to the door and sent Fanny's escort to get Johnny.

"You don't need Johnny to change a dressing," Fanny said. "I can help you." She looked at me with an air of indignation. "I've always wanted to, you know. Always wanted to help you in your profession."

We unfastened the long cotton wrap that was tied at Crazy Horse's stomach and peeled it back on both sides. I lifted him up while Fanny slid the dressing out from under him. Only a little blood showed until the dressing was totally revealed in the lamp light. It was not as bad as it could have been, but it was clear that clotting was not proceeding normally.

"Will you stitch the wound?"

"Can't be done," I said. "I'm afraid the bleeding is coming from inside. If I closed the wound he would bleed into his body cavity."

Fanny was rolling a fresh dressing from the pile Johnny had left on the desk. Her head tilted to the side, a sign she was considering seriously what was being said. "The bleeding is coming from somewhere inside? A muscle?"

"No. Deeper. I believe now that the bayonet pierced a kidney."

Fanny continued to think. "Poor thing," she said almost to herself. Crazy Horse was staring again at the ceiling. She shook her head but continued to prepare the dressing the way she had learned while volunteering at a hospital in Washington the year before. We were silent as we rewrapped the lean, muscular body in cotton. Crazy Horse tried to hold himself up as we worked, but I had to supply most of the support. I laid the chief down on his back as Fanny refolded the blanket under his head, then tied a square knot to hold the dressing in place and checked his pulse. There was a stethoscope on the desk but I'd never liked them. It was better to lay my head on Crazy Horse's chest and listen intently.

Fanny remained on the floor, stroking Crazy Horse's head, her skirts billowing around her. It was impossible not to think that some of the other officers, and particularly their wives, might think this scene unseemly. My temper still rises at the thought, but back then I wasn't sure why I felt such anger. To hell with them, I thought. Fanny was beautiful that way, caring for an injured man, be he white or Indian. But Fanny was not merely womanly. Her brow was knit in thought and I knew she would eventually speak what was on her mind.

From the first days of our courtship she had been outspoken. Not boisterous, but when she had something to say, she said it. I received a letter from her only two days before the Rosebud Fight. "The papers are full of nothing but Colonel Custer. Colonel Custer this, Colonel Custer that. They say he will run for president if he is successful with the Sioux—as if he were the only soldier out there. I believe he is little more than a boy, out for a good time!" It was something she would never have said in public. Her comment was no doubt motivated by a feeling that I had been indirectly slighted by the newspapers' coverage of Custer. But it was also something that was whispered around Crook's camp. Within a month Custer's presidential hopes were crushed. He lay dead and decaying on a hillside above the Little Big Horn River.

The battle that the Sioux call "Where the Girl Saved Her Brother" we call the Rosebud Fight, and it was a defeat for the United States. In smaller engagements the weeks before, Crook had been successful. Perhaps he was overconfident. Or perhaps he was simply outgeneraled by Crazy Horse, who laid a trap for us that Crook did not see coming. The Crow and Shoshone warriors who had just joined us proved to be more frill than fight. Their discipline broke down with the first counterattack, and their effectiveness dissolved. The man who lost his arm came in early in the fighting and I stitched his bloody stump the way an old woman would sew, to calm her nerves.

Johnny Provost had been assigned to me when I joined Crook's camp. He performed well but needed my encouragement. There was constant danger that our hospital would be overrun and I kept my revolver close at hand, because we had no guards. In fact the hospital was makeshift; most men were simply laid on the ground. An hour into the engagement all romance had drained out of warfare for me. I had never seen so many men who needed my attention. I had never seen so much blood. And by the time I had commanded the wounded train in the three-day retreat, watching men die who shouldn't have, I had never been so tired. We retreated to Little Goose Creek to lick our wounds and restore order to our ranks. A deep lethargy set into the command, though. Neither Crook nor his troops seemed inclined to move.

Somewhere to the north Custer, Gibbon, and Terry were closing in on the same band that had fought so well on the Rosebud. No one knew exactly how large the band was or exactly where it was camped, so there was the fear of a great unknown. But Crook and his officers seemed to have forgotten the war. They sent parties north to try to make contact with the other arms of the pincer; every group came back without finding any white men. What they did find were Sioux and Cheyenne. The enemy seemed to control all the country north of Little Goose Creek. Through Fort

Fetterman mail reached us from the south, and a sorrow, fueled by that connection to civilization, settled into the daily routine. Crook hunted in the mountains as if the war had stopped; most of the men played cards or fished, which I could not bring myself to do. Some caught hundreds of fish a day, as if they were taking their frustration out on the land, draining it of its nutrients.

I tended the wounded from the Rosebud Fight and fought the sensation that something was happening that I was missing. Some days I rode Buford out into the hills, to the edge of safety, and stared off to the north hoping for a clue. No one in Crook's command had any idea that Custer was moving steadily toward the Little Big Horn; still, like an animal, I sensed that something was about to happen.

As I watched Fanny nursing him now, I wondered if Crazy Horse knew that Custer had been approaching his camp that sultry summer day in June. Did Crazy Horse play the pivotal role in that catastrophe, as some said? Or was all that part of a grand nascent myth?

"Will you try to remove the damaged kidney? Stop its bleeding?" Fanny had characteristically focused directly upon the dilemma that had been working on me for the last hour.

"It's not something that is generally done," I said.

"But it was described in that paper you read to me." She looked up at me more like a comrade now than a wife.

"It's something to consider," I said. "But I'm not sure yet. We need to watch his pulse for a while longer. If he starts to fail, surgery could be an option."

Fanny nodded. "You could do it," she said.

Just then Johnny came softly through the door, and Crazy Horse made a low sound like the beginning of a song. The chief's eyes came open to find Fanny watching him. A tiny smile pulled at his mouth. He let his eyes close again, and Fanny reached out to touch his face. She let her hand trace the white scar that ran from his upper lip, along the cheekbone, to near his left ear. The room was still. Again she moved her fingertips over the scar.

From the back of the room came a voice like the sound of a thousand horses running in the distance. *"Mazasu,"* it rumbled.

Disoriented, Fanny and I looked at each other. Simultaneously we realized the source of the voice and turned our heads toward Touch the Clouds. He sat as straight as the shaft of a lance. *"Mazasu,"* he said, gesturing to Johnny.

"The scar is from a bullet wound," Johnny said.

"Tatanka sapawi hignaku ta mazaha ki."

"From the gun of Black Buffalo Woman's husband."

23

Fanny's eyes were wide, her mouth slightly agape. There was something in the way Touch the Clouds had volunteered his statement about Crazy Horse's scar that told us both he wanted to say more. It struck me immediately that the chief wanted to talk about his friend. "Black Buffalo Woman?" I asked.

He began to answer my question and Johnny related the story to us. "Crazy Horse and Black Buffalo Woman were friends from childhood," Johnny said in halting English that matched Touch the Clouds's speech. "She was the niece of Red Cloud." Touch the Clouds's head nodded slightly and his eyes narrowed with what might have been the memory of the days when they were all young. "But he could not marry then because he had vowed to protect all the helpless ones." Fanny let her hand stroke Crazy Horse's head. He was resting, perhaps asleep, and not unlike a child.

"And she married another," Fanny said.

Her comment was translated and Touch the Clouds began to nod. "Yes," Johnny said. "When Crazy Horse was fighting the Crows. The man was No Water."

I recognized the name. It was No Water who had ridden two horses to death pursuing Crazy Horse the day before. Fanny's features had softened with Touch the Clouds's words, and I was sure she had no idea how tangled the story was. I was also pretty sure that she would try to untangle it.

"And why did he shoot Crazy Horse?"

Touch the Clouds did not answer immediately. He waited until it seemed he would never go on. "In the end," he finally said, "their attraction was too great. They ran away and No Water should have let her go. It is our way. But he did not. He burst into their tepee and shot for the face."

"And the woman?" Fanny asked.

"Her nose is cut away but she lives still with No Water. Here on Red Cloud's reservation," he said.

Fanny's face contorted with the coldness of Black Buffalo Woman's punishment. Then she thought of Crazy Horse's wife and shock came over her face. "My God," she said. "Does Black Shawl know what's happening?"

"She may by now," I said. "I imagine word has circulated back to their camp."

Fanny stared. "Will she come?"

I shrugged because I had no way of knowing. "I'm sure she is at his camp."

Fanny looked to Touch the Clouds. "Will Black Shawl come here?" There was urgency in her voice and Touch the Clouds's stoic stare seemed a cruel response as he listened to Johnny's translation.

"I'm sure she'll come," I said to reassure Fanny.

"No," said Touch the Clouds. "It is not safe. Only me. And Worm, the father of Crazy Horse, if his son dies."

We all looked back to Crazy Horse. His eyes were closed but a wave ran through the muscles of his jaw to show that the pain was still with him. Fanny seemed to know my thoughts. I was chilled to think of a man suffering alone with his wife so close. I thought how I would need Fanny if I were in Crazy Horse's situation and I felt the tragedy of the politics that could force such an unnatural separation.

"He could die at any time," Fanny said to me.

"Yes, it is quite serious," I said dumbly.

"And how do you plan to treat him?"

"Well," I said in a low voice, "I'm not sure what is wrong with him so I have no idea what to do about it." I pulled at one side of my mustache, a bad habit I still have, and let my eyes shift away.

"My God, Valentine," Fanny said. "You could do anything you wanted to do. Why do you hold back?" She looked at me and I could see that she was confused and somehow disappointed.

She stood and moved toward the door. "You have opportunities to affect events. I can't see why you don't grab on to those opportunities."

She opened the door with a bemused look on her face. "I should get back to Lucy," she said mostly to herself. The waiting corporal came to attention. "I'll be back for the dishes," she said. But she gave me one last hard look before the door closed.

24

There was a light film of perspiration on Crazy Horse's forehead but when I felt him, he was not overly warm. He was so damned healthy I knew he'd be hard to kill. When I pressed a finger into a bicep, it sprang back like a teenager's. The muscles stood out in sinewy relief. I've often wondered how many times they'd pulled back the string of a stout Osage orange bow, how many deer and elk they had killed. I still think of those things; the remembered sounds of buffalo piked from horseback and the pounding of their hoofbeats sends a tremor through me yet. I can almost dredge up the vision of warriors riding full speed, bareback, lying along their horses' necks, swooping down on our confused column when we finally did venture into the field again.

Sitting back in the chair, I looked over my patient to Touch the Clouds. "Tell me how he fought," I said in poor Lakota. "Tell me how it was."

Johnny came to my aid. *"Tasanka witko tó ske wica kiza hwo?"*

The faint smile came again to the chief's face as if he, too, could hear the charge of unshod horses. "Was he as good as some say?" I asked.

Touch the Clouds hesitated in the way of the Sioux and I wondered if my meaning had gotten across. Johnny nodded to tell me that it had. The chief's eyes squinted as he thought. "He never tied up his horse's tail," he said. Then he nodded his head as if the image of his battle captain was coming clear. "He didn't care for the decoration of knots and feathers. He thought a horse needed his tail free for balancing his jumps and for killing flies." There was a pause; I suspect that the three of us were all thinking fondly of horses.

"And what kind of man is he, really?"

"It was all in his childhood vision," Touch the Clouds said. His voice trailed off into a tantalizing pause.

I couldn't wait. "Vision?" Crazy Horse had never

mentioned a vision, but I was familiar with this custom of seeing one's future in a dream. It is a marvelous notion; I wish Presbyterians had some similar magic in their doctrine. Life might have made sense to me earlier.

"He was an unusual child. Always alone, kind to the horses, and very quiet. Very good at the games we played. Always games of war."

Sioux boys were known for their skill at riding, shooting arrows, stealing meat from the drying racks. I'd watched them in their camps and knew Touch the Clouds was right, it was all training for war, horse thievery, endurance, and courage. *"Woihambli ki tuku hwo?"* I said. What about the dream?

"Woihambli ki tuku hwo?" Johnny said, with stress on different syllables.

A distant look came into Touch the Clouds's eyes and I regretted I'd been so insistent. I was suddenly afraid that Touch the Clouds would go silent. But the chief was only gathering his thoughts. Perhaps he was thinking back to the time when he and Crazy Horse, still just boys, had gone to the hills in search of wisdom and prophecy from the spirit world. All that was new to me then, though I've seen many mystics and vision questers among the Sioux since. From Sun Dancers to Ghost Dancers. The visions are mostly a mix of flimflam and exhaustion that induces hallucinations. Like all religion it is nonsense, except that it often works.

"Conquering Bear was dying," Touch the Clouds

began. I was caught off guard and had to think hard to recall that Conquering Bear was the first chief selected by the army to be the chief of all the Sioux; in some ways he was Red Cloud's progenitor. He was given power over the annuity goods that the United States traded for peace. The concept of a *supreme chief* was not understood by the Sioux but the army insisted upon it. The military thought it was an honor. It did Conquering Bear little good. He was mortally wounded by a volley from thirty army muskets fired at point-blank range. All the riflemen and their commander died at the hands of Conquering Bear's warriors minutes after their leader was gunned down. It was the initial clash of the first Sioux War. And as with seemingly every important engagement, Crazy Horse, though he was a boy, had been there.

"Crazy Horse fasted for three days, and on the third night a man in plain leggings and simple shirt appeared from the depths of a lake. He rode a fine horse but neither the man nor the horse were painted. He wore only a single eagle feather in his hair. And a small brown stone tied behind his ear." We all looked to Crazy Horse. The brown stone of the dream was the same stone Fanny had touched only minutes before.

"It was the man he would become?"

"It was the man he is, but it was a teacher, too." Again Touch the Clouds hesitated, and I was tempted to urge him on. But I didn't have the proper words, so I held my tongue and waited.

"He taught Crazy Horse how to dust his horse and his body for battle so that no bullet or enemy could kill him. He showed Crazy Horse how to ride through his enemies, how to keep his horse fresh. He told Crazy Horse that his own people would pull at him and try to bring him off his horse, but that he should always be kind to the helpless ones. He should take no scalps. He should give everything he won in battle to others. He should hunt for the people and be the last to eat." Touch the Clouds had been staring off into space as if he saw something invisible to me and Johnny. He let the room go silent then turned his eyes directly onto me. "All these things, he has done," Touch the Clouds said. "Only one prophecy remains."

"And what would that be?"

"He taku hwo?" Johnny asked.

When he is finally killed," Touch the Clouds said, his arms will be held by friends."

"No matter how he dies," I said, "he will be remembered as a warrior."

"He has always been a warrior. He killed many men. Crow, Shoshone, Omaha, Pawnee."

"White?" I asked. *"Wasicun?"*

"Han," Touch the Clouds said. *"Ska wica 'sa otapi yelo."*

I looked to Johnny for the translation. "Yes," he said. "Many. Many whites."

25

Southern Michigan in the middle of the last century was a civilized place with cities and institutions that exemplified the best parts of our country. It was a seedbed for politicians, educators, thinkers, and, perhaps most of all, for defenders of the Union that had recently been preserved through warfare like the world had never seen before. Fanny and I were pedestrian products of that culture. During the Civil War, and for years after, the most visible citizen of that heartland was Bvt. Gen. George Armstrong Custer.

General Custer and his wife, Elizabeth, lived in Monroe, Michigan, a scant thirty miles south of Detroit. The Custers were an ideal model for many younger couples during and after the War of Secession. We were no exception. I was just a boy when Custer earned the rank of brigadier general, and he, only a few years older than that. The dashing soldier took command of the First Michigan Volunteers at the age of twenty-three and in the midst of the Civil War became an instant hero. His courage and his exploits on and off the battlefield were well known to all through intense newspaper coverage. He was a man who inspired tremendous confidence in those Union ideals that so many had died defending. When I found out that, during the Yellowstone Campaign, Custer would be commanding the Seventh Cavalry under the overall command of Terry, I was thrilled; it meant I would be serving in the same campaign as my childhood hero. I did not yet know the difference between a hero and a murderer legitimized by war.

I even wrote Fanny a giddy letter predicting that, when the three columns met up, I would have the distinction of meeting George Custer face to face. The possibility that Custer would be dead, stripped naked, mutilated, and buried in an unmarked grave never could have occurred to me.

Crook's column had moved out from our sanctuary on Little Goose Creek and into a terribly hot July. One morning somewhere in the broken country along the Powder River a messenger arrived at Crook's tent from the north. It was the first contact we'd had from the other columns since before our defeat on the Rosebud. The camp began immediately to buzz with rumors that the hostiles had been located, that Terry had engaged them, and that there were huge casualties. Word eventually seeped out that the invincible Custer and over three hundred troopers had been killed. The news was profoundly demoralizing. In an effort to hold ranks together, Crook pronounced the account of the battle unreliable. Still, when we began to make our way north, we moved with uncertainty.

Crook was cautious and halting in his command for a week before he could get a messenger to Terry. During that time Sioux warriors were sighted on our flanks nearly every day, and everyone believed an attack was imminent. Deep in our hearts all of us knew that the rumor was true. Custer, a demigod with many times the skill and courage of any of us mere mortals, had died at the hands of the enemy that surrounded us. The professional officers maintained their air of confidence but, as a surgeon, I was asked to counsel several young troopers who were so afraid that they could do little more than clutch themselves, rock back and forth, and sob.

One evening the Shoshone scouts brought in scalps of Sioux they had encountered. They paraded through the camp with their bloody, flyblown prizes held high on lances. I had a chance to speak with a young warrior who claimed to have taken one of the scalps. He smiled and shook the blood-matted hair in my face. It was hard to tell what he was saying—something about his bravery, about how the sight of him had terrified the Sioux and they had run from him like antelope. Though I could not understand everything he said, I did recognize that the bravado in his voice reflected the terror in the young man's heart. It was the talk of a frightened boy, and the scalp he was so proud of, I can assure you, was that of a woman.

On the eighth of August we marched through an immense deserted Sioux village on the Little Big Horn River. Several thousand Indians had camped here. It took nearly an hour to march from one end to the other. The day was intolerably hot; dust from the horses' hooves rose and hung in the air so that half of every breath was earth. The eastern horizon was obscured by a curtain of black smoke, for the Sioux were burning the prairie to sterilize the ground and discourage pursuit by destroying all forage. The column rode through the ghost village for miles. Tepee rings and racks for drying meat stood eerie and useless, along with the expendable personal effects of the Indians who had fled. I didn't realize it then, but now I know I was riding through the remains of an entire culture. Never again would this many Indians camp in one place.

The column passed hastily constructed burial scaffolds and a tall, bare pole used for a Sun Dance. Dried rawhide ropes that had recently held dancers by wooden pegs forced through their flesh dangled twenty feet long in the furnace-hot wind. At the top of the pole a doll hung from a strap of rawhide. It was a figurine of a mounted Sioux warrior, riding naked, his exaggerated phallus erect and rising in front of him to head level. A lowly trooper leveled his rifle and shot the phallus away to the cheers of the entire command. An officer near me spit out his disgust with his tobacco. "Devil worshipers," he hissed. "Imagine a religion symbolized by such a thing." At the time I foolishly agreed with the man, but now I'm not so sure a phallic icon is any worse than any other religious symbol. At least it makes some sense.

On the night of the ninth of August the weather changed. The next morning, the day we finally met up with General Terry, frost lay thick on the sleeping men and a chill seeped up from the ground. That afternoon we saw where Terry had buried the 311 officers and men who had died with Custer on the Little Big Horn.

From the men who had found them I heard of the ways they were mutilated, the fingers, genitals, even heads severed with crude axes. Hundreds of arrows protruded from nonvital parts of the bodies; there were marks in the dirt where the troopers had crawled, vainly trying to escape their tormenters who, undoubtedly, walked along behind, laughing and betting on how long the man could remain alive. They said it was the women who performed most of the atrocities, but everyone seemed certain that it was Crazy Horse who led the attack.

In the late afternoon I stood over the grave said to hold the man I had grown up admiring. Gloom settled on me. I wondered what could possibly have gone so wrong. Some said Custer died a hero's death and others said he died a coward and a fool. If that were true, or even if it weren't, what of all those things he stood for? What of the Union, what of emancipation, the Constitution, courage, and honor? Had something changed? Were the laws of nature different on the western side of the Missouri?

After walking over the battlefield and imagining what it must have been like, I looked again to the east—to where the grass fires were taking away the grazing for any column that might try to chase Custer's killers. Hundreds of thousands of acres smoldered between me and the Black Hills, a couple of hundred miles southeast. The Sioux were turning the country they were fighting for into a wasteland. A chill shot through my body like an arrow—for two reasons. First, because I had come to think of that growing wasteland as my land, too, and second, because I was nearly petrified with fright. Crook would have to go after those Indians. I did not want to go along. Now, many, many years later, I know it was Crazy Horse moving in front of that wall of fire. Had we known that at the time, our fear might have been complete. There might have been mass mutiny.

Even in that ignorance there were other cowards not strong enough to conceal their stripe. And there were soldiers who were showing signs of emotionally breaking. It was at the camp on the Little Big Horn that Private Holden was first sent to see me. His sergeant had told him to come talk to me, but Holden didn't seem to know just what he was supposed to talk about. I was busy with dysentery, malaria, and wounds of men from both Crook's and, now, Terry's commands. My coat and hands were bloody, and several men called deliriously for me from their cots. But I nodded to Holden, letting him know it was all right to speak.

"Sergeant Arnold said I was talking crazy," Holden said. "He sent me to the chaplain but the chaplain's a Lutheran. He really didn't want me around."

I rolled the white sleeves of my coat in preparation for the next patient. I tried to maintain a professional presence even under those extreme conditions. But of course the coat had not been washed for a week; there were stains where my sweat had collected the dust from the march, a button was missing, there were spatters and smears of blood. It bothered me, though I was certain no one noticed. I had already asked Johnny Provost to wash my second shirt and coat when he got a chance. But Johnny was working shoulder to shoulder with me in the heat of the tent awning, and even if no more casualties came in it would be another couple of days before either of us had the time to do laundry.

"What seems to be the matter?" I asked Holden. I was debriding an infected arrow wound on the thigh of a young, curly-haired trooper.

"I guess it was mostly a political difference between me and the sergeant."

"Political difference?" I spoke absentmindedly, concentrating on my patient, who was doing his best to quietly endure the scraping of my scalpel. The dead tissue was coming away, exposing the pus underneath, and the trooper was trying to smile. His blond hair stuck to his forehead, where perspiration caused by heat and pain stood out in tiny droplets. "Political differences are not usually a medical problem."

"Well, it's really not so much political as social."

The precision of that comment got my attention. I took my first real look at Holden. He was neat and handsome; he carried a perpetual smile on a broad, square face. From what I had already heard I knew he was more articulate by twice than any enlisted man I'd met since I left Cheyenne. Filtering through my fatigue was the thought that, had we been in a civilized place, with time to spare, it might have been pleasant to spend an evening chatting with the man. I've always enjoyed evenings like that, a cigar, a glass of port perhaps, Fanny at my side, a fire. During the Yellowstone Campaign I longed for such an evening. It would have been nice to take a long walk with Holden and learn all about the difference of opinion he had with his sergeant. But I was too busy with men like the young trooper grimacing on the cot in front of me. Instead of my usual curiosity about the discussion the sergeant had had with this private, I felt an irritation at the sergeant for even sending the man to me. "So what exactly did you say that upset your sergeant?"

"Not rightly sure, sir. We were talking about what happened to Custer's Seventh and I said it was understandable."

"None of us should attach blame, soldier. It's not our place."

"I don't mean I understand how the engagement came to happen. Engagements just happen. I mean about what happened afterward."

By then I was dressing the trooper's wound. Johnny had finished with another man and come to help. He mopped the soldier's brow. "What afterward?"

"I mean the butchering. I told the sergeant I could see how those Indians would want to cut pieces off the men they killed."

The curly-haired trooper leaned slightly forward and tightened. He pulled himself to one elbow and stared at Holden. Emotions were running far too high to let

Holden continue talking in the presence of a man who could easily find himself in exactly the same situation as the men of the Seventh Cavalry. "That should help, soldier," I said to the wounded man. "The corporal here will issue you some salts. Do as he says." Johnny read my mind and hustled the soldier to his feet, away from Holden. I walked out from under the tent awning and Holden followed. Even though the nights were freezing, the noonday sun was as hot as a campfire. We moved to the shade of a cottonwood tree and I took a canteen from where it hung on a broken branch above a crude table.

"Tell me more," I said. I motioned for the soldier to sit down as I poured water into a basin set on the table. He spoke while I washed my hands.

"Not much more to tell, sir. I can just see that a man, any man, might get mad enough to do some pretty nasty things if he was put in the position of these Indians."

I moved to where the private was sitting and settled down on a wooden keg beside him. "Where are you from, soldier?"

"Connecticut."

"And how long have you been on the frontier?"

"About a year."

Holden was younger than I but not much. He had a slightly wild look to his eyes yet I felt an immediate kinship with him. "You like it out here, don't you?"

"Yes, sir. In some ways I like it out here fine. I would think everyone would like it some. I mean, look at it." Holden swung his arm to the rolling, grassy hills that surrounded the camp. He was right to see beauty in those hills, and I was ready to agree with him. Then Holden laughed in a way that made me hesitate. The laugh was a little too shrill, and Holden's eyes danced under raised brows. "Christ, Doc, Custer was damned fortunate to be gutted and skinned in the midst of all this."

26

Holden's cackle rings in my ears to this day. When I sit alone at night like this I can still see the delight in his eyes and the bright white teeth of his smile. There had been no choice but to send Holden back to his company. We were hundreds of miles from any kind of permanent settlement and thousands of miles from any facility that could give Holden the care I suspected he needed. We were the army of the United States and we had just suffered the worst defeat ever sustained at the hands of Indians. Perhaps worst of all we were still deep in the land of the enemy with no force on the planet that could help us. There was no way to know what adversity lay ahead of us, and I already had too many men to take care of. For his own good I advised Holden not to discuss his opinions with any other soldiers. He would have a tough enough time in the next battle to keep from catching an arrow in his chest. A few more comments like the one he had made to me and I would have expected him to turn up with a bullet in the back of his head as well. But I'm getting ahead of myself.

The lamp on the adjutant's desk needed trimming, and I stood up and went to it. As the light came up the face of Touch the Clouds came clear again. Crazy Horse's eyes were open but drugged. I stretched and took my watch from my coat pocket. It was nearly nine-thirty. Crazy Horse had lived for four hours and seemed about the same. Who could have said but there was a chance he would live forever?

I went to him and checked his pulse. Slow but steady. His breathing was shallow, perhaps due to the morphine. The wound was still bleeding, though—not profusely, but something was keeping it from clotting. I laid my hand on Crazy Horse's head and searched for a temperature. Both of us closed our eyes as I tried to feel what was wrong inside this patient. I concentrated and let myself drift into something of a trance. Over the years I've learned that the science of medicine is really more of an art. I didn't know that then; but I must have sensed it, because I expelled all the air in my lungs and visualized the hand laid on the chief's forehead slipping beneath the skin, past the skull, and into the great puzzle that constitutes human health. I felt for the rupture that was making this man so sick.

I was roused by the opening of the door behind me. I kept my eyes closed until I heard Johnny's quiet voice. "Your missus sent a message," he said. "She says we're needed up at the Cheyenne camp. She asked me to bring the birthing equipment and said she'd meet us here."

My eyes snapped open and I took a moment to regain my professional dignity. Facing Johnny but still not looking him in the eyes, I spoke matter-of-factly. "What's the trouble at the Cheyenne camp?"

Johnny shrugged. "It's Willow Bear's sister. She's in trouble with a bad delivery." He held up the canvas bag that held the little-used obstetric kit. The last person to need it had been Major Flannery's wife. Fanny and I had helped her deliver twins not a month before.

"She expects us to leave here to deliver a Cheyenne baby?"

Johnny shrugged again. "She sent a message to meet her here with the tools." Again he held up the canvas bag.

"I don't see how we can leave." I spoke more to myself than to Johnny and turned my attention back to Crazy Horse.

"And how's he doing, sir?"

"Not much change, I'm afraid." I caught myself shaking my head. It was not good bedside manner and, even though Crazy Horse would not mind, I stopped myself immediately. "About the same," I said.

Johnny hesitated before he spoke. "Are you considering going inside?" he asked. It was a surprising thing for Johnny to say. He spoke it in a reverent voice.

The tone of the question made me wonder what

Johnny imagined a kidney operation to be like. He had no medical education and I was aware that his Indian side told him the body cavity was a sacred place. He had never seen the insides of a living man; he must have equated such an operation with field-dressing an elk. "Where did you get the idea I was thinking of operating?"

"Mrs. McGillycuddy mentioned it when I escorted her to your house."

"Well," I said, "don't believe everything my wife says." I spoke too sharply. It was not my intention to give Johnny the impression that Fanny and I were in public disagreement. If we ever disagreed, which throughout our life together we did very seldom, it was no one's business but our own. "And I wouldn't let that sort of wild talk get around the camp."

Conversation came from outside the room. We heard the sentry greeting Fanny, and then the door opened. "Mrs. McGillycuddy to see the doctor."

Fanny came in wrapped in a dark purple shawl. Her hair was tucked up under a hat that tied under her chin. She carried two mason jars in her hands and, as she had done on her last visit, she embraced me and looked square into my eyes to be sure I was all right. This time she saw that I was slightly perturbed with her but enduring the larger situation. "How is he?" she asked. I nodded and she understood that as a neutral sign. She moved to Crazy Horse and looked down at him with deep scrutiny. "I brought him more broth," she said absently.

"What is this about the Cheyenne camp?"

Fanny's head jerked up as if she had nearly forgotten why she had come. "A woman has been trying to give birth for over twelve hours. Her brother came for your help."

"Fanny." I held my hand out to Crazy Horse. "This man can't be left alone."

"Of course not. That's why I'm here. I can stay with him."

"Nonsense," I said. "You can't stay here with two hostiles."

"They hardly look hostile."

"Well, they are. Or they were. No, it's out of the question. I shouldn't leave him, anyway. And besides, it's not safe traipsing around the Indian camps tonight."

"Going to Indian camps has never bothered you before."

"Crazy Horse was never stabbed by a white man before."

"But the woman. And what can you do here?"

"I can watch. I can be here."

"Then let Corporal Provost watch and be here. I'll go with you to help the woman."

It took an effort to hold my temper but the sense of what Fanny suggested was impossible to dispute. I looked at Johnny. "Would you feel comfortable, Corporal?"

"Certainly, sir. I'll keep a close eye on him."

"And you'll send a messenger if there is even the slightest change?"

"I can do that, sir. Shouldn't be any problem to send someone up the hill to find you."

I squinted but nodded, then I looked to Fanny and around the room. Touch the Clouds stared straight ahead. Crazy Horse's eyes were open again, and I went to check him one more time. His forehead was perspiring. I mopped it with a towel that lay across his chest. Then I felt his earlobe for any sign of excess heat. The touch of my hand caused his head to turn and we stared at each other. Neither of us moved until Crazy Horse spoke. "Go," he said. "Go help the Cheyenne woman."

27

Fanny and I, in the company of a small squad of troopers, were halfway across the parade ground, a quarter mile from where the woman lay in prolonged labor, when the meaning of what Crazy Horse had said began to register on me. I had not spoken to Fanny as we walked and just then, even though she was speaking to me, I was dumb as I sorted out what it took for Crazy Horse to send us to the Cheyenne camp.

It was well known that Crazy Horse had spent a great deal of time with the Cheyenne when he was a boy, and that they had fought side by side during the worst of the Sioux Wars. But the winter before, when Col. Ranald Mackenzie, serving under Crook, struck the Cheyenne village of Dull Knife, everything had changed. It was the coldest part of a horrendous high plains winter. Above the Powder River, where Dull Knife was camped, the wind was ceaseless and cut through the men's clothing like hypodermic needles.

Crook and our column had been rescued six weeks earlier from our fateful Starvation March and, after a period of recuperation, I had already escorted Private Holden to an insane asylum in Washington. Fanny had joined us on the way to the capital, so we first heard of Mackenzie's success at a Washington, D.C., cocktail party three weeks before Christmas. The regiment had captured 205 Cheyenne lodges, all filled with the necessities of war and life. The site of the battle was well known to me. Even there at the party I could imagine the tepees, strung out along the Powder River among the giant, ancient cottonwoods and the sagebrush peeking up through the snow like dark green fingers. Certainly the entire scene was tortured by icy wind.

On the subzero morning of November 25 Mackenzie struck with the full force of his cavalry and hundreds of Pawnee and Shoshone scouts. In addition Mackenzie enjoyed the services of a meaningful contingent of disaffected Sioux and Cheyenne, who betrayed their people with a savage glee. Schuyler, who led these turncoats, later told me that the men under his command were fighters first, members of a given tribe or race of people second. It made no sense to me at the time, but now I see that most soldiers are the same.

The Cheyenne were driven from their tepees and into the freezing winter with nothing but the meager clothes in which they had slept. In addition to Chief Dull Knife there was Little Wolf, one of the bravest in battles where all were brave, and Standing Elk, known for his coolness and determination in hot action. These were some of the best fighters on the plains but their prowess did them no real good against Mackenzie's stealthy night fighters. The counterattack never materialized; the action was a complete success.

Some women and children were taken prisoner, and 705 ponies were captured. That night, after the fleeing Cheyenne warriors had gotten their remaining women, children, and elderly into the hills, they were forced to kill the ponies they had managed to take with them—for food and for the meager warmth their body cavities could offer the feet and hands of the weakest. Even among the captives in Mackenzie's charge, fourteen babies froze to death in their mothers' arms.

Before the tepees were burned, along with all the stores of food and clothing the Cheyenne had amassed to get them through the winter, the camp was searched. Among the plunder was a buckskin bag containing twelve of the right hands of Shoshone babies lately killed by the Cheyenne. The dreadful bag was given to Mackenzie's Shoshone, who wept and wailed over it all night. They refused to be comforted, and declined to join with their Pawnee comrades in the festivities celebrating their brave battle feats. In other tepees were found gauntlets, hats, saddles, and silk guidons marked with the names of United States soldiers and the insignia of Custer's Seventh Cavalry.

It was the discovery of these grim artifacts that interested the guests at the Washington cocktail party most. They asserted that their existence in the lodges of the Cheyenne proved these people were directly involved with Custer's massacre—as if this fact justified any action of the army. Fresh from the front and still being kept awake by dreams of my ordeal with Crook, I knew more about the situation on the plains than any man at the party. I had no doubt that the Cheyenne had helped kill Custer. But that meant only one thing: They had fought with Crazy Horse in the most stunning military victory the plains Indians had ever achieved. And that is why it seemed so cruel that after the destruction of Dull Knife's village, his frozen, suffering band of survivors made its way to Crazy Horses's beleaguered camp hoping to be taken in. But Crazy Horse could not take care even of his own. He turned the Cheyennes back into the icy darkness, where Mackenzie's troopers coursed for their prey like savage lurchers.

28

No one slept in the Cheyenne camp. Deep drums rumbled from near the many fires that sent sparks up and into the stars. Some of the young men danced to the drums. They strutted stiffly and leapt through the firelight, casting wild, feathered, Platonic shadows against the hide walls of the tepees that were their homes. “Stay close,” I told Fanny. She held her head erect, her back as straight as one of the lances that jutted from the earth in front of each lodge.

“You needn’t worry,” she said.

One of the camp criers noticed our little party approaching from the army camp. He let out a shout as if to warn the camp, but his main intention was to draw attention to himself. With a few of the closest warriors watching, he began a ritualized march to meet our band as if we were dangerous intruders.

The corporal commanding our escort moved to intercept the man. I held him back. “It’s just for show,” I said. “Let him have his moment.”

The campfire at the crier’s back lit the huge wooly head of his buffalo helmet. The horns curved in an arch that could have been mistaken for a halo, but the scene was so very pagan that any Christian could only think it a crude mockery. The crier carried a painted war club with long spiked feathers dangling from the handle. He held the weapon high in one hand and rattled its heavy, menacing head between the buffalo horns. “Steady,” I whispered. “This is a kind of game.”

The warriors for whom the performance was being staged moved up behind the crier. I addressed a question to them. “The woman who is giving birth? We’ve come to see her.”

“The sister of Willow Bear.” It was Fanny. Her voice

was surprisingly strong.

None of these Cheyenne spoke English so I tried again in a combination of sign and Lakota. The young men, dressed in finely tanned buckskin and with the figures of animals painted on their faces, had been resolute in their aloofness. But, they understood enough of my signs to respond by dissolving into animated, giddy chatter. Now they realized who this long, lanky, mustached man was. It was the white doctor, and his huge canvas sack was his medicine bag. They waved for us to follow and we left the crier, still strutting and shaking his war club. As we moved past one tepee after another more warriors joined. Older women fell into line, and a ball of nervous children circled us like small human satellites.

Fanny watched the children. "They're wild," she said.

"Confused," I replied without altering my gait. "Not only the children. This is a night they will all remember, even if they never understand what is happening."

Fanny must have known by the distance in my voice that I was struggling to understand what was happening myself. Initially, she might have believed it was simply a matter of another war chief stricken out of ignorance, perhaps the death of another friend, the birth of a baby. But there was something more going on that night. We all felt it and were all trying to get our minds around it. Fanny was an attentive woman; as I watched her from the corner of my eye I saw that she had resolved to pay close attention, to be ready for whatever was ahead.

The birthing tepee was set off alone at the end of the camp. A campfire glowed fifty feet to the north, and a half-dozen old women sat on the ground chanting to a beat that we could not anticipate. These women were likely relatives of the woman who was laboring inside the tent. Farther into the darkness, at the end of the camp, alone and rigid, stood a young man. He was hard to make out in the poor light, but he faced away from the others and looked up at the sky. He was motionless with his hands down at his side and his fingers spread so they looked disproportionately large.

From the shadows to the young man's left came a boy. It was Willow Bear and though his face was held tight, we could tell he had been crying. He spoke in Cheyenne; I was able to understand only that he was talking about his sister. Then the boy motioned toward the tepee. He spoke again and I believe he said, "High Wolf is with her."

As if cued for an appearance, High Wolf sprang from the tepee entrance. He was completely naked except for two long trains of feathers braided into his hair and dangling to his knees. Black and white lightning bolts of greasy paint slashed his chest and face, and his eyes were circled in blood-red vermillion. The rattles in his hands whipped from side to side. He uttered a catlike sound that sent a visible chill up Fanny's back. Again the corporal of our escort moved to protect us, but I held him back. "Easy, soldier. Easy,

Fanny. This is High Wolf, the medicine man."

Neither Fanny nor I let on that High Wolf's appearance had any effect on us. Fanny averted her eyes from High Wolf's nakedness but held her ground as the medicine man swirled around. He shrieked and held the rattles close to my face. They were made of some canine skulls sealed at the eyes and mounted on flexible wooden shafts. They were ghastly, with the mouths of the creatures sewn up like trussed turkeys.

None of this surprised me. It was to be expected from a medicine man in the throes of plying his art to save a mother with child. Such shenanigans were particularly predictable from High Wolf, who had a reputation for theatrics and the grotesque. It was well known that he had been relieved of a necklace of human fingers after Mackenzie struck their village the winter before. The relic had fallen into the hands of Captain Bourke and, on the same trip that had escorted Private Holden to the insane asylum, I delivered the necklace to the National Museum in Washington. High Wolf had no idea of the fate of his talisman and continued to lobby Bourke for its return as if it were a sentimental article of memorabilia. Unfortunately, Fanny had suffered seeing the thing. Now that she knew this was High Wolf, she put the two together. A look of disdain came over her face, and she stared right through him. I paid no attention to the medicine man's attempts to intimidate us. He made one more round and stopped, stock still, pretending to be in some sort of a trance. I motioned for the escort to take positions on each side of the tent then took Fanny by the hand and led her around the staring sorcerer into the tepee.

An old woman poked the coals of a low fire with a charred stick. The fire was in the center of the tent and popped to life at the woman's touch. The walls of the lodge danced with shadows. A few sparks ascended toward the chimney hole at the top of the tepee. The old woman turned her head halfway toward us, the creases in her cheeks creating their own maze of shadows. She was dressed in worn buckskin; one of the thongs that wrapped her braids had come untied. She stirred the fire one more time then moved to the back wall of the tent, where she looked on with the same passive stare that Touch the Clouds employed to watch over Crazy Horse.

Outside the tent flap High Wolf wailed, and a choir answered from the fire at the edge of the camp. Fanny went rigid at the frenzied sound. I tried to assure her by simply clearing my throat. "Pay them no attention," I said as I removed my coat. "See if there's water in that canteen, Fanny. Give the poor thing a drink if she'll take it."

I tried to keep the urgency out of my voice but it's hard to tell how successful I was. The girl looked dreadful, and the moment Fanny saw her ashen face she forgot about High Wolf. She found water in the canteen and poured some into a ladle. When she knelt beside the laboring woman, she shook her head. "Oh," she said, "she's so young." It was true. Her smooth skin testified to that fact, though her face was thin and her eyes sunken. She was barely half Fanny's age. "Too young," Fanny said, "to be a mother."

There was fear in the girl's eyes but she was too exhausted to resist us. Fanny settled beside the frail figure and offered the ladle of water. The girl stared up at her with hollow eyes but did not move. It was impossible to tell if she wanted the water or not but, when Fanny put the ladle to the dry lips, they parted. Most of the water trickled down the girl's throat, but a dribble ran from the corner of her mouth. Fanny mopped it with the hem of her dress then felt the pale forehead. "She's burning up, Valentine."

"I should think so." I had raised the woolen blanket that covered the girl and was inspecting the process of the birth. "The baby is breached. It's trying to come backward, sort of a footling breach." I sat back on my haunches and rolled up the sleeves of my white shirt. When I leaned forward and tried to manipulate the child I expected the girl to wince with pain, but she lay still, as if she felt nothing. "She's too tired to help," Fanny said.

She was correct. The baby was not going to come into the world easily. I rose and looked around the tepee. An iron pot hung by its handle from one of the tepee poles. "Let's get some water boiling in that pot," I said. "Hand me the bag." Fanny passed the canvas bag we had brought and I set it on the buffalo-robe-covered floor, unfastened the brass snap that held it closed, and gazed at the crude obstetric tools of a frontier army camp.

While Fanny poured the remainder of the water into the pot and set it to boil, I stripped off my shirt. In my military-issue underwear I set the implements contained in the canvas bag on the tanned side of an antelope hide. Fanny was afraid to ask, but she had to. "Is the baby still alive?"

I was placing the shiny tools in a precise order. "I'm not sure," I said absently. Fanny forgave my insensitivity immediately; she knew I was thinking about the baby. When I looked up and found her staring at me, I tried to smile. "We'll try to take the baby by cesarean. Give that canteen to the old woman. We're going to need more water."

When Fanny held the canteen out to the woman, I spoke in my elementary Lakota. *"Mni. Ota mni."* The woman must have understood, because she took the canteen from Fanny and slipped out under the tent flap.

Next, I stripped off my underwear shirt to reveal my white, bony chest. I've always been thin, with stringy muscles—not a sight to stimulate most women—but I found Fanny looking at me in a curious way, a smile curling her lips. I carefully poured the powdered contents of a small vial into a larger bottle. She let her eyes drift up to mine as I mixed the fluid by restoppering the bottle and shaking it vigorously. I answered the question in Fanny's eyes. "Opium and alcohol. It will help her with the pain."

I measured half the bottle into a small, engraved

pewter drinking cup. "She needs to take this."

Fanny took the cup, knowing instinctively that it was her job to see that the girl took the medicine. She sat by the girl's head and tried to elicit a smile by smiling herself. The girl couldn't return it, but there was something good in her eyes that had not been there a few minutes before. When Fanny held the cup out to her the girl took it, inadvertently touching Fanny's hand. From the corner of my vision I saw the tenderness in the touch and my eyes filled instantly with tears. But the laudanum was bitter and the girl wanted to gag when she swallowed. Fanny held the cup tight against her mouth until all the liquid was gone.

"We need to wash her belly." I slowly pulled the blanket away to expose the abdomen. With her tiny strength the girl clutched at the blanket, and though I could see that Fanny wanted to turn away out of modesty, she eased the girl's weak fingers from the coarse wool to leave the body exposed. The belly was swollen, the skin stretched tight over the unborn infant. The girl's legs looked thin in contrast, and there was almost no hair around her dilated vagina. One knee of the baby that was trying to be born was visible.

I called for the hot water and washed my hands in the steaming kettle with rough, government-issue soap. Then I soaked a sizable section of gauze in the water and soaped it well. Fanny took the gauze without a word from me. She began to gently wash the girl's belly and most private areas. Those Great Plains were such a land of extremes. Not a year before, after Crook's battered column set off after Crazy Horse, I was ready and willing to fight at the Slim Buttes. Untrained in marksmanship, I took a rifle and scabbard from the saddle of a wounded officer and tied it to Buford's saddle when the scouts reported hostiles in the area. But now my wife and I were caring for a girl as if she were our own child.

It was the same contradiction Fanny had witnessed on the train from Chicago to Washington, when I snapped at poor Private Holden. I told the private, in no uncertain terms, that he was to stop frightening my wife with stories of the Starvation March we had endured together under the command of General Crook. Later, though, when I thought she was asleep in the berth, Fanny caught me speaking with Holden quietly, urging him to talk freely about the heretical opinions that had caused him to be declared insane.

The old woman reappeared with a fresh canteen of water. Right behind her was High Wolf. Now he wore a loincloth, but his skin was still painted with the black and white lightning bolts. He was no longer in an otherworldly state. In fact he seemed almost civilized. He shook his rattles over the girl but did not venture to chant. We ignored him and the medicine man paid little attention to us.

High Wolf and I plied our trade independently of the other until I slid a scalpel from its leather case. The sight of what must have seemed a sinister small knife set High Wolf off again. He leapt in the air and spun in a circle. Then he stood perfectly still and pointed to the scalpel. "You will kill her," he said in an understandable mix of sign and Cheyenne.

I had made a point of not looking at High Wolf since he'd entered the tepee. Now I raised my eyes with theatrics to match his. I spoke deliberately. "Perhaps I will," I said, raising the scalpel so that its sharpness hung between us like a threat. "But if I don't use this, she will die for certain."

"No," High Wolf said.

"Yes. She will die and, if the baby is not dead now, it will die, too." We stared at each other over the blade and for a moment neither of us was sure what would happen. Then the old woman, who had been standing on the other side of the tepee fire, spoke in Cheyenne. There was a question in the unintelligible speech. High Wolf answered her with words and sign language.

In my clumsy sign I gestured to the woman. She grunted and stepped up between us. The tepee was quiet, and she began to nod her head. *"Ina pa yo,"* she said, and High Wolf exploded with a tirade of excited sounds. The old woman held her ground, though, and unleashed her own tongue. She squealed in High Wolf's face. When he tried to speak again, she dug her claws into his chest.

An old woman could never hurt a warrior like High Wolf. Still, he stepped back, and the woman came away with the black and white greasepaint, skin, and blood under her fingernails. She said softly but with intensity, *"Iya yo,"* and High Wolf was forced to retreat from the tepee. When he was gone she turned to me and, with a look of exhaustion, nodded her old head. She looked at the girl. *"I glustan,"* she said.

29

When I drew the scalpel lightly down the midline, the belly skin peeled back like the petals of an emerging rose. There was only a trace of blood, and Fanny wiped it away almost before I asked. From habit I spoke in a clipped, precise way. Fanny obeyed me very much as Johnny Provost would have.

The girl did not move. Her eyes were glassy from the laudanum but she certainly felt the pain. "The muscle layer is next," I said. "Keep her as still as possible." Fanny didn't know what to do. She reached across the girl's body to where I knelt between the thighs. "No," I said. "I can handle the legs. Just keep her arms from flailing around. I don't want her to hit the hand with the scalpel."

Fanny nodded but couldn't speak. She was no doubt imagining an arm getting loose, driving the cold steel into the girl's abdomen and into the child. She lay across the girl's bulging breasts and gripped the wrists above hands that again clung to the woolen blanket. She must have felt the yearning in the breasts and was moved to mutter a prayer for the survival of the baby.

When the muscle layer began to split, the girl rose

up under Fanny. The poor thing's strength was incredible and her arms threatened to break free. I was not sure if Fanny could hold her down, but I was too busy to help. She tried to push the wrists against the floor of the tepee but they rose up until the old woman came to Fanny's aid. The two women lay across the girl's upper body, Fanny squeezing her eyes tight to focus her strength and prayers. The girl never made a sound, but the power inside her rolled like a tremendous serpent. Fanny opened her eyes long enough to watch me slice the uterine wall. Bloody fluid gushed from the incision and I pushed on the upper belly. The girl twisted beneath her and Fanny closed her eyes that much tighter.

Then the tepee was filled with the girl's screams and the women had to fight to hold her. It was like restraining the Devil. Fanny told me later that when the screams began she thought High Wolf had again begun his demonic singing. Then the serpent inside the girl went limp. When Fanny looked up, the baby was being wiped clean by the old woman and I was busy stitching as quick and neat as a tailor.

"He's alive," I told her. "Weak, but alive."

The placenta had been removed and lay limp and useless on the tepee floor. The uterus is fragile tissue and must be sewn outside the body. But this is not difficult; it takes only a moment. I tucked it back inside and started on the abdominal muscle layer, with Fanny helping where she could.

The girl was drained but her thin lips tried to smile.

Fanny wiped away the blood on her stomach and thighs with soapy gauze. There was a stain on the front of Fanny's blouse, and I saw her wipe at it as if it were blood. But it was not blood. It was mother's milk from her struggle with the girl and when Fanny realized this, and that it was soaked warm against her own skin, her lower lip began to quiver.

She put more water on to boil and prepared a stack of dressing material while I cleaned the instruments. The old woman had wrapped the baby in an animal skin with fur so soft that it felt like rose petals. The boy was small and pink and Fanny assumed he would be put at his mother's breast, but he was taken away. "To a wet nurse," I explained. "They believe colostrum is poison." I shook my head and checked to be sure the incision had been washed carefully.

I examined each stitch closely, engrossed in the work of finishing the operation properly. But by the time I painted the incision with gentian violet and began applying the dressing, I was smiling slightly. When Fanny finally caught my eye, we both burst into broad grins. Then a soldier suddenly appeared at the doorway.

"Corporal Provost sent me," the trooper said. "He says for the doctor to come."

I was on my feet before the man had finished his sentence. "Is it an emergency?"

"I'm sorry, sir. I couldn't say."

"I want you to come with me, soldier. The escort waiting outside will see that Mrs. McGillycuddy is delivered back at our quarters." Buttoning up my shirt I turned to Fanny. "Could you finish with the dressing?"

Fanny nodded. "Yes, I think so."

"I should hurry. I'll instruct our escort to see you home."

"Of course." She looked at the girl. "We'll be fine here."

"Thank you, Fanny." I gathered up my coat and bent to duck out the door. But before leaving I stood back upright. "Thank you for everything," I said. "You know I have tremendous admiration for you."

That was about as intimate as my talk got in those days, and it took Fanny by surprise. She stared at me. There must have been a great deal that she wanted to say, but it wouldn't come to the surface. All she could do was tell me to be careful. "I don't know what I'd do without you, Valentine."

30

The bright belt of Orion was just appearing over the butte to the east of the camp. As my guard and I hurried past tepees and small groups of Cheyenne, I tried to remember if this was the first time I'd seen the constellation that autumn. Orion is a celestial sign that always raises my spirits. The sight of "The Hunter" in the east means the summer is over, and the time of making meat has arrived. Unfortunately, because of the city lights it is impossible to see from within Oakland, California—impossible, I should think, from any city. That is a shame, because it heralds a time of year that should stir the primal juices in every man's gut.

Like many Michigan boys, I hunted with my father, but he approached hunting as if it were a job to be accomplished. For him it was a question of the product, how fast and much could be collected from God's bounty. In my boyhood the process of hunting was never considered, and so the significance—the core excitement and virtue—of the hunt never dawned on me until I came to the Great Plains.

As I moved to the edge of the parade ground that first night of Orion's fall reign I noticed the fires of the anxious Lakota in the distance. They were Red Cloud's people, and it was hard to guess how they might respond if Crazy Horse died—hard to guess what they'd do if he lived. When I saw the reinforced guards at the government buildings and heard the mingled sounds of both camps, it occurred to me that I could just keep on walking. I could order the trooper at my side to go back to his unit and proceed alone, across the corner of the parade ground, past the camp's perimeter and into the hills to the north. I could walk into those hills and hunt the animals that lived there. I could find water to drink and I could sleep soundly under the stars. I could survive on my own. I could flourish. That knowledge, that feeling of confidence and access to the bounty of the Great Plains, was a secret that I have always kept just for myself. Even before my introduction to the plains I might have tried such a thing, and I would likely have failed. But by the time that night came around I knew I could actually do it. I had learned such confidence from the inhabitants of the plains. It was like finding something valuable that I had lost without knowing it. There is still a rightness about going forth to gather the sustenance of life without the aid of agriculture or trade. It is not hard to understand why the Sioux did not want to give up hunting buffalo for the plow. A large portion of the trouble that engulfed that camp, those people, and the entire northern plains was a result of a particular promise unkept. It was about buffalo—the promise Crook had made to Crazy Horse that he and his people would not be deprived of their autumn hunt—that finally convinced the chief to surrender. But rumors that Crazy Horse might not return to the reservation from the hunt frightened Crook and Sheridan so much that they simply canceled the hunt.

What Crook should have known is that he had promised Crazy Horse a chance to take his people, men, women, and children, north to perform the essential sacrament of their lives. It had been denied like a parent would deny a child a stick of candy. It was Crook's greatest failure. The breaking of that promise was the cruelest deception of all. It was the beginning of the intrigue that finally led to the bayonet thrust that put Crazy Horse into my care.

The pull of Orion was great, but not nearly so great as the pull of my duty to my patient. I got to the adjutant's office just as another officer appeared from the darkness of the west parade ground. It was Philo Clark, but I hesitated only an instant to let him catch up.

Clark's face showed concern. "I heard there was a problem."

"I don't know any more than you do," I said as we pushed open the door together.

Touch the Clouds sat very straight on the floor where I had left him. His eyes were steady; his mouth revealed nothing. Johnny was bent over Crazy Horse, mopping the chief's face with a damp rag. His head snapped around when he heard Philo and me come in, and I could tell that Crazy Horse had taken a turn for the worse. "His heart's gone weaker. The bleeding just won't stop."

Johnny stepped aside to let me kneel beside the patient. Crazy Horse's eyes stared toward the ceiling, his lips were parted, and his breathing was shallow. "McGillycuddy," he said. "Is the Cheyenne woman safe?"

"Yes. I think she will be all right."

"Hoksicala ki tan yan hwo?"

"The baby is alive." Crazy Horse nodded then winced with pain. "Damn it all," I hissed.

"What is it?" Philo was close by my side. "Is he dying?"

"Not yet. But he's failing."

"You have to do something, Mac. We can't let him die under these circumstances."

"We might not have any choice." I rolled Crazy

Horse onto his side. The dressing was soaked through with blood.

"Jesus," Philo whispered at my ear. It was not an expression of revulsion; Philo had seen many wounds bloodier than this. It was his frustration coming to the surface. "Is he going to die on us, Mac?"

"It doesn't look good. Something is damaged inside. The wound's not going to clot on its own."

"What can you do?"

"I'm not sure."

"Well, you can do something, can't you?"

I was peeling away the fouled dressing and Johnny was doing his best to help. I shook my head. "Perhaps," I said.

"It's important, Mac."

I looked up at my friend. "Of course it's important." My tone conveyed impatience, and Philo pulled back to let us work.

We redressed the wound and administered more morphine. Crazy Horse's pulse was erratic, his heart weak. When I finally stood up I looked at Philo, then at the other two faces in the room. "I wonder," I said as my gaze returned to Philo, "if we couldn't have a word outside?"

Philo nodded and preceded me out onto the small porch of the adjutant's office. Soldiers stood on each side. We stepped out into the shadows cast by the quarter moon rising in the east.

"They're organizing a Sun Dance for him," Philo said, as much to himself as to me. This was the

Sioux's most sacred ceremony. Philo was no doubt concerned that it could excite the tribes. "There's legislation in Congress to outlaw it," he said.

Even then it seemed a travesty of law to prohibit a religious ceremony but I was focused on my own duty and so didn't bother to comment.

I fished the last of my cigar out of my pocket. As if we had rehearsed it, Philo drew a heavy kitchen match from his own pocket and snapped it with a thumbnail. The phosphorus flared and illuminated our faces. I leaned toward the light, drew on the cigar, and let the smoke out slowly. "He's got one chance, Philo, and it's not a very good one."

"Go on."

"I'm convinced now that the bayonet pierced his kidney." I paused, thinking just how to say this. "Kidneys are delicate things. There's almost no chance it will stop bleeding on its own. He's lost a lot of blood already and the fact is, he's bleeding to death as we speak."

Philo folded his arms over his chest, exhaled, and looked down at the ground. "This is not good for anyone," he said. "Our friend, Lieutenant Lee, is charging around this camp stirring things up with a stick. I received a telegraph from General Crook ordering me to do everything possible to see that Crazy Horse stays alive. He ordered me, Mac. Can you imagine that?" Philo reached into the breast pocket of his coat and brought out a pewter flask. He unscrewed the cap and raised it to his lips. I could smell the whiskey and it smelled heavenly. It's hard to imagine being ordered to keep a man alive, but I had no trouble imagining how the whiskey felt against Philo's tongue. His Adam's apple bobbed once, twice, and when the flask came down I was caught looking on longingly.

"Would you like a snort?" Philo held out the flask. I took a close look at the battle scene engraved on its side. It was very much like the flask that Private Holden had with him on the trip to the insane asylum. I had drunk from Holden's flask and that drink had led to my vow of temperance.

"No," I said.

"You said he had a chance."

"I said he had a poor chance."

"And what would that be?"

"It's hypothesized that a kidney might be repaired with stitches. It's also hypothesized that a damaged kidney could be removed and that the human body might function perfectly well with the services of only the remaining kidney."

"Hypothesized?"

"There is literature on the subject. Rumors that such operations have been performed in Europe."

Philo's voice revealed his excitement. "And you could do that to Crazy Horse?"

"It's a very long shot."

"But it's a potential avenue of action."

"That it is. But I can't hold out much hope that the results will be any different from simply letting him bleed to death."

"But you have to try, Mac. You doctors have an oath to that effect."

"The oath is something like that. But the first principle is to do no harm."

"Well, allowing Crazy Horse to die would do a great deal of harm." Philo paused in an attempt to let that statement soak in. But I wasn't yet ready to see, beyond the ending of an imperiled life, how Crazy Horse's death could do harm. I wasn't sure what Philo was getting at. But I knew it was not the time to press him for details.

"Could we move him to the hospital?"

"I don't think so."

"Well, if it's so vital that we try this, why is it not vital to give it the best chances of succeeding?"

"It's vital to Crook. It's vital to me. But Bradley has his orders and Calhoun can't be expected to forget that his widowed sister-in-law was the sister of Custer. Can't it be done in there?" He motioned toward the adjutant's office.

"It could be that it can't be done anywhere."

We fell silent and, after a few seconds, Philo put a hand on my shoulder. "Give it your best, Mac. For me, for Crook." He paused. For Crazy Horse."

My head began to nod. "Sure, Philo." I went on nodding, thinking. "You know me. I always do my best."

31

Johnny's eyes became huge when I explained what I planned to do. On a piece of paper from the desk, I carefully wrote down all the equipment I thought would be needed. The usual clamps and forceps, a selection of scalpels, all sorts of suture material. A lot of what I asked Johnny to fetch was guesswork, because I had never invaded the body cavity of a living human in this way. Johnny looked at the list and shook his head in wonder. "You're going to cut right into his back?"

"The side, I think. Go on now. It will take you some time to gather up all this. If anything else comes to your mind while you're over there, bring it along. I trust your judgment, Corporal."

Johnny straightened up and gave me a crisp salute. "Thank you, sir. I appreciate that, sir."

"Go on." I waved him out the door and rubbed my hands over my face. Good God, I thought, what was I contemplating? With the heels of my hands I rubbed my eyes and let myself feel the pressure. When I opened them, they focused on Touch the Clouds, still motionless, unfathomable, and exuding the rawest kind of strength.

I seated myself in the chair on the other side of Crazy Horse from Touch the Clouds. My elbows found their places on my thighs and I laced the fingers of my right hand into those of my left. "Well, you enigmatic son-of-a-bitch," I said to Touch the Clouds, "do you think you could tell me something that I've been wondering about for over a year?"

Touch the Clouds had no idea what I was saying so I pointed to him and to Crazy Horse. "You two," I said. "The Big Horn Fight?"

Touch the Clouds nodded ever so slightly.

"And when the camps broke up you set off in what direction? Afterward? *Toketki ya hwo?*"

"Wiyokiyapata kiya."

"Toward the morning sun?" I made the sign for east and south.

"Han," Touch the Clouds said.

"The southeast."

Touch the Clouds nodded again. He knew already what I was getting at, and I knew he might use our lack of good communication as an excuse for not telling the truth. "Was Crazy Horse in charge of your march?" I reverted to basic sign language.

"There were several bands," he signed back.

"But the band you were with. Was Crazy Horse leading?"

"Han."

"And you were heading southeast."

"Han."

"Toward the Black Hills. Paha Sapa." There, I'd said it. I watched Touch the Cloud's eyes for a glimmer of deception but detected none. "There were a couple of thousand settlers in the hills. Were you marching to make war on them?"

"Paha Sapa was granted to us in the treaty" Touch the Clouds's hands flew angrily and I had trouble getting his meaning.

"The treaty of '68?"

"The treaty signed after Red Cloud's war. If we rode for Paha Sapa, it was our right."

The chief's huge hands came up and crossed in front of his chest as if he were cold. Then they loosened again and in flowing gestures told me, "The miners had no right to be in our hills." He added, in slow deliberate movements, "They were tearing the insides out of the earth."

What Touch the Clouds was saying was true enough. It's hard to imagine what those desperate days after the Big Horn Fight must have been like for the victors. Certainly they were exciting, heady days. Was Crazy Horse full of himself? Did he taste invincibility on the wind? Were his intentions what Crook feared, the annihilation of the civilians in the Black Hills?

My eyes swept the prone figure laid out in front of me. Even in his diminished state, there was still that same equine smoothness to his muscles that I had been drawn to from the first day, in the cool waters of the Knife River. "So that is where you were going when we ran into you in the Slim Buttes."

"We had already been there," Touch the Clouds signed.

I was sure that Touch the Clouds had misunderstood me. The Slim Buttes are 150 miles from the Black

Hills. In September, near the middle of our Starvation March, when the troops had begun to despair, we stumbled onto some Sioux holed up in the rocky cliffs of the buttes. It was a ghastly affair—they turned out to be mostly women, children, and old men. On the second day of the siege warriors appeared on the horizons but I doubted that they were Crazy Horse's.

"Our women and children," Touch the Clouds signed. "That is why we returned. We had been to the hills around your Deadwood City. We were returning. You did not catch us. You caught our women and children. They were hiding in the Slim Buttes."

It was a massacre—cold-blooded and motivated by fear and fury. The camp's occupants who didn't die in the initial charge found refuge in caves where they suffered a prolonged hail of bullets until they were rooted out. Philo's troopers were like caged animals, teased by the defeats and deprivations of the campaign. Now on the offensive, their blood lust could not be assuaged. The screams of women and children prompted Crook himself to shout an order to cease fire. But it was ignored. In the end there was a pile of bodies seething in agony and gore. The last to come out of the caves was the old chief, American Horse, walking upright and with dignity, but he could not raise his hands in surrender. They were occupied with keeping his slippery intestines from falling onto the ground. I did my best to save him and others that night, but he died an ugly death. And all the time more and more warriors appeared to keep up a harassing action against our rear guard.

"It was you and Crazy Horse firing on us? How could you have been to reconnoiter the Black Hills settlements and back?"

Touch the Clouds didn't understand me but he gazed with a mixture of contempt and humor. "We traveled fast," he signed. "We followed Crazy Horse, running the ponies downhill and walking them up. It took us three days to find your stinking towns." His hands were gaining speed; I was having trouble following. "We watched your miners, and Crazy Horse killed two who were digging in a stream." The hands stopped and we both looked down at Crazy Horse. Then they began to move again, more slowly now. "The miners cried like children. They were cowards and Crazy Horse chased them down and killed them with a knife. They called out to your God, but it did them no good."

The image of Crazy Horse chasing two white men, probably boys, as they tried to escape across a knee-deep stream they believed held gold haunts me to this day. I can sometimes almost hear them sobbing, begging for their lives. The second to die no doubt prayed for deliverance as he watched his companion being butchered. It was the nightmare that must have plagued Crook as he drove us, a starving column of exhausted men, toward the Black Hills.

If the Lakota plan had been to wipe out the settlements in the hills, it would easily have been the greatest disaster the white race had ever experienced at the hands of the red. They had been scouting for an attack that might have killed a thousand people. I realized all at once what they had forfeited when they abandoned the fight and returned to the Slim Buttes because we had stumbled onto their women and children.

Touch the Clouds let his eyes drift away and into the dark corner of the room. He swallowed slowly, with the bitter memory. "We wanted to fight," he signed. "But Crazy Horse always protected those who could not protect themselves." I can't imagine the same would ever be said of the leaders I served under. "When *you* fight, you leave your women and children. Ours are always with us. It is the only reason you ever catch us."

There is no question that Touch the Clouds was correct in this assessment. The trip that he described taking three days had taken Crook's suffering column weeks. We had been on a mission to save the settlements in the Black Hills from attack and, in a fraction of the time it took us to reach the hills, the warriors we were chasing had traveled back and forth and defended their village in the bargain. Those were easily the toughest times I have ever known. They must have been at least as tough for the quarry we pursued.

There was sadness and defiance in Touch the Clouds's face but nothing of the horror and suffering that we experienced on the Starvation March to the Black Hills—and nothing compared to the suffering of the Sioux women and children who died at our hand. Survivors suffer differently than did those they mourn. But sometimes survival seems no gift when I consider the goblins that infested the minds of men like Pvt. John Holden.

32

To a casual observer Holden did not appear to be mad, and I have suffered some guilt for being the one to declare him so. Though a burden, it was only right that I was directed to deliver the man to the National Asylum for the Insane. Perhaps if he had been put on permanent sick call after his condition was discovered Holden would have avoided the incidents that sealed his fate, but those months after the Custer massacre were the most horrible times the Yellowstone Campaign was forced to endure. To avoid active duty a man had to be dead or dying, so I insisted that Holden remain with his unit.

It was not so much that Holden's actions were unique; many soldiers reacted poorly to the deprivations of that campaign. His refusal to stop firing once the command was given was understandable and common. The taking of scalps was prohibited but ignored. More unusual was his distracted, chillingly calm way of talking about the battles on the eve of their commencement. But his greatest offense came at the end of a particularly repugnant fight when he built a solitary fire for himself, stripped naked, and danced around the flames with fresh scalps tied around his neck. Blood was smeared on Holden's arms and chest and some of the other troopers concluded that the Devil had seeped into his body. Malnourished and exhausted, they grumbled that he should be hung; I had to intervene to keep them from doing something we all would have regretted. From that time on, until we were rescued by a relief column sent north from Crook City, Holden stayed close to me.

Crook's men stumbled into Camp Robinson two weeks later. Then, after another week of recuperation, on an early-November morning Holden and I hitched a ride on a freight wagon deadheading to the rail station in Gordon, Nebraska. The road was rough and rutted from a full summer of transporting supplies, both for Crook's starved army and for the Lakota who were trickling back to the Red Cloud Agency from the war in the north. Freight wagons moved in squads, back and forth, with strings of mules or oxen jerking them through the ditches of standing water during the middle of the day and over curbs of rock-hard, frozen mud when the night's chill was still on the land.

The bullwhacker was part Negro and wore a tightly curled beard under red eyes that had seen too much August sun. He knew he was transporting a surgeon and a soldier who had gone mad on the then-famous Starvation March that had concluded the Yellowstone Campaign, and he was loathe to speak to either of us. He called to his oxen and let his long whip snake out and crack over their heads, but he kept those smarting eyes on the road ahead, except to quickly survey the ridges. He did not believe that the Indian troubles were over.

A Pullman car was reserved for army use and Holden and I carried our own bags aboard and stored them above our seats. At Omaha the conveyance would become more comfortable, but that first leg of the journey was spartan. It was still the frontier, and even the train seemed to declare that the pretensions of civilization were ridiculous in that setting.

There were no porters to seat us. The locomotive simply blew its whistle and began to lurch forward. Last-minute cargo and passengers were hurled aboard as the steam pistons began to pop and suck. I sat back in my seat and observed Holden as he watched the sandhills of central Nebraska begin their eternal roll just outside the window. Holden was handsome in a classic way. His features were sharp, his eyes keen. He had black hair and a clean-shaven face. Like me, he was dressed in the uniform of the Second Cavalry. He was freshly bathed and gave no appearance of suffering from a mental disorder. Dried bluestem grass spiked the sandhills to infinity. Holden pointed out a small group of antelope moving away from the train with a motion as erratic as a flock of phalaropes. Above the grass a seasonal swirl of sandhill cranes spiraled up for another downhill glide toward their wintering grounds.

There had not been much time in the weeks before for diagnostics, and I did not feel qualified to judge insanity anyway. I was much more at home with the tangibles of gangrene, malaria, and bullet and arrow wounds. I had asked Doctor Munn and a Deadwood surgeon in private practice to confirm my suspicions. Their judgment came back unanimous: Holden was the victim of battle fatigue, delusionary, out of touch with reality—crazy as a coyote.

But Holden didn't look any more fatigued than any of the other hundreds of men who had survived Crook's foodless march to the Black Hills. In fact by then, after a couple of weeks of good rest and nutrition, Holden looked positively fit. He folded his arms across his chest, leaned his head back on the worn leather seat, and smiled as the treeless hills of bluestem moved past. He rolled his head over to look at me. "I bet the buffalo got fat as barn cats on that pasture," he said.

"It's beautiful range," I agreed. "They're already moving huge herds up from Texas."

Holden laughed. "Cows," he said. "Dumbest damned notion yet."

This gentle belligerence was part of Holden's malady and I knew better than to incite him, yet I wanted to be sure the private understood me. "It's a great boon," I said passively. "These prairies can support hundreds of thousands of cattle. They have the potential to change the economics of the entire country."

"These prairies supported hundreds of thousands of buffalo just twenty years ago." Holden laughed that chilling laugh again. "And besides," he said suddenly, "who wants to eat meat that someone else killed for you anyway?" The question was rhetorical and I knew not to answer it. "You've eaten buff, haven't you, Doc?"

"I have."

"Like it?"

"It's excellent, yes."

Holden smiled. "You ever kill one, then eat it?"

I nodded as the memory of buffalo hunting stirred inside. I'd been just a year older than Holden was then, surveying the border between the United States and British America. It was the time when I felt most at home on the grasslands, only a month after meeting Crazy Horse for the first time. "Yes. I've killed several for the pot."

"Off a horse?"

I smiled back at Holden. "I tried," I said. "I wasn't successful from horseback."

Holden laughed again. Was that laugh part of what had convinced the others that he was mad? "Tell me about it," he said.

"There's not that much to tell," I said. "It was in the northern part of the Dakota Territory, and there were lots of animals. We lived off them for months."

"Ah, come on. Was your first kill out of a big herd?"

"No. It was a group of about fifteen. They'd issued us one large-caliber Sharps. We had a hunter, but he was glad to take one of us along when he went out. I guess he got tired of killing buffalo."

"You don't believe that."

After thinking for a moment I had to agree. "No, I guess I don't believe that. I suppose he just wanted someone to come along. I was keen enough to go. In fact I went with him every chance I got."

"But your first buff. Was it a bull?"

"No, a dry cow."

"Finest kind," Holden said.

"Indeed. She was at the head of the herd as they grazed the wheatgrass from a wide, flat draw. We came up from the downwind side so they didn't know we were there."

"Nothing like a breeze in your face and the smell of buffalo close up." Holden closed his eyes as if he were savoring the smell of morning coffee. I was, at first, disturbed by this nearly perverse exhibition of the sensual.

Then I recalled that smell myself. It is musty and rich and the best parts of it are indeed like the smell of perking coffee. The memory of that wild odor still causes my mouth to water. The taste of buffalo hump roasted slowly over a green ash fire has no equal and I wish this damned hotel could procure some for its house doctor. After Holden's hedonistic display my own eyes narrowed (much as they are narrowing now) and I found myself reveling in memory just like the madman sitting in the train seat beside me.

I was brought to my senses by the conductor, who stopped beside our seats and made a notation in his book of two soldiers riding the train to Omaha. He tipped his hat and I thought, with some distress, that he raised his eyebrows.

For the rest of that first leg of our trip, I declined to engage Holden in conversation. We pulled into the station on the outskirts of Omaha in the twilight and disembarked to stretch our legs. We were only stopping for fuel and to pick up a few more passengers. The city was young but growing; I was disappointed that we had no time to take in the sights and perhaps sample the fare at a local restaurant. Holden just shrugged. He was perfectly comfortable to wait and walk along the tracks that converged at a point miles into the prairie from which we had come.

In Omaha the train picked up three officers and a group of enlisted men who, like Holden and myself, planned to ride the train to Chicago. Fanny was waiting to join us there for the trip to Washington. For several hours, the officers drilled me about my experiences in the Sioux War. At the back of the Pullman the enlisted men were doing the same to Holden. There was drinking going on at both ends of the car. I could only imagine what Holden was telling these men, who had spent the war in domestic positions at army headquarters in Omaha. I knew the whiskey was loosening my own tongue but I could never have explained to the officers, who hung on my every word, what war had really been like.

It was nearly midnight when we reached Des Moines, Iowa. The locomotive stopped to take on more fuel and water but no one got off. By then the drinking had taken its toll. Almost all the men were asleep when we set off into the black Iowa night. I was responsible for Holden and, throughout the drinking session, had placed myself so that my charge was not out of sight. Then late, with the lantern swinging in the center of the car trimmed low and the subtle shadows rocking like the ocean, I moved to a seat beside Holden. There was no reason to think that he was dangerous; still, it would have been a terrible embarrassment if he'd disappeared somewhere between the frontier and Washington, D.C.

Settling in beside the man I was surprised to find him awake and still fairly sober. "Get some sleep," I said. I tried to make it sound like I was prescribing sleep as a remedy for what ailed him.

But Holden shook his head. "Not sure I can." He shrugged and grinned in his boyish way. "Little trouble sleeping without cold air on my face." Then with open, questioning eyes he added, "You know how it goes?"

We looked at each other in that dull swaying light and our smiles grew conspiratorial. "Yes," I admitted. "I guess I do." Then I tried to turn the conversation to a lighter track. "But don't tell my wife."

Holden laughed out loud, then settled back into his seat. "Tell me about her," he said. He stared at the ceiling like a child waiting for a bedtime story.

"Well, she's only been my wife for a year."

Holden's head came up and he looked at me, startled. "You were with that cursed campaign for a year."

"Damned near."

Holden's head settled back down. "I guess you'll be glad to see her."

"That I will."

The train rattled on into the night and I let my eyes nearly close. "You're a lucky man," Holden said. "I don't reckon I'll ever know a woman. I reckon they'll keep me locked up inside some building for the rest of my life." I wanted to avoid that conversation and watched Holden through one squinting eye that I knew he thought was closed.

Holden glanced at me and accepted that I was asleep. He swung his gaze back to the rushing blackness beyond the window. "It's the worst punishment they could think of," he said softly. "Especially for a man who knows what we know."

33

Then Holden went silent but I knew he wasn't sleeping, either. There was something to what he'd said about cold, fresh air against your face being an aid to sleep. It has been years since I actually spent a night out-of-doors but occasionally I take a blanket out onto the broad porch that this hotel is known for and doze in a chair until the security guard comes and chases me inside. This need to strip away the insulation of buildings was one of the emotions I struggled to explain to Fanny when I returned from that first grand adventure of mapping the Great Lakes.

It seemed trains were always bringing me and Fanny

together or taking us away from each other. At the conclusion of that first aquatic survey, my crew tied the government bark to the public dock in Milwaukee, Wisconsin, and signed it over to the Port Authority there. Every man went his own way. I was entrusted with the field notes and celestial calculations that would eventually be turned into maps. They gave me five days to report to the Geodetic Survey Office in Washington, D.C. Another train would take me there, but first I would go to Detroit to see two people: Doctor McGraw, to explain something that had become apparent to me during the months of the survey, and Fanny Hoyt, for reasons I could not easily admit to myself.

I had written her several times after our meeting at Otter Point, but before mailing the letters, as I reread them in the light of the campfire on some desolate island or barren shore, they sounded stiff and wooden. Once, late at night, with the rest of my crew asleep in their blankets in front of a fire built on the shore of the Keweenaw Peninsula, I threw a particularly lifeless letter into the flames and tried again. What I wanted was precision and wisdom. I tried to concentrate but the Keweenaw Peninsula juts out into Lake Superior and when I looked out over the black, icy water with pinpoints of light reflected from above, a meteor sliced in from the east, flared with great intensity, and extinguished itself on the watery horizon.

I leapt to my feet and turned with excitement to my crew, but they were all asleep. No one had seen the meteor except me. It was gone forever and there had been no one to share it with. As I came to realize that fact, a sadness that I had never known before settled over me. After the meteor the night was intensely black. Then slowly the brightness of the stars returned and I noticed them as if for the first time. When I went back to the stationery I'd laid out on the portable camp desk, thoughts of Fanny pulsed in my blood like never before. Words poured from my mind, through my pencil, and onto the page. A description of the meteor appeared. I compared it with the way fiery thoughts of her surprised me every day. I told her how the taste of her at Otter Point lingered on my lips and how I longed to breathe in the smell of her. Words as ripe as October fruit continued to come and the letter grew to ten, eleven pages. I wrote through the night and on into the gray light of dawn.

But as the crew began to ease awake under their blankets I silently reread a paragraph here and there and found the words shocking. It was not a letter fit for a doctor to send to a lady of culture. By the time the cook had stirred the fire to life, I was embarrassed by what I had written. When no one was looking, I committed the letter to the flames. It was impossible for me not to see the campfire as a metaphoric Hell. My silly, repentant hope was that that fire would kill my passion. And with that thought to guide me, I jotted down a few benign lines and slipped the letter into the mail pouch headed for Detroit.

In the sanitized letter I informed Fanny when I

would be back in Detroit. Two days were allotted in Detroit to see McGraw and I told her that I hoped to see her, too. I never expected Fanny to be at the station when I arrived, but when I stepped off the train her face tilted up at me from under a white straw hat in that curious way I had dreamed of since we'd last met. "So, Doctor," she said, "you look hale and hearty. Did sleeping under the stars agree with you?"

My eyes would not come away from her. I nodded dumbly. "Yes," I said, "I suppose it did." Then my tongue took off on its own. "You look beautiful," I said. It was something I would never have said six months before, something I wished I could retract before it was fully out of my mouth. But Fanny smiled and off my tongue went again. "I missed you," I said. "And I wanted to apologize for what happened at Otter Point."

"No apology is necessary," she said as she took my arm. "You feel strong." She laid her white, delicate hand over my bony, sunburnt one and gazed at the contrast. Her shoulders came up in a shiver and she smiled like a schoolgirl.

"Is that all the luggage you have?" she said, pointing to the leather valise in my hand.

"Yes."

"You travel light, Doctor." She steered me through the station and to a waiting carriage. "I hope you don't think me too forward," she went on as the hack driver opened the door, "but I thought we could eat dinner together. A family of Italians has opened a fashionable new restaurant on the Deerborn Road."

A year later I was on another train headed for another rendezvous with Fanny. All I remembered then and all I remember now of that dinner on Deerborn Road was a piece of bread soaked in garlic butter and held to my mouth by Fanny. My taste buds exploded like a thousand tiny comets and every nerve ending clamored to be noticed. I was appalled by my thoughts and fought to hold them in check. But once Fanny was my wife and we had spent nearly a year apart during the Sioux War, the passion created by the prospect of meeting her in Chicago was impossible to repress. I longed to taste garlic on her lips. Even now, thirty years since I lost her, when I eat alone I sometimes rub a clove of garlic on a piece of bread and eat it as slowly as possible.

Arrangements were made to leave Holden in the temporary custody of surgeons at General Sheridan's Chicago headquarters. The staff at the army hospital had not seen action in an Indian war and they would treat him like a simple madman. My sense of guilt for leaving my patient was doubled because I was motivated by desire to be alone with my wife. It was a day of guilt: about my lusty feelings for Fanny and about my decision to leave my patient in the charge of strangers. But it was just for one day. The three of us were scheduled to start for Washington in the morning.

Outside the hospital I stepped into the street to hail a carriage. It was nearly dark and I was already late for our rendezvous. We were to meet at the Drake Hotel on the corner of Michigan and Walton Streets. Fanny would have arrived from Detroit two days before and would be waiting for me.

The hackman was an old, white-haired German who spoke poor English and was in no particular hurry. The horse was old and gray, too, and the man refused to use the whip for anything more violent than swatting flies from the animal's rump. I was tempted to jump into the front, take the reins from the old man, and wake the nag up. But what was a few more minutes after nearly a year away from my bride? In many ways this would be like our wedding night. There was no sense rushing it.

Fanny and I had, of course, been together long enough to consummate the marriage, but we were both inexperienced and shy and our first year of marriage had been carried on mostly by a series of letters. Fanny had written Ito letters over the months of war. I had counted them and kept track of my own, so I knew I had written her nearly as many. Sometimes, when duty allowed, I had written two or three a day. Her letters remained with me through the entire campaign. They were prim letters, filled with news and good cheer. Fanny knew I was made nervous by too much emotion. But occasionally I detected a word with a double meaning or a joke with a warm and slippery edge. In spite of myself, between operations or after long marches, I read those particular letters many times. A few were thin and tattered.

When the great hotel came into sight, I suffered a tremor of doubt. What if something had changed? What if the woman of the letters was not the woman of the flesh? The old horse pulled the carriage along the curb and stopped without a cue from the German. "Sixty-five cents, please."

I tossed my valise to the ground and jumped to the cobblestones. Before hitting the ground I was digging into my pocket for my purse. But I found only fifty cents and a small roll of bills. The hackman had no change and in frustration, I thrust a dollar at him and told him to keep the whole thing. A porter stood at the curb and, when I turned, he reached for my valise. I waved him away and bounded up the granite steps with my own meager luggage to the brass-plated revolving door.

Once in the lobby I reined myself in. Willfully slowing my pace, I approached the desk with a forced air of nonchalance. The clerk was a swarthy man with spectacles hanging on the end of his nose. He glanced up with what looked like disdain until I told him my name. Then a broad smile broke across the man's face. "Doctor McGillycuddy, of course. Your wife has been down twice to ask about you. She instructed me to give you this key." He handed the key over the desk and the smile grew so broad that I was embarrassed. "Room 415. Right at the top of the stairs. Would you like a porter to help?"

"No," I said. "I've carried this bag six thousand miles by myself. I can make it up a few flights of stairs."

"I'm sure you can, sir." The clerk gave a little salute that I nearly returned. "If you need anything, you'll be sure to call."

"We will."

I took the stairs two at a time. So fast, in fact, that I was winded when I came to room 415. I held my hand up over my mouth and breathed deeply. The feel of my mustache and beard startled me. Had I mentioned in a letter that shaving in the field had been difficult? I couldn't remember if I'd told Fanny what I looked like now. Perhaps she would be repulsed by the whiskers. I contemplated finding a washroom and shaving quickly, but there was a sound on the other side of the door before I could move. The knob began to twist and suddenly Fanny was standing not a foot away.

The figure of a man standing at her door was startling. Her hands came to her chest and her eyes came wide open. But it took only an instant for the eyes to soften and her to throw her arms around my neck. "Oh, Valentine. You've come."

The valise dropped to the floor and my arms took her in and lifted her upward. I buried my face in her hair and breathed her scent the way I had so often dreamed. I pulled her tight, wanting to feel her breasts against my rib cage and, even though I was afraid of hurting her, my arms and shoulders continued to pull her tighter. When I finally made myself try to let go I felt her pulling at me for more.

It was as if her response caused an animal to wake inside me. A guttural sound issued from my lips and into her ear as I took her backward and into the room. When Fanny's back hit the bed her legs spread easily and I took her head in my long hands and bent it back to get at the whiteness of her neck.

Late that night, with Fanny curled and sleeping against my chest, I tried to forget how I had torn her dress, how I had pressed my face into her breasts and licked the hard red nipples. The memory of Fanny scratching at my clothes, her own mouth hungry, sent a chill through me. I tried to blame it on the war, tried to see our actions as a natural ritual of war's end. Surely there had been scenes like this since the very beginning of time. But that was not reassuring. I wondered about my sanity. Like the young idiot I was, I vowed never to let the beast get the upper hand again. But no sooner had I made that vow than I felt Fanny's leg over mine and her wetness burning my thigh. I moved away and closed my eyes tight.

When the eyes came open again, nothing had changed. The gaslight from the street came through the lacy curtains and cut across the bed. The bareness of Fanny's back glowed white beneath my sun-scarred arm. I became frightened and verbalized the cowardly sentiment that had invaded my brain. "I should never have left the hospital in Detroit," I whispered.

To my surprise Fanny's head began to shake in semi-conscious disagreement. "I'm glad you left," she whispered dreamily. "I want to go with you next time." She snuggled tighter against me then went limp again with sleep.

I told myself that she was dreaming of the life ahead of her. The war was over and we could let this night be the end of it. In the morning we would depart for Washington, D.C., and Fanny would be exposed to the events and characters that a woman like her deserved. Washington society no longer held any allure for me, though. I had been changed by the war-torn plains and felt an eerie certainty that they were not done with me yet.

34

After the Big Horn Fight morale was the lowest any of the officers had ever seen. We were two hundred miles from any sort of civilization and already worn out from three months in the field. Crook's vitality had been sapped by the news of Custer's massacre and when I observed him, sometimes playing cards with no zest for the game, sometimes sitting alone and staring out over the prairie to the east, I saw a man in the throes of self-doubt. For most people suffering such melancholy, I would have prescribed rest and a combination of salts. But Crook was a warrior. The only real remedy for his malady was retribution in battle.

On the fifth of August, with the unrelenting sun pushing the temperature to 105 degrees in the shade, Crook issued the orders for all tents, bedding, and baggage to be stored in the 160 wagons of the supply train. Each trooper was to draw 150 rounds of ammunition, a blanket, a greatcoat, and four days' worth of rations. The wagons would be left behind in favor of a faster-moving mule train. Crook had become convinced that the Lakota were moving to the Black Hills, where they would brutally evict the miners who were there in violation of the treaty of 1868. He was ready for action and intended to march east and catch Crazy Horse and the other killers of Custer before they reached the mining camps. But his zeal had clouded his reason. He planned for no supply line. He left us exposed to the elements of the Great Plains in an act of hubris that we would pay for dearly.

Like everyone else, Johnny and I were issued 150 rounds of ammunition and carbines to fire them through. Neither of us had signed up to fight, but the events of the last month had cast a desperate pall over everything. Even the wind and swaying grass of the prairie seemed ominous. By now we were willing, if it came to it, to take our turn at battle. In addition to the ammunition and rifles, we were given a pair of mules to carry medical supplies. Johnny was issued four pairs of saddle horses, because the ambulances would be left behind, too. If there were wounded—and there would be—they would be transported by horse-drawn travois. I was still riding Buford; the big horse seemed more than willing to carry me and my newly issued rifle for another thousand miles if necessary.

We rode at the rear of the column that snaked away from the Big Horn Mountains for miles into the morning sun. The fine red trail dust kicked up by the horses and mules would not have been tolerable had I been forced to endure it from the seat of the ambulance. I'd never gotten used to riding on the medical wagon and was glad to have Buford between my legs. I leaned forward, stroked his neck, whispered that he was a good boy, and smiled at the ears twitching, first this way then that, alert for whatever was ahead.

It was good to be on the move again, and though I felt some shame admitting it even to myself, there was something exciting and satisfying about setting off in search of the murderers of the Seventh Calvary. With the exception of the Crow and Shoshone scouts and a few half-breed Frenchmen, I was the only man of the two thousand who had traveled through this country before. In fact the map that General Crook rolled out on his field table every morning was a copy of the one I had drawn from notes of the boundary survey in the summer of 1873. But oh, how the land had changed from those halcyon days. Now the tall, swaying wheatgrass was gone, reduced to sooty ash by the fires set by the fleeing Sioux. These hills were no longer the nubile land that had enchanted me three years before. They were barren, cruel, and seemed to roll on into oppressive infinity.

Before the war I had tried to explain this land's seduction to Fanny one night as we lay in bed. I had done my best to describe the land's beauty in letters and, from written words, she must have come to understand part of my attraction. But when I spoke, soft and low in the darkness of our bedroom, I was afraid she would feel that the prairie had seeped into me like the love of another woman. I asked her not to imagine the land as a siren luring me but to see it as something she, too, could love. I asked her to come and see for herself, and she agreed that she would. But what would she think, I wondered, if she were to see the land as it was after Custer's massacre, a simmering wasteland through which a bedraggled, beaten, imperiled, white man's army marched?

The ash and dust rose under the horses' hooves and clung to their lathered flanks. When they passed a low pocket of earth that had escaped the fires, the horses strained for the meager grass that had survived. In accord with Crook's orders, only twenty mules carried forage for the horses. Everyone believed we would march out of the burned prairie and onto healthy sod where the horses could eat at their leisure and where we could hunt for our meat. But for the first two days there was no pasture for the animals, no game for the hunters, no relief from the searing sun. The heat of those first few days drained the juices from horse and rider. Buford and the government horses were used to getting grain, and the occasional tufts of grass were not enough to maintain their weight. They lost ten, twenty, thirty pounds a day.

When merciful night came, men were sent to the mule train for horse feed—and given only two cups of grain per animal. It was barely a mouthful for a hard-working horse, but the mule train was being managed like an East Coast railroad. There were no exceptions.

The mules were rotated under their loads. Sore backs were treated properly and I was called upon for advice. The train was always ready to move when the order was given, it always kept up with the column, no loads were lost. The train was run with such competence that it has become for me a symbol of the culture that was moving into the land, displacing and destroying the plains Indian culture and its democratic disorder.

The mule train was most efficient, but every part of Crook's command functioned well. As we approached the confluence of Rosebud Creek and the Yellowstone River a great cloud of dust was sighted; rumors that the Sioux were just ahead ran through the column. Crook deployed an advance skirmish line and set scouts north to investigate. They found no Sioux—only skirmishers deployed by General Terry's command in the belief that Crook's column was the enemy. The armies had found each other.

But where was Crazy Horse? How could he and thousands of warriors and noncombatants have slipped away? Crook and Terry were infuriated and took up Crazy Horse's trail with a vengeance. We turned southeast, across more ground that had been burned to discourage pursuit, and extended the marches to nearly thirty miles a day. By the time the two columns separated, Terry to his resupply on the Yellowstone River and Crook into the heart of the Dakota Territory, horseflesh was melting like snowdrifts in May.

From Terry we took a week's rations. The coffee, which our column had gone without for days, gave the men some heart. But then the weather turned cold: from temperatures too hot to bear in the daytime to freezing rain and hard frost at night. The rains came and the bivouac ground flooded to a depth of two inches. Because the tents had been left behind, there was no shelter. One trooper pulled the saddle off his gaunt mount and flopped it down into the water. He sat in the saddle the way he had all day and covered himself with his greatcoat. One by one the other two thousand followed suit until an area of a hundred acres became a field of solitary, miserable, little camps from which reins snaked out, anchoring equally miserable horses to their spot in the driving rain.

We did our best to sleep sitting up, praying that the dawn would bring sunshine. But in the morning the sun was dim and the horses bogged down in mud. Their feet balled up to the size of a man's head and their already compromised strength was taxed even further. Seeing their mounts suffering lowered the morale of the horse soldiers. Many chose to walk, and their own feet became as ponderous as if they wore a ball and chain on each ankle. It was as if the high plains were testing us, were throwing obstacles in the way of any retribution for the destruction of the Seventh Calvary. It all began to seem fruitless. Hope was fostered only by the knowledge that Sioux were suffering even more.

35

Looking into the face of the man who had been our quarry during those weeks of the previous autumn, I wondered how he had managed to drive his people on. Crazy Horse's eyes were squinted in pain and I thought that the image of those desperate times might be floating through his tortured mind. He had somehow stimulated his people—women and children, old and infirm—to go on through the same elements that had demoralized our column. They carried their tepees and possessions with them. And still they stayed ahead of us.

Touch the Clouds stared over Crazy Horse's body with the incomprehensible expression I had come to expect. "Christ," I hissed to myself, "what's keeping Provost?" I took my watch from my coat pocket and looked at it without noticing the time.

On the nights of August 20 and 23 the sky opened up with hail as hard as bullets. The wind sliced from the north with nothing to stop it but the men's soaked greatcoats. There was no wood to build fires, and many men were sick with dysentery and rickets. We desperately needed fresh meat and fruit, but for another week there was nothing but half rations of raw bacon, hardtack, and coffee boiled in cups over dried grass withheld from the horses.

We could have gone on to Fort Lincoln on the Missouri River but Crazy Horse's trail was warming and turning southward. The trampled ground and travois scrapes were a quarter mile wide. At the Grand River household goods began to be jettisoned. The Sioux were lightening their loads so they could stay ahead of the army that grew more excited for blood every day. Just past the Grand River the trail split. It was the work of Crazy Horse the tactician. All the experienced officers knew that the trail would split again, and again, and again, until our massive, stumbling, starving army was in pursuit of a single Indian. The killers of Custer were sifting away, into the arms of a land that was increasingly hostile to us.

On the morning that the column found the spot of the fourth split Private Holden seemed to lose control of himself. His laughter could be heard throughout the filthy, famished camp. He danced with more energy than the entire rest of the command had left. "Now," he cried, "now our mettle will be put to the test!" And that afternoon the horses began growing too weak to carry the troopers. Before nightfall six single shots had been heard. With each lethal crack the horse soldiers' morale slipped a notch. By the middle of the next day Crook ordered an end to shooting horses. "It's like murder," Lieutenant Schuyler said. "They've carried us, with courage, into raging battle."

And with courage the crippled and famished mounts denied the dignity of a bullet continued to limp after the column. They stretched out for miles behind us; a rear guard had to be deployed to keep troopers from quitting the column to be with their discarded and doomed mounts.

Malaria riddled the camp and Johnny and I ran out of quinine. The sick and wounded bounced on travois, alternately shivering and soaking their stinking blankets with feverish sweat. There was nothing we could do but listen to their ravings and lay a hand occasionally on a tormented shoulder. To discourage rickets I ordered the hunters, who were finding no game, to gather wild onions, chokecherries, and plums. But there was not nearly enough of anything, and half the column complained of painful joints. Yet even the worst cases, the soldiers whose bones actually began to bend and break under their weight, were refused berths on our travois train. We simply did not have enough healthy horses to pull people who were not completely disabled. Those unfortunate soldiers dragged themselves along like the string of crippled horses that snaked behind.

The hospital train grew until I was in charge of a significant portion of Crook's command. By then neither Johnny nor I was sleeping more than a few hours a night. Everything was filthy. My clothes felt like greasy sandpaper against my skin; everyone needed something that I didn't have. But still I endured. Endured the sorrow of it all until the afternoon I felt Buford begin to limp.

When a gallant horse begins to go lame it is as if your heart has begun missing beats, the precursor of a heart attack that will hollow you out like a burning firebrand. Of all the suffering of Crook's Starvation March, this was the worst. I sit in this rocking chair and recall every painful step as I walked beside Buford. It began as a hitch in his right front leg that in any normal situation might have been a stone or a bruised frog. He did not lurch like the hundred or so other horses that were following the column, and I fostered a hope that he would recover. On the day that Crook rescinded his order to cease shooting horses I mounted Buford again and rode until after six shots had sounded. That evening the hungriest of the troopers ate horseflesh. It was the first good food they had had for weeks.

The next day I was walking again and trying not to believe that Buford could no longer hold his head high. Johnny begged me to ride his horse, one of the few that could still carry a rider, but I refused. To do so would have been a grave infidelity.

All of that went through my mind as I stood above the stricken Crazy Horse. I thought of infidelity and stared straight ahead, toward Crazy Horse but not seeing him. I was having a difficult time coming back to the present. I could still hear the faint squeak of worn leather and smell the scent of men and horses. I saw the hungry, battered column of angry men, wandering south toward the Black Hills, more in the grip of the enemy's land than in meaningful pursuit. To this day I can see the herd of miserable horses doing their best to stay with us. I can hear the rifle shots that culled the worst of them for the evening meal.

36

That's the way Fanny and Jesse Lee found me, bent over my patient and staring into the past. When Fanny's hand touched my shoulder, I assumed it was Johnny and brought myself back to the present with a head shake and a snort. But when I turned and found anxiety in Fanny's face, I knew that something was amiss.

"Are you all right?" she asked.

"I am. What is it?"

Fanny drew back. "I think you should talk to Jesse. He's found out something that you should know."

Jesse Lee stood with his arms folded across his chest. His eyes were narrow and his jaw was set. "Is he any better?" he asked through his teeth.

I shook my head. "No. We are about to take some extreme action. Just waiting for Johnny to come with the equipment." The tension in Jesse's eyes made me stand and turn him away from Fanny. "What is it, Jesse?"

We leaned against the far wall of the cabin. Our eyes met and our voices went low and secretive. "It's a tangled intrigue," Jesse said, "and your friend Philo Clark is at its center." I did not respond. "The interpreter, Billy Garnett, has told me that two days ago there was a clandestine meeting in Colonel Bradley's quarters. Bradley wasn't there but Crook and Clark were, along with a rogue's gallery of reservation Indians. They made sinister plans, Valentine. Plans not worthy of the United States Army."

Although Jesse's eyes were very serious, something about the words made me smile. "And what sinister plans are you talking about?"

"They agreed to assassinate Crazy Horse."

My smile faded but all this intrigue still seemed vaguely amusing. "This was no assassination, Jesse," I said. "I saw what happened. So did you. The private who stabbed him was there by sheer serendipity."

"Yes, yes, I know. The plan was aborted for some reason but Clark offered three hundred dollars and his running horse to the man who would kill Crazy Horse."

I shook my head. "This is a serious charge. And you say it happened in the presence of General Crook?"

Jesse nodded. "In the presence of Crook," he said. "With the blessing of several of the reservation chiefs."

I was stunned. I turned my head from Jesse and my eyes fell first on Fanny, then Crazy Horse, and finally Touch the Clouds. I watched Touch the Clouds move forward and mop the sweat from his friend's forehead. "But the plot dissolved."

"Yes," Jesse said. It was called off, but before it was called off forty Oglalas were armed to carry it out. It set the scene for what happened. The conspirators are as guilty as the poor dupe who made the bayonet thrust."

That was hard for me to take and I shook my head.

"No, Jesse. It must have been called off in favor of a more prudent tactic. Things just got out of hand."

"I would admit that things got out of hand," Jesse said. "But as for your belief in a prudent tactic, think about this." He lowered his voice even further. "I don't know why, but our friends, Philo and his comrades, in their great wisdom, decided the best thing to do with Crazy Horse was not to kill him, but to send him to prison in Florida."

"To the Dry Tortugas?" I was incredulous.

"Or Saint Augustine. There is a train waiting in Omaha at this minute to take him into that forsaken swampland. No doubt he will serve a life sentence, without trial—without even charges—in the midst of common cutthroats, thieves, and rapists." Jesse exhaled venom. "My God, I think I prefer Clark's first plan."

We were standing near the door and when it opened, Jesse jerked back. But I stood still, thinking about what it would be like for Crazy Horse to spend his life in prison, in a hot humid land, antithetical to the prairie he'd fought for since he was a boy.

Johnny stepped into the adjutant's office with a canvas bag under one arm and a pair of saddlebags under the other. Immediately he was aware of the extra tension in the room. "I'll just lay the surgery tools out on the desk," he said. "I brought everything I could think of."

I was still lost in thought and am not even sure if I acknowledged him. What if there really was a train in

Omaha waiting for Crazy Horse? A poetic thought ran through my mind then that has been with me ever since: Was imprisoning a man like Crazy Horse for defending his people and land any different than caging an eagle for the impertinence of flight? What is the reasoning? Where is the justice?

Jesse clamped a hand on my shoulder. "I thought you should know," he said. "Now I'm going to get out of here and let you work. I'll go talk to Bradley, but I don't think it will do any good."

37

After the door closed behind Jesse I could hear Johnny preparing for the operation. I wanted to help him with the equipment, but I couldn't pull myself to the task at hand. Fanny told me later that I squinted as if looking to a distant horizon, like I'd found something in my mind both fascinating and frightening. She had seen such a look on my face once before and hoped she would never see it again.

Clacking of steel wheels beneath the floor. Gentle swaying as the train took the curves of Pennsylvania's hills. We were on our way downcountry to Washington, D.C., late at night only a month after the Starvation March had ended; we were due to arrive in the capital in the morning. For some complicated reason I have always imagined that Fanny was dreaming of a man, smooth, hairless skin stretched over granite muscles, the smell of wood smoke, grease paint, and the feel of oiled, braided hair. It was certainly not me she dreamed of in the upper berth of that rocking train and now that I am old and less ignorant, it doesn't matter. I like to think that Fanny wanted that man to be me. She would have felt the man's smooth leg against her own, and the tiny, imagined friction of it might have been what brought her closer to consciousness. More swaying. The clack of iron wheels. And she came awake with a light film of sweat covering her entire body.

There was no light in the tiny bedchamber, so she would have felt clumsily into the darkness beside her. Perhaps it had crossed her mind as she slept that she would like to move her hands across my body. It's pleasant to think that there was something attractive in my scarecrow strength. Maybe my complete lack of body fat and the soft hair of my chest had mixed themselves somehow into her dream. But the berth was empty. She told me that her hands scurried over the sheets again and again as if I could be hiding in a fold, but as she came fully awake the chill of the cotton registered and she knew that I had slipped from the bed hours before.

The old fingers of fear caught her as she sat up in the shaft-black berth. She had awakened with this sort of dread hundreds of times during the years when I was surveying and almost every night of the Sioux War. But rock, rock, and more clacking of iron wheels. It was the train to Washington, to parties, to the theater, and to recognition for the two of us. There was nothing to worry about, yet still the choking feeling made her need to slide the curtain away and to peer into the less perfect blackness.

A lantern swayed in the car ahead of the Pullman. The yellow light came through the windows, causing gray shadows to float on the curtains and ceiling above Fanny's berth. Projected against the back wall a shadowy hand swung grandly, and Fanny would have known in an instant that it was mine. She'd seen that gesture a million times, when I told her stories of the plains, when I talked of endless grass and men moving unconfined by roads or fences. She found her housecoat at the bottom of the bed and slipped it on. Going into the lounge car so scantily dressed was a bold thing to do but she knew then that I was in that car and that the only other passenger who would be up so late and listening to me would be Private Holden.

She left the Pullman and stepped onto the platform between the cars. The swaying of the train was jointed there where the cars met, and she would have taken a moment to enjoy the sense of one foot on each car. If it was a smooth piece of track the motion would have been gentle, like being between two noisy but benign worlds. The air was surprisingly warm that night, so she would not have hurried to open the door to the lounge car. She always liked to put her fingers to panes of glass and try to feel what was going on behind them. All she would have seen was two men, sitting beside each other, facing away. She would have tried to understand our conversation through her fingertips, but there was no way for her to know what we were talking about. She could only see the backs of our heads: Private Holden's hair long and mussed into a cowlick from the headrest; my head, six inches higher, with a thinning reddish mop uncombed since I'd slipped out of bed to banter with the private.

That thinning hair had made me self-conscious and when Fanny told me that she liked it, I was only more embarrassed. Sometimes I would have to cover my head with my hand if I thought she was looking at my hair. Now if I had it to do over again, I would undress Fanny slowly and rub this old pate over every inch of her.

Fanny must have felt like a little girl, slipping into the car without either Holden or myself knowing and listening, secretly, to us talk of war. She loved to listen to men, especially older men. She always hoped that she would become privy to mature events and situations to which only the very wisest and experienced had access. I imagine she was often disappointed.

A thin blue haze of cigar smoke filled the car and, coupled with the smell of whiskey, created an atmosphere that Fanny told me seemed intensely male.

I held the flask up and shook it to see how much remained inside. Then Holden's hand came up to take it away. I watched the flask's bottom come up and imagined an amber bubble twisting up into the chamber of air within the metal. After Holden took his swig he passed the bottle back to me. "The one good thing about this is that my mother has moved to Philadelphia." Holden's voice sounded very young. "It's not that far from Washington to Philadelphia, is it, Doc?"

"No," I said. "She should be able to come and visit you. If you give me her address I'll see that she knows where you are."

Holden didn't respond quickly. His head began to nod but still he didn't speak. Finally, the thin voice drifted up and back to where Fanny sat unnoticed. "That would be nice, Doc. I'm sure she's worried." Then some of the vitality came back to Holden. "She'll believe you when you tell her where I've been. She'll be disappointed 'cause she always wanted me to get educated, but she'll say I'm my father's son. The bastard went to California in '49 and we never heard from him again. I was less than a year old." Holden laughed and went on with childish excitement. "I guess he got one look at the mountains and forgot all about the East Coast. Up until he lit out he worked in a foundry. Imagine that, a foundry! Casting frying pans and wheel bearings."

"It's noble enough work."

"Ha! It's slave labor. Everyone I knew growing up worked in that foundry six days a week. They never went anywhere, they never saw the sky when it was daylight, they spent their lives arguing with their neighbors. Maybe I am my father's son. Maybe we all are."

"Easy, Private. Don't get yourself all upset." I meant

it as a joke and the whiskey made me laugh.

"Well, I can see why Dad left. Mom was always mad at him for going, but I could see his reasoning."

The flask passed back and forth again. Back and forth, back and forth. What is it about whiskey that makes it such a universal touchstone for men? The taste is foul, the effects numbing. Why are men so intent on turning the clear air around them to fog? "I know what you're saying, Private. I don't think a person can know himself in a city." I paused and cleared my throat. "I certainly became someone different after I left Detroit."

Fanny must have leaned forward then. She would have wanted to hear more about me, but Holden took up the theme. "I didn't know my own mind from a bucket of oysters," Holden said. "Never knew what I was made of till I crossed the Missouri River." That made us both laugh, and the laugh was no doubt hard for Fanny to understand.

"Absolutely," I said. "I'm afraid I frightened the man who was responsible for me leaving Detroit. A fine old man, Doctor McGraw. He was so excited when I returned from that first surveying trip. He believed I was there to go back to work at the hospital." I probably took a sip of whiskey just then in memory of Doctor McGraw. "Maybe I did intend to go back to work at the hospital. I'm not sure now. But McGraw's face turned so worried when I told him about the survey that I knew I could never take my old job again."

Holden laughed the laugh that some took as a sign of his condition. "So what did you tell the old boy, Doc? Did you tell him how a person can get to craving a drink from a mountain stream like it was a woman? Did you tell him about that relic Captain Bourke gave you to deliver along with me?"

"No. This was long before I met Captain Bourke. Long before the plains exploded into such confusion and cruelty."

"Come on, Doctor, you and I both know it's less cruelty than reality. What did you say that scared the old doctor?"

"It was innocent, really. I simply told him that I had learned something about myself and that I thought it was important. I told him that I had learned to smell rain on the wind."

Holden had been staring at the ceiling but when I said that, his head turned to me and his deep eyes looked at me with the recognition that we shared a secret. "We're like brothers," he said.

I refused to acknowledge that I, too, felt the kinship. Again the bottle passed and Holden laughed. "And the fact that you could smell rain like a buffalo or an antelope gave the old bird the heebie-jeebbies."

"It did. He believed in the steady march of human progress. I suppose sniffing weather seemed a bit of a retrenchment."

"The steady march of progress, horseshit!"

"Now, now. That belief is not simply horseshit." I wasn't ready to accept Holden's cynicism, and his madman's certainty was unnerving. In defense I fell back on something that had stuck in my mind since childhood. It came from my father, who had once taken me by the ear and dragged me out the back door of our house in Detroit.

He had just heard of a fight I'd been in at school. "We'll have no shanty Irish in this house," he said. He stood me up against the back of the house and told me to take off my shirt. "This family left all that when it boarded the ship in Galway." As he spoke he peeled the branches from a willow stick. "If I must, I'll beat the brute out of you." And as the switch came down on my back my father hissed the same words I spoke to Holden. "Our purpose in life is to strive for civilization."

Holden let out a sharp laugh. "If we're so civilized, why did we fight each other for the meat of the horses that carried us through Hell?" This stopped me then, and stops me now. I try not to think of the power and the pain of hunger. It is a fact of life but one I try not to think of because when I do, it throws all belief into question. I watched Buford weaken until his once-velvet nose brushed the ground. When the order came that he should be shot for the evening meal, I was sick with grief. I tried not to eat that night, but my hunger drove me to chew on Buford's flesh like a hyena. "That little march Crook took us on put civilization in its proper place," Holden said. "Right behind the ache of an empty stomach."

Now I think I sensed Fanny behind us, leaning forward, trying to understand all she could. "Extreme situation," I said in self-defense.

"Life is extreme."

Holden was right, but I couldn't quit. "That was an isolated incident," I said.

Another laugh from Holden. "Yeah? Pull out that necklace again. Let's take a look at your steady march toward civilization."

"That's exactly what we're fighting against."

"Come on, Doc. Pull it out. I won't get a chance to see anything like that where I'm going. Hell, I'll bet it'll get put away in a box in that museum and no one will ever see it. They'll all forget. Come on, pull it out."

I felt Fanny rise to her feet and start forward. Yet I couldn't resist Holden's challenge. I reached into the inner breast pocket of my coat and brought the necklace of mummified human fingers into the light. "It was found in a captured Cheyenne camp," I said. Fanny moved closer, drawn by the ghastly relic. "It's a talisman for us all."

Holden grunted. "It might as well be our altar."

At that Fanny rushed forward and slapped at my shoulder. "Stop it, Valentine. Stop it. Put that horrible thing away." I turned to face her and the expression on my face seemed to frighten her more than the artifact I held twisting in front of me.

Later that night I collapsed into an ocean of self-recrimination. The whiskey was deep into me and I begged Fanny drunkenly for forgiveness. I talked of the Devil and swore that I would never drink again. Fanny shook her head. She claimed not to blame me. She was afraid of what she'd seen but glad to have seen it. She clung to me and told me it was all right. It was not the whiskey, it was the world. When she said that, I began to sob. She had seen me cry over a sad story or a song, but never like that because she'd never seen me so frightened. Pain came out of me in convulsions. I bucked and babbled apologies for being what I was. She held my head tight between her breasts and rocked me. "It is all right," she said. "It's all right. All right," she said. "All right," until I was asleep.

At the gate of the asylum the next day I tried to pretend that nothing had happened. I acted as if my behavior the night before had been solely the fault of alcohol, and because I had sworn never to drink again I was saved. A stranger would have seen nothing unusual in the way Holden and I looked into each other's eyes. But there was unusual strength in our long embrace.

Empathy filled Fanny's eyes as she watched me in the shadows of the adjutant's office. Lost in such thoughts I must have seemed oblivious to the critically ill man on the floor and Johnny fussing over the surgery equipment. My eyes were seeing things she could not imagine or understand. She reached out and touched my shoulder and after an instant I looked up. We stared through each other's eyes, deep into the other's thoughts and emotions. When a sad smile came to her face I was able to return it, a perfect replica, as if we were both looking into a mirror.

38

"Could you have a look, sir? Tell me if there's anything else you'll need."

Puffing myself erect, I stepped toward the desk where the instruments were laid out in two parallel rows. Fanny tried to catch my eyes, wondering, I suppose, what I had been thinking, but I had left all that in memory by then and couldn't let my eyes dwell on her. Now I was focused on the intricacies and theory of what I was about to do.

Kidneys, I recalled from my medical school experience with a cadaver, were bean shaped and surprisingly diminutive. They lay along the vertebral column at the small of the back. In the body I studied the left kidney was slightly higher than the right, but I had no way of knowing whether my cadaver was normal or an anomaly. It was something of a moot question, since I would have to explore for the damaged kidney in any case.

Repair or remove, I thought. Once we were inside it could be that the tissue would be too flimsy to stitch. If that was the situation, I planned to remove the kidney and do my best to suture whatever arteries and ducts connected it to the rest of the urinary system.

That sort of operation is done with some regularity now, though at the time I sincerely hoped I wouldn't have to try it on the floor of the adjutant's office at Camp Robinson. It was hard then to believe that a human body could get along without one of its organs.

Imagining the path I would have to take, through the skin, muscles, ribs, and connecting tissue, was standard. Before every operation I tried to go through the stages of the procedure, anticipating what might be found, what might go wrong, and which instruments would be best for every contingency. Johnny had laid out a selection of scalpels on the top row. Those would do for the dermis and the muscle layer below. Two bone saws, one shaped like a carpenter's miter saw and the other like a keyhole saw, were next in line. I took the larger, miter-style saw away and placed it at the back of the desk. There would be no room between the ribs to operate a saw with such a wide blade. There was an array of clamps and retractors, a device that might do for separating and spreading the ribs. On the lower line was the magnifying glass, a half-dozen needles of different shapes with suture material already threaded through their eyes, a hypodermic syringe, a glass-stoppered bottle of pure water, a mound of swabs and sponges, and a huge vial of morphine sulfate—the camp's entire supply. In the center of the desk stood the ubiquitous bottle of whiskey.

I ran my hand over every instrument, the morphine vials, the swabs, the gauze, and finally the whiskey bottle and glass. I went through the procedure in my mind one more time, then nodded my head. "And you've brought the chloroform and mask?"

"Yes, sir. Right there in that bag. I can mix it up in a shake."

I nodded again. "Very well done, Corporal. You've done an excellent job, as usual." Johnny looked down at the praise and was able to mumble only a thank-you. But when I knelt to look at Crazy Horse, a smile spread across the corporal's face. He made a few tiny adjustments to the instruments laid out on the desk.

Crazy Horse moaned when he was rolled onto his side so that I could look into the wound. It was difficult to discern anything of value, because the laceration was weepy with watery blood. The skin along the edge was curled up, thrusting the muscle out like an erupting spring shoot. "My God, Valentine." Fanny was at my shoulder. "I'm so glad you've decided to do this."

"We should bathe this area in gentian violet," I said to Johnny.

"Yes, sir. I've mixed up a batch."

He went to work quickly and, when he had finished cleaning Crazy Horse's wound, glanced up to see what I wanted next. "That's good, Corporal. I want you to go find Lieutenant Clark. I think he should be here for this."

"Yes, sir." Johnny got to his feet and straightened his uniform. "I'll bring him right back, sir."

"Thank you, Corporal. Now Fanny, let's secure the patient on his side and prop his head up where we can administer the chloroform."

I had arranged Crazy Horse's legs and arms in such a way that he was stable enough on his side to take chloroform and would not move when we began to operate. I adjusted one blanket under his head and drew a second to help keep him warm.

I glanced at Fanny as we worked and could tell that something was on her mind. I smiled in an attempt to keep things light but Fanny's face was filled with question. "Doctor?"

I looked at her as if I was surprised that she had spoken. "Yes?"

"That day at the asylum, when we left Private Holden?"

I fiddled with Crazy Horse's blankets. "Yes?"

"He whispered in your ear, didn't he?"

"Ah, yes, I think he might have." I was assembling the hypodermic syringe, pretending to concentrate on what I was doing.

Fanny wouldn't let me get away with the deception. She stared at me until I spoke. "I don't know if you'd understand it, Fanny," I finally said. "I'm not sure I understand it myself." The syringe was assembled and I held it up in front of the lantern, checking to be sure it was functioning properly. A thin stream of morphine ejaculated into the air. "We'd been discussing the fact that he would likely be inside that fence for some time. Holden was quite concerned about his loss of freedom, but he was an intelligent and brave man. He knew he didn't have much choice."

"What did he say?"

Again I hesitated. It was hard to tell her. "You might recall that we embraced," I said to gain some time. "When his head touched my shoulder he said for me not to worry." I looked right at Fanny. "He said he wouldn't tell the doctors that I was still loose." A tiny laugh came out of me then. "He was so gloriously insane," I said.

"It was from the ordeal of that horrid march."

"Partly. That march made us all a little mad." I looked to the back of the room and there, in exactly the position he had been in for hours, sat Touch the Clouds. "We must have been quite a sight, Chief. I imagine the two of you would have found humor in our plight if you had not been in a similar one." There was a moment of silence in the room, but it was clear that Touch the Clouds had not understood and would not speak.

Crazy Horse squirmed on the floor and a low moan issued from his dry lips. "Could you bathe his head, Fanny?" I removed the ground-glass stopper from the bottles of morphine sulfate, measured enough for a very strong dose into a dish, and added purified water. I stirred the mixture with a glass rod, then sucked it into the syringe. The syringe could hold ten cubic centimeters; one centimeter would be enough. Mixed as strongly as possible, it could deliver fifty milligrams of morphine, enough to ease the pain of a dozen recent amputees. When I held the syringe up to the light the morphine took up only a small portion of the glass tube.

Fanny held Crazy Horse's arm as I slipped the needle into the muscle. She let her hands slide down and I noticed that her left touched Crazy Horse's right. Their hands were nearly the same size, but Crazy Horse's were hard with strength along the inside of the fingers. There were calluses and scars where the world had fought back. I noticed her run her fingertips over one of Crazy Horse's fingers as the syringe emptied. But I was not offended and was pleased to see Crazy Horse's eyes come open. He was exhausted and weak in the extreme. "McGillycuddy," he said.

I patted his arm. "Yes, it's me. We're going to try to fix you."

The chief tried to speak but the sound was faint. Both Fanny and I had to lean close to hear him. "Will I fly again, McGillycuddy?"

Again I patted his arm. My eyes blinked quickly. "I hope so," I said. "And if you do, I hope to fly with you."

Crazy Horse smiled thinly. "It is all I ever wanted to do," he said.

39

There was only an instant of silence before the door came open and the room filled with the distant sound of a drum and the keening of women. Philo came through the doorway, Johnny a step behind. They were quiet, and Philo removed his white Stetson as he would coming into the sickroom of any man.

The morphine was beginning to take hold of Crazy Horse. His eyes were again closed. Fanny knelt beside him, mopping his brow. I stood at the desk honing a scalpel. Before greeting Philo I tried the scalpel on the back of my hand. Three red hairs came off without the slightest hesitation of the blade.

"The corporal tells me you're going to operate," Philo said.

"That is our intention." I removed my coat. "It doesn't appear that the damage will heal itself. I'm convinced now that it is a kidney. The tissue is very fragile." I laid my coat over the adjutant's chair. The watch chain made a metallic click against the oak.

Philo stood over Crazy Horse with a bowed head and deep concern in his face. When he looked up, he saw the bottle of whiskey on the desk. He gestured toward it. "Would you mind?" I shook my head, picked up the bottle, and handed it to him. He took a swig and offered it back. I stared at it intently and felt Fanny watching me consider Philo's offer.

Now I know that the Devil is not in the bottle. Now I know that it isn't that easy. But then I could only stare at the whiskey. Finally, I nodded toward Johnny. "Have a shot, Corporal. You've earned it."

Johnny's head bobbed and he poured an inch of whiskey into the glass. He tipped the glass up and swallowed the liquid in one gulp. "Thank you, sir."

"I suppose we should begin," I said. "But Philo, I'd like to speak with you first."

Of course," Clark said.

“Could we step outside?” We looked at each other and Philo nodded. “Corporal, please prepare the chloroform,” I said. “We’ll only be a minute.”

Fanny was up, standing beside me, and when we moved toward the door she moved with us. She might have thought she would be asked to stay inside, but if Philo had that intention he quickly read the veto of it in my eyes.

The night had cooled. Across the parade ground small fires burned where the extra guards huddled to warm their hands. Farther east fires projected shadows on the tepees of Red Cloud’s Oglalas, the Cheyenne, and the Brules. In the dark hills to the north points of campfire light mixed with the stars, making it difficult to tell where the lodges of Crazy Horse’s people left off and the sky began. The air was still and cool and, as Philo and I knew so well, those conditions on the prairie gave sound the ability to mock distance. A scrape of a ladle against an iron kettle came from the Brule camp, a soldier snorted at the comment of a friend, a horse pawed the ground in the hills. And over it all was the hollow, distant drum and the plaintive wail of a lone singer.

“Is she mourning Crazy Horse?” I asked.

Philo cocked his expert ear and listened for a full minute. “Perhaps,” he finally said. “She’s singing about buffalo and the migration of waterfowl.”

“There’s something I need to know, Philo.”

“I thought there might be. I’ve been following Lee around for five hours, trying to make sure he gets the correct information."

"The correct information or the most expedient information?"

Philo rubbed his face before he answered. "I suppose that was a fair comment. But so is this: I'm no more happy with what's happened to these people and this land than you are. There have been mistakes and we're all a party to them. But there is no sense pretending that this could all have been worked out at a tea party. There are no innocent participants in this affair."

"But you schemed to murder a man."

"That was Red Cloud's idea. His jealousies are as Machiavellian as any European monarch's."

"Did you offer your own horse to the successful assassin?"

Fanny stared at Philo. He removed his hat, looked up at the stars, and exhaled. "I did. I believed the Indian who told me Crazy Horse intended to kill General Crook, and I wanted an end to all of it. I wanted this land to be peaceful, the way you described it the first time we met. My consent to that plot was one of the mistakes I spoke about. When I realized it, I canceled the plan."

"I know that, Philo. I just wanted to hear you say it." The three of us were leaning against the wall looking out over the parade ground. Fanny was near me and I surprised her by reaching out, putting my arm around her waist, and pulling her close against my side. "Jesse told me something else," I said. "He claims that if Crazy Horse lives, you intend to send him to prison."

"Lee's thorough," Philo said. "I'll say that for him."

"Then it's true."

"He can't stay here, Mac. He drives the other Indians crazy, either with fervor or envy."

"But Florida? The climate alone will kill him. It would be like uprooting a tree."

"It's a matter of necessity."

"Necessity?"

"It has to do with myth and legend, Mac. If Crazy Horse had died at the Little Big Horn, we would barely recall his name. If he lives to die in prison, his fame will fade and finally die with him." He stopped abruptly and let what he'd said soak in. Then, with a chill in his voice: "What frightens me, Mac, is that he will die now, of this stupid wound delivered by his enemy. If that happens, he might live forever. We may be fighting the myth of him for a thousand years."

Fanny looked to me and found my face set in a numb stare focused on what must have seemed nothing. She had been silent to this point, but what Philo said troubled her as it troubled me and she spoke for us both. "And what about the good in him? You all admit that he embodies what we profess to be good: bravery, charity, responsibility." Her voice trailed off as two figures appeared from the darkness on the far side of the parade ground.

The figures were hunched up and came slowly toward the adjutant's office. They clung to each other, casting pale shadows in the starlight. It was an old Indian couple out much too late on a night when everyone should have been close to their fires. But the old people moved doggedly toward where we stood with frozen expressions on the porch of the adjutant's office.

When the couple were twenty feet away, they stopped. They seemed frightened. Still, the old man, leaning now on a crooked cane, took two steps forward. He planted himself and made a sign with his hand. Philo signed back easily. The old man leaned his cane against his hip and launched into a swirl of signals. Philo understood him completely and returned the signals with tiny, perfect gestures. "They are the parents of Crazy Horse," Philo said. "They have come for their son."

Both Philo and Fanny looked to me. "Tell them to wait, Philo. There should be some news in a short time."

Philo spoke to the old man in Lakota too fast for me to follow, but both the old man and his wife nodded their heads. "I told them you are going to make their son live."

When Fanny turned to gauge my reaction, she found my face as hard and textured as the sandstone buttes that surrounded the camp. My thoughts could have been among those buttes or in the tall, pulsing grass beyond. "I said you were going to make their son live," Philo said again.

My head began to nod slowly to the beat of the distant drum. "Live?" I said. "Tell them I'll try." I didn't look at Philo but reached out and wrapped Fanny's arm around my own. "Have them wait, Philo." Fanny and I looked at each other and she realized that I was angry, a little confused perhaps, definitely fearful of what might happen. "Even better, Philo. Wait with them. They deserve that much from us."

40

Johnny had turned up the wick in the lantern so that his form cast a crisp shadow against the back wall as he fussed with the instruments on the desk. Touch the Clouds and Crazy Horse were illuminated by the indirect yellow light at the edge of the lantern's sweep. There was a slow pulsing of light as the flame consumed the impure lamp oil. Touch the Clouds swayed back and forth as if he could feel the light come and go. His eyes were closed and he hummed in a low, soft rumble. The words of his chant were unintelligible to us as we stood around the desk draped with a linen cloth to keep the surgical instruments clean, but it was clearly a prayer.

I fondled the instruments but my mind was still far away. I looked down at Crazy Horse and found him sleeping but taut. When I glanced back at Fanny, I saw that she understood I was teetering on the edge of a decision. "Corporal," I said, "would you be so kind as to hand me my watch?" I pointed to my coat, hanging over the adjutant's chair.

Johnny removed the watch and handed it to Fanny before going back to preparing dressings. She looked at its face. The delicate, gold second hand snapped another step in its endless circle. "It's eleven forty-five," she said. Our eyes met over the desk.

The lamp light froze the whole room in its gently strobing light. I might have appeared to be deep in thought about Crazy Horse's condition but surely Fanny knew I was far away, surrounded by rolling plains, folded into a million miles of waving grass, and moving under an endless sky. Finally I came to the decision that I have kept secret all my life and my head began to nod almost imperceptibly. Fanny understood. Her steady eyes and determined jaw assured me that I was right. Without another instant of hesitation I took up the vial of morphine, but I did not mix the powder in water until Fanny had moved discreetly between me and Johnny. When my movements were shielded I dumped the entire contents of the vial into the pure water, shook it quickly, and loaded the syringe with all it would hold.

When I knelt at Crazy Horse's side I did not let myself falter. I eased the needle into his arm and pushed the plunger until the last drop of deadly morphine disappeared into his body. By then Fanny knelt beside me. With my right hand I reached out and held Crazy Horse's arm firmly. Fanny took my left hand into her own smooth hand and, with her other, she clutched Crazy Horse's left arm. She stroked us both with her fingertips but only I felt the caress. It did not take long. Together we watched the features of Crazy Horse's face go limp and pale.

When Johnny looked down he knew immediately that the chief was dead. "Oh God," he said. The tone of his voice alerted Touch the Clouds to what had happened. By then Fanny and I had risen and stood beside the desk. Without fanfare, Fanny poured an inch of whiskey into the glass. Her index finger pushed the glass in my direction and I watched it come. Without a word I took the glass and raised it to my lips. I closed my eyes and let the amber liquid slide slowly down my throat.

Touch the Clouds stood to his full height and moved to stand over Crazy Horse. He bent at the waist, elegantly, and touched his comrade's head. "It is well," he said in Lakota. As he passed on his way to the door, he touched my shoulder with his long, broad hand. "*Pilamayaye,* McGillycuddy," he said. You are a friend."

Johnny followed Touch the Clouds out the door and Fanny and I were left staring at each other over the desk. I heard Philo swear and the parents of Crazy Horse cry out. Immediately, as if the news had been transmitted by lightning, the wails from the surrounding camps and buttes rose until the night was nothing else. It was the most mournful dirge the high plains had ever heard. As Fanny watched me, my eyes filled and overflowed. She touched my face, her hand hot with a passion I have never forgotten.

41

Since that day the Great Plains have writhed and twisted under the white man's yoke. For a while I remained in that country but eventually, after Fanny's death, I couldn't stand it any longer. Cattle moved in from Texas to replace the buffalo; steel plows were buried deep in the prairie's flesh. I traveled to the Rocky Mountains, then Nevada, Alaska, and finally California. Time slipped away as if nothing had happened. For many years I heard nothing of those people and those times; Philo's prediction of eternal life for Crazy Horse did not materialize.

Then one day, when I came back to the hotel from my morning walk, the bellman pulled me aside and motioned toward a man standing near the street. "I asked him to wait for you there," the bellman said. "He was insistent and the manager wouldn't let him into the lobby."

When I looked at the man, I felt a shift in my core. I did not recognize him but there was something familiar about the way he stood, unsupported by lamppost or building. He was in his sixties, and his full-length dark overcoat and brown derby hat were worn. "I can chase him off, Doctor."

"No." I moved away from the bellman and slowly down the front stairs. It had been so long that at first I thought the man might be Chinese, but he was too tall. His face looked as if it had been sculpted by huge, gentle hands. Beneath the tattered hem of the overcoat I saw a fine pair of beaded moccasins.

I am an old, scrawny man with short white hair and thin whiskers but the man recognized me. "Doctor McGillycuddy?"

"Yes."

"I am Willow Bear. You nearly electrocuted me one day. You delivered my nephew that day, too. It was the day Crazy Horse died."

I stood dumbstruck. "Yes," I said, "I remember. What are you doing here?"

Willow Bear smiled. "I came here with the Wild West Show. We've toured the country and Europe. I am leaving them here. I have one more performance, then I'm going back to the reservation. I would like to borrow a few dollars for the trip."

"Certainly," I said, and fumbled for my wallet. "But how could you know that I was here?"

"Everyone on the reservation knows where you are. The Indian agent tells us where you go. People talk of you at night. They remember you fondly."

I gave Willow Bear all the money I had, twenty-five dollars. He thanked me and pressed an envelope into my hand. "They need me on the reservation," he said. "The people have been sleeping but now they are waking up. They want to Sun Dance. It has been outlawed and there are few of us who remember how it is done."

I shook my head and thought, *Great God.* But I couldn't speak.

"My nephew," Willow Bear went on, "the boy you delivered that night, will be the first to dance in many years." He smiled. "He will dance in the spirit of Crazy Horse." Then he raised the fist full of money. "And he will dance for you, McGillycuddy."

My silly, old chin quivered as Willow Bear took my hand and gave it a firm shake. I wanted to say something but couldn't.

"I must go," he said. "My last performance is at one o'clock. I ride a big white horse with bright red paint and get chased by six cavalry officers." He laughed. "They ride like farm boys."

Then he was gone and I was left on that city street looking after him, wondering if I had imagined the whole incident. But inside the envelope Willow Bear had given me was a ticket to the Wild West Show. That afternoon I took in the matinee.

Some would say the performance was tawdry and melodramatic. There was a great deal of galloping back and forth and lots of blank ammunition fired into the air. The cavalry did indeed ride like farm boys. But as grist for an old man's memory-mill, that afternoon has served me well.

Now when I sit in this rocking chair watching the lights of warships in the bay, I can start with the thought of Willow Bear on that big white horse. He charges around the arena in my mind. They gain speed with each lap. So fast that the horse loses the gaudy paint. Then its whiteness fades until finally it is a hard, brown pony with a single eagle feather braided into its mane. There is no saddle, and the nearly naked rider is lean and trim. His hair is long and flows out behind. Around the arena they go until the spectators and the walls of the building melt away. I can hear the hoofbeats and feel the prairie tremble. I can smell the grass and taste the wind in their faces. Long strides. Faster. Faster. Until the horse's hooves leave the ground. When they begin to fly I can close my eyes and be sure that sleep will finally come.

Center Point Publishing
600 Brooks Road • PO Box 1
Thorndike ME 04986-0001 USA

(207) 568-3717

US & Canada:
1 800 929-9108